Rhinegold Study Guides

A Student's Guide to A2 Performance Studies

for the **OCR** Specification

by John Pymm and Gail Deal

Rhinegold Publishing Ltd
241 Shaftesbury Avenue
London WC2H 8TF
Telephone: 01832 270333
Fax: 01832 275560
www.rhinegold.co.uk

Rhinegold Performance Studies Study Guides
A Student's Guide to AS Performance Studies for the OCR Specification
A Student's Guide to A2 Performance Studies for the OCR Specification

Rhinegold Drama and Theatre Studies Study Guides
A Student's Guide to AS Drama and Theatre Studies for the AQA Specification
A Student's Guide to A2 Drama and Theatre Studies for the AQA Specification

A Student's Guide to AS Drama and Theatre Studies for the Edexcel Specification
A Student's Guide to A2 Drama and Theatre Studies for the Edexcel Specification

Other Rhinegold Study Guides
Students' Guides to AS and A2 Religious Studies for the AQA, Edexcel and OCR Specifications
Students' Guides to GCSE Music for the AQA, Edexcel, OCR and WJEC Specifications
Students' Guides to AS and A2 Music for the AQA, Edexcel and OCR Specifications
Listening Tests for Students for the AQA, Edexcel and OCR GCSE and A-level Music Specifications
A Student's Guide to Music Technology for the Edexcel AS and A2 Specification

Rhinegold Publishing also publishes Teaching Drama, as well as Classical Music, Classroom Music,
Early Music Today, Music Teacher, Opera Now, Piano, The Singer, British and International Music Yearbook,
British Performing Arts Yearbook, Rhinegold Guide to Music Education, Rhinegold Dictionary of Music in Sound.

First published 2005 in Great Britain by
Rhinegold Publishing Ltd
241 Shaftesbury Avenue
London WC2H 8TF
Telephone: 01832 270333
Fax: 01832 275560
www.rhinegold.co.uk

Rhinegold Publishing Ltd has used its best efforts in preparing this guide. It does not assume, and hereby
disclaims, any liability to any party for loss or damage caused by errors or omissions in the guide whether such
errors or omissions result from negligence, accident or other cause.

You should always check the current requirements of the examination, since these may change.
Copies of the OCR specification may be obtained from Oxford, Cambridge and RSA Examinations at
OCR Publications, PO Box 5050, Annersley, Nottingham NG15 0DL
Telephone 0870 870 6622, Fax 0870 870 6621.
See also the OCR website at www.ocr.org.uk

A Student's Guide to A2 Performance Studies for the OCR specification
British Library Cataloguing in Publication Data.
A catalogue record for this book is available from the British Library.

ISBN 1-904226-49-3
Printed in Great Britain by WPG Ltd

Contents

The authors

John Pymm is Associate Dean of the School of Sport, Performing Arts and Leisure at the University of Wolverhampton, where he is responsible for undergraduate and postgraduate degrees in dance, drama and music. Prior to this, he was Performing Arts Coordinator at Rowley Regis College. A graduate of the University of Birmingham, John also holds Masters degrees from the universities of Exeter and London, and has spoken at numerous conferences about performance studies. He is chief examiner for A-level performance studies and has overseen the development of the syllabus since 1994.

Gail Deal is a senior examiner for performance studies with OCR, an examiner for dance with AQA and an examiner for drama with IGSCE. She trained as an ice skater, coming fifth in the World Professional Championships in 1974, and has taught ice skating and dance in Barcelona and London. She has taken dance classes in a variety of styles including tap, disco, modern, contemporary and flamenco. She studied French and German at university and has a masters degree in literature and culture. Gail is head of performing arts and music at Esher College in Surrey, where she also teaches media studies and previously taught English.

The editors

Emma Whale (project manager), Charlotte Regan (senior assistant editor).

Acknowledgements

In the writing of a guide such as this many people have contributed. The authors and publishers are grateful to the following people for their specific advice, support and expert contributions: Hallam Bannister, David Dalton Leggett, Joanna Hughes, Lucien Jenkins, Ruth Lyon, Louise Powell, Elisabeth Rhodes, Elizabeth Rogers, Susan Segal, Bev Sokolowski and Abigail Walmsley. In addition, the authors would like to thank the following students: Francesca Bellmonte, Scarlett Brooks, Rachel Cox, Richard Dinsdale, Lucy Dolman, Louise Evans, Hayley Green, Jessica Goodchild, Josie Haworth, Sophia Hooper, Vicky Jessup, Emma Johnson, Jane Lawes, Emma Leone, Sam Margetts, Cristina Rapacioli, Elle Saunders, Natalie Smith, Sarah-Jane Tiffin, Mirijiana Vasovic, Kate Watson and Hayley Worth.

The authors are also conscious of having drawn on a lifetime's reading. More recently, the growth in use of the Internet has made an unparalleled amount of exciting information and challenging opinion widely available. Although every attempt has been made to acknowledge both the primary and secondary sources drawn on, it is impossible to do justice to the full range of material that has shaped the creation of this book. The authors would therefore like to apologise if anyone's work has not been properly acknowledged. They would be happy to hear from authors or publishers so that any such errors or omissions may be rectified in future editions.

Introduction

You've chosen to carry on with A-level performance studies at A2. This probably means that you're happy with the grade that you got in your AS units and you feel that you have a good chance of being successful at A2, perhaps even going to university to study a related course. You probably don't have quite as many questions as you had when you started your AS course, but there may be some things that you'd like to get sorted out before the start of the A2 units.

You need to be honest with yourself about your strengths and weaknesses before you start your A2 course. Look back at your grades for individual units in the AS and ask yourself whether there is a real area that you struggle with – written exams, coursework or even practical work. If so, you need to discuss this with your teachers to try to improve in that area.

In particular, you need to review how your skills are developing across the three art forms. You may not have studied dance, drama and music together before you took performance studies, and you may feel there is still one art form in which you are not as strong. You might be tempted to ignore that art form and concentrate on the two that you feel confident in. We would really encourage you not to do that. You will find the whole experience of taking performance studies to A2 much richer if you work at all three art forms. All three of the units involve working across the art forms, so it's best to embrace it enthusiastically rather than grudgingly.

You might also be thinking about the balance between practical work and written work. This is exactly the same in A2 as it was in AS: 30% coursework, 30% written examination and 40% practical assessment. There is slightly more group work at A2 – you'll be working in groups for the whole of two of the three units.

You may have been using your work from performance studies to provide work for your Key Skills assessment. The key skills for all subjects are the same as they were before:

➢ Communication
➢ Application of number
➢ Information technology
➢ Working with others
➢ Improving own learning and performance
➢ Problem solving.

Communication is easily delivered through performance studies, as it includes discussions, presentations, reading and synthesis. Equally, the last three of these relate almost exactly to what you'll be doing in your work in this subject. By now you'll be able to see how useful the creative group work is in balancing your portfolio. There should be plenty of examples already of how performance

At the end of the two-year course, the marks for the six units are added together. Each unit is worth a maximum of 100 marks, and it is the total mark out of 600 that will decide your final grade.

Further reading

Throughout this guide, we refer to the AS companion *A Student's Guide to AS Performance Studies for the OCR Specification* as the *OCR AS Guide*.

Skills

Group work

At AS, were there group sessions that went particularly well or badly? What can you do to improve your work for the benefit of all members of the group?

Key skills

group work to improve performance techniques. Make sure that you use the profile you've started to build up to prepare yourself for university interviews during your A2 year.

Can I get into university with it?

Performance studies is recognised by all universities in the United Kingdom as an approved A-level specification. However, as with all A levels, it depends on what course you want to study as to whether you can use it as an entrance qualification for a specific course. Similarly, you need to be clear about the purpose of this subject in comparison with A levels in specific disciplines. If you want to be a music teacher or play in an orchestra, performance studies will be a very useful subject for you to study, but it won't replace music: if your ambitions are to work solely in music, you need to take A2 music as well as A2 performance studies. The same principle applies to dance and drama as well.

The A2 units

Let's look through the three units that you'll be studying for A2 performance studies. You can find out much more about them by looking at the specification in full, but it's helpful to have a summary to give you an overview of what to expect.

How A2 follows on from AS

You'll find that in the A2 units, some of the activities will seem similar to things that you have done in your AS course. This is deliberate. The idea is that you will do similar things in much greater depth so you will build on the foundation of the AS course. There are three units in A2, just as there were in AS and for each type of activity, there is a direct link.

Web link

You can find the whole specification on the examination board's web site: www.ocr.org.uk. Download a copy for yourself. There are also quite a few other resources on the site that you may find helpful as you move into the A2 course.

AS units	A2 units
Unit 1 **The Language of Performing Arts** (90 marks)	Unit 4 **Community Performance Project** (90 marks)
Coursework	*Coursework*
Worth 30% of the marks for AS	Worth 30% of the marks for A2
Unit 2 **Contextual Studies 1** (90 marks)	Unit 5 **Contextual Studies 2** (90 marks)
Written Examination Paper (2 hours)	*Written Examination Paper* (2 hours)
Worth 30% of the marks for AS	Worth 30% of the marks for A2
Unit 3 **Performance Realisation** (120 marks)	Unit 6 **Student Devised Performance** (120 marks)
Practical Examination	*Practical Examination*
Worth 40% of the marks for AS	Worth 40% of the marks for A2

You'll see from this that your A2 year in performance studies could be structured in a similar way to your AS year. Obviously the details will depend on the teaching staff at your school or college but the assessments are very similar and the weightings for coursework, written examination and practical work are the same as at AS.

The crucial thing is that the work will be pitched at a higher level so you need to be prepared to work harder. If you want to improve your grades, you need to remember that the standard is higher.

Let's have a look at specific requirements of the three units for A2. We'll refer to them as units 4, 5 and 6 because they follow on from units 1, 2 and 3 at AS.

Unit 4 Community Performance Project – Written (30%)

This unit builds on the work you did for unit 1, The Language of Performing Arts. As in that unit, you'll be assessed on your written commentary where you'll discuss your performance work.

There are three aspects of unit 1 that are intended as a basis for the work in the Community Performance Project. These are:

Building on unit 1

➢ **The performance process**. You'll need to be completely familiar with the approach of improvising–rehearsing–performing. You used it as a basis for creating the four short pieces in unit 1 and the devised piece for unit 3. Now you'll have to go through the same process to create a much longer piece.

➢ **The technical skills and vocabulary**. You have acquired a number of skills and the ability to discuss these using technical language. It will be assumed that you are able to produce more demanding performance work and discuss this with an even greater degree of technical insight.

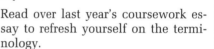

Tip

Read over last year's coursework essay to refresh yourself on the terminology.

➢ **The ability to link the art forms**. In unit 1 only one of the pieces – the integrated piece – involved working in all three art forms. You now have to work in at least two art forms throughout and it would most effective if you thought in terms of using all three.

The practical work for the Community Performance Project is straightforward. You need to work in a group to produce an original piece of about 30 minutes in duration. There are three crucial aspects of the piece that you will need to be aware of throughout the devising process:

Practical work in unit 4

➢ The style or genre of the piece and what it's about

➢ Where you are going to perform it

➢ Who the performance is intended for.

The same rules about group work apply as before. You will not be allowed to work alone for this unit but the size of the group is not prescribed. You need to decide what size of group best fits your decisions about style, content and venue. A piece intended for an intimate performance space is unsuited to large numbers of performers.

These questions are interrelated and some of them will be decided by your teachers. Nevertheless, you need to know the rationale for these decisions and how you moved forward in each stage of the work.

Your written work is what you're going to be assessed on. You need to produce a written commentary of 3,000 words in total on the extended piece that your group has devised. Your work will be marked by your tutors and they will then send their marks off to OCR for external moderation. This means that the final mark you receive for the unit may be the one awarded by your tutors or it may be moderated to bring it into line with national standards.

Written work in unit 4

Unit 5 Contextual Studies 2 – written examination (30%)

In Contextual Studies 1, the focus was on individual pieces; now you study a whole genre. There are four aspects of Contextual Studies 1 that you will be expected to understand and use. These

Building on Contextual Studies

If you know people in the years above you who took Performance Studies, you may notice that what you're studying for Contextual Studies is different from what they did. This is because the exam board changed the specification. The first examination on the revised requirements is June 2006.

move from the specifics of individual works to the genre as a whole. Here's a reminder of what you did at AS:

> **How pieces are constructed**. You won't be analysing pieces in as much detail for A2 but you'll be expected to pick out the most important aspects of the extracts you study.

> **How a practitioner makes use of technical aspects**. Rather than looking at just one work, now you'll need to be able to compare how technique is used in three pieces by each practitioner and you'll be expected to compare and contrast how this works in the different art forms.

> **Stylistic influences**. This will become much more important at A2. At AS, you focused on a single work to comment on a practitioner's style. Now, you'll be expected to explore the range of influences you can see on a range of works and compare them across the art forms.

> **Cultural, historical and social context**. This will now be central to your study and will shape the way in which you understand the individual extracts.

What do I have to do?

In Contextual Studies 2, you need to show that you have a detailed knowledge of a topic that you have studied. You will be assessed on your study of one topic that brings together all three performing arts. You will study three extracts from works by a choreographer, three extracts from works by a composer and three extracts from works by a playwright.

You will have two hours to complete the written examination paper. The paper will contain a choice of **two** questions on the topic you have studied. The questions will be fairly broad and will not make specific reference to the titles of any of the pieces you have looked at. In your answer to each question you will have to show that you thoroughly understand the topic through your study of the nine extracts, as you will be writing for two hours about it. Your answers will be marked externally by examiners from OCR.

From June 2006 onwards, the choice of topics will be as follows:

> Topic 1: Postmodern approaches to the performing arts since 1960

> Topic 2: Politics and performance since 1914

> Topic 3: The 20th-century American musical.

You will have to memorise any quotations that you want to use in the written paper as you will not be able to take copies of works studied or any of your notes into the examination room.

Unit 6 Student Devised Performance – Practical (40%)

Building on Performance Realisation

In your AS work, you focused on performing a piece of repertoire from the work of one practitioner and devising your own performance in the style of another. There are two aspects of this work that you will develop further:

> Your performance standard. During the second year of the course you must really push yourself to develop your techniques in the art forms and to make sure that you are performing at a higher level than at AS.

➢ Your ability to devise sophisticated performance material. For your devising work at AS, you were copying the style of a practitioner you had studied. The test at A2 will be whether you can devise an original piece from a commission and maintain a coherent style and message for the piece as a whole.

In this unit you will take part in one group performance and the whole of the marks will be awarded for your work in that piece. You will work in a group of between **three and seven** in total. As at AS, the length of your piece is related to how many people there are performing in it. Everyone must have five minutes of exposure during the piece and – as a broad guide – the total length of time allowed for each performance is therefore the number of people multiplied by five minutes. The maximum time allowed for a group of seven candidates is 30 minutes, though, so if your group contains the maximum number of people, you will need to make some efficiencies in time.

There are three aspects to the assessment of your work in this unit.

➢ The commission. Your group will have to choose a commission from a list of 20 set by the exam board and devise a piece that reflects this commission in a meaningful and effective way. Everyone in the group will be awarded the same mark for this. This mark is out of a maximum of 25.

➢ Your individual role. You will be awarded an individual mark out of a maximum of 25 for your role within the piece.

➢ Your performance skills. You will be assessed on the quality of your performance on the day. The examiner will expect to see you perform in at least two art forms. You will be awarded a mark out of a maximum of 50.

Your performances will be assessed by a visiting examiner from OCR. The examiner will meet with your group prior to the performance and have a short discussion about the piece you are about to perform. This discussion may last up to 30 minutes (depending on the size of your group) and, although it is not assessed, the examiner will be quite probing about how you have explored the commission and the individual roles that you have created within the piece.

What do I have to do?

As the discussion is not assessed, you may take your working notes along to refer to so that you do not get flustered or forget what you've done.

Community Performance Project

We're assuming that you haven't started the piece yet and that you're reading this as you prepare to work on it. However, you may already be quite a long way into the process, or have even performed the piece. If that's the case, read this chapter through and make sure you've covered everything.

What do I have to do?

At AS, you will have worked in groups to devise some original performance pieces. In this unit, you'll need to build on the skills that you developed at AS and show that you are able to perform to a high level in at least two art forms. You'll also be expected to produce a longer piece than before – about 30 minutes in total.

Even though you will spend a long time devising this piece, you will not be assessed on your actual performance of it. This is a coursework unit and it works on the same principle as the Language of Performing Arts unit at AS. If you think back to that part of your AS work, you'll remember that even though you spent quite a lot of time devising the practical pieces, the actual assessment was based on a written commentary of 3,000 words that you produced once you had finished the practical work.

That's what will happen here. You will work in a group to devise and perform a practical piece and you will then work on your own to write up your commentary on what took place. It sounds quite straightforward when put like that, but obviously this unit is pitched at A2 level, so examiners will be expecting to see quite a lot of knowledge and understanding of what you've done when they read your commentary.

Getting started

Imagine that five friends are asked about a performance they've just seen. Each person is told that they can only say one sentence about the piece and that it has to be different from what the others have said. Here's what they come up with:

'It was a piece of pantomime – a great example of that genre.'

'The performance was in the Grand Theatre – it holds 950 people.'

'The audience was mainly children under the age of 11.'

'The piece lasted for over two hours – it was great!'

'There were over 50 performers.'

Try to imagine the specific questions you'd need to ask to get those responses. They might be along these lines:

➢ What sort of piece was it?

➢ Where was it held?

➢ What was the audience like?

➢ How long did it last?

➢ How many performers were there?

Notice that the answer to the first question determines the answer to most of the others. For example, suppose the answer to the first question was 'a piece of street theatre'. It would be extremely unusual for such a piece to be performed in a traditional proscenium-arch theatre, attract an audience of 950 (mostly children) or last for two hours. The number of performers would also be far too many since a company of 50 people performing in the street might prove overwhelming (and possibly intimidating) to the passers-by who were meant to watch it.

Now imagine the piece was a cabaret. Cabaret shows are generally performed to audiences seated at round tables that are placed informally in a large flat performance space, possibly with a stage at the front. The audience size might be between 100 and 200 and there could well be some interaction between the performers and the audience, especially if requests were invited. A proscenium-arch theatre would be useless for this type of performance as the raked seating is normally fixed and the audience could not be seated appropriately. Furthermore, a venue that holds 950 people is not likely to feel suitably intimate for this type of show.

> **Tip**
> The style of the piece should determine everything you do.

Before you start work on the practical piece, you need to be clear about the answers to these types of questions. If you've finished your piece and you still can't answer them, then you need to do some serious thinking about what you've been trying to do for the last few weeks – more importantly, you need to ask what your audience thought you were trying to do. So let's go through the questions in detail.

Be clear

What sort of piece is it?

As we have just seen, this is the most important of the questions about the piece, but in some ways it's also the most difficult because your mind will tend to be drawn to what the piece is about – its subject matter – rather than the style or genre it's in. When your group first gets together, it's quite likely that you will have all sorts of ideas concerning what the piece should be about. Suppose, for example, you have decided to produce a piece about the life of someone famous from your area. Let's imagine that your school is in Coventry, so you decide to make your piece about the city during the blitz. A lot of students might decide to bring the story to life in a naturalistic way but this could create difficulties in including dance and music. It's also likely to mean that you are unclear about the style. It's therefore better not to start with the content. There are lots of different ways of treating the same story or event, so **decide on the style first**.

> **Tip**
> Don't start work until you're clear what performance style you're working in.

> Theatrical naturalism originated in the work of playwrights such as Ibsen and Strindberg as a challenge to the non-realistic melodramatic forms of theatre that preceded them. They looked to the new ideas coming from biology – most notably the work of Charles Darwin on natural selection and evolution – in order to create their characters.

The exam board provides some recommended examples of styles and genres that you could use as the basis for your piece, although the list is not exhaustive or compulsory. In the end, the decision on which style to go for will be left with your tutors, as they will be delivering taught sessions about this style. This may not seem very democratic, but obviously they will want you to work in a style in which you can do your best – and you need

The exam board recommends that you avoid work that is highly improvisatory or informal, as this is unlikely to meet the demands of the unit and will therefore be unlikely to score highly.

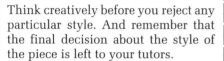

Tip

Think creatively before you reject any particular style. And remember that the final decision about the style of the piece is left to your tutors.

You are not allowed to use Theatre in Education (TIE) as a style for your piece because the focus on education may mean that the performance is not the major element of that style.

Pieces in more than one style

to bear in mind that it may be one that you wouldn't necessarily have chosen yourself. Although you don't have to go for one of the ones suggested by the exam board, you should consider them seriously. The list is as follows:

➢ Cabaret

➢ Commedia dell' Arte

➢ Folk music and dance

➢ Pantomime

➢ Pageant

➢ Performance art

➢ Melodrama

➢ Street theatre.

Each of these represents a style or a genre – you may not be familiar with some of them, but that's no reason to dismiss anything at this stage. It may become obvious fairly quickly that one of these would be ideally suited to something you could use – especially as they are styles that build on the skills you learned at AS.

There are lots of creative ways of reworking styles. For example, a pantomime on a contemporary political theme might be ideally suited to a working men's club, and you could have great fun adapting some stock characters to create satire. Imagine the story of Cinderella set in a block of flats. It could feature an unemployed young woman unable to afford an expensive dinner and night out because her income support was cut after she refused to go on a government scheme. The performance could have all the usual stock characters, costumes, slapstick, songs and exaggerated movement, while still making heavyweight political points about housing, questions of work and employment, and state intervention in the lives of individuals.

Your tutors may suggest another style or genre for you to work in that is not listed here. For example, it may be that you want to work on a piece for a specific festival, such as a mystery play for performance at Easter. This would provide plenty of scope for working within a genre and would allow you to include all the art forms.

You'll notice that all of the examples so far assume that the piece has a single style that does not change during the course of the piece. However, it may be that your piece is **eclectic** – that is, it brings together a number of different styles. This is quite possible. The exam board states that this unit is intended to be **synoptic**, which means that it is intended to test your understanding of all the things that you have done throughout the whole course.

How can it genuinely sum up all the whole range of styles you have already studied? Think back to the different practitioners you studied in your AS course. You may have spent time learning how to realise drama in the style of Bertolt Brecht and compose songs in the style of George Gershwin. They appear to have very little in common at first, and you might wonder how you could use either in a piece. Obviously, you can't use work that you've already done before, but you can draw on the skills you have picked up on the performance studies course so far, to write new songs in a related style, or use a similar structure but adapt it for a new piece.

The most important thing is that your piece is coherent. This means two things:

> ➢ The work in each art form must be coherent: for example, don't mix styles in your drama – Stanislavski and Boal have different aims in creating drama, for example, and don't work well together.

> ➢ The overall piece must be coherent: for example, a piece that uses physical theatre techniques but where everyone breaks into song every few minutes is likely to be amusing or baffling for an audience.

Obviously, the style of the piece needs to be related to the content. Don't choose content that is likely to be undermined by the chosen genre. If your piece is about the life of an important war hero, then a piece of Commedia dell' Arte is likely to look like satire, and an audience might think you were not in support of the subject of the piece. On the other hand, a piece of epic theatre could heighten the sense of gravity of the piece.

Where are you going to perform it?

You'll find that within your area there are quite a few places where you could feasibly perform your piece. There are, however, some places where the exam board says you must not hold the performance. These are:

> ➢ Your own school or college

> ➢ Primary schools

> ➢ Senior citizens' homes.

Remember that the unit is called Community Performance Project. While schools and residential care homes do lie within your community, they provide what are essentially captive audiences, who are unlikely to be able to leave if they do not like the performance. In other words, there is no risk involved in giving the performance. Your performance must expose you to the risk that the audience could leave or express disapproval. Exposing yourself to this risk will provide you with a greater sense of satisfaction in a performance that successfully attracts and retains an audience.

Your tutors will be responsible for locating a suitable venue for the performance, but talk to them about the choice that is made. You can run through this list of questions with them to make sure that everyone is clear about the suitability of the venue:

> ➢ Is it appropriate to the style of the performance?

> ➢ Is it appropriate to the content of the performance?

> ➢ How local is it and can we get there easily?

> ➢ Will we have to pay to use it, and if so, who will pay?

> ➢ Is the venue keen for us to perform there?

> ➢ Are we able to get access to the venue for rehearsal purposes?

The content of the piece

> **Tip**
>
> Don't get too bogged down in local issues. You have to do research to inform your work and this will involve much historical exploration, but remember that your research is not a history exercise.

Risk

> **Tip**
>
> There may be other questions that you need to consider that are unique to your school or college. Try to answer them now rather than leaving things to later. It goes without saying that putting on a performance in the community needs much more planning than putting on a performance in your own theatre – so plan ahead.

- Is it possible for an audience to come to the venue on the day of the performance?
- Is the venue accessible for people with special mobility needs?
- Are there suitable facilities available – toilets and so on?
- Has a risk assessment been undertaken for the performance?
- Has the necessary paperwork been undertaken to allow you to work off-site as a group?
- Are the school management supportive of the project?

For whom is the performance intended?

The most important thing about your performance is that you actually manage to get an audience at all. This is part of the risk that we spoke about before – your performance might fail to attract anyone's interest or attention. This is always the greatest challenge for anyone devising a piece: has this piece got anything to say to an audience? A fundamental question you need to ask is: who is likely to want to watch our piece?

Let's ask some hard questions about targeting an audience for the performance:

The exam board states that 'a decision needs to be made early on in the work as to who should attend the performance, bearing in mind that in an open-air performance the audience may be anyone who is passing by and stops to watch'.

- When and where is the performance going to be held and will this affect who can attend?
- Who is the performance likely to appeal to?
- Is the appeal of the performance wide enough?
- How do you know that that your target audience wants to see this performance?
- How are you going to publicise and promote your performance?
- Is there a local group that has a particular interest in your piece and can help you to promote the performance?
- Will the audience be charged admission?

Remember also that you will need to make a video so you can watch the final performance when you come to write up your documentation.

How long will the piece last?

This question is easier to answer. The exam board states that the final piece should last for about 30 minutes. This length does not depend on the number of people in the group: the 30-minute rule applies whether you have three people or 30 people in your group.

Thirty minutes is quite a long time for a devised performance. You may have taken part in scripted performances – a school production, for example – in the past, but this is different, as in those cases you won't have had to devise your own material and you probably had a director. You'll have seen already that we think that every minute of performance you devise will take you about one hour's work, so you'll need to devise a rehearsal schedule to make sure that you allow 30 hours for the practical work. That is probably about 60 per cent of the time available for the unit (this will vary, depending on how the timetable is organised at your school or college). Allow approximately two or three weeks at the start of the unit to consider all of the things we've mentioned so far, and another two or three weeks at the end for you to complete the written commentary.

> **Tip**
>
> Agree on the production schedule with your tutors before you begin the practical work. As a group, commit to this schedule and agree how you will deal with any member of the group who turns out to be unreliable.

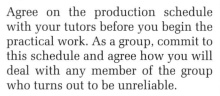

We've mentioned already that this unit is synoptic – it sums up all the things you've learned in the course. At AS, you learned about the performance process of improvising–rehearsing–performing. Don't forget that process now. In particular, allow plenty of time for your group to rehearse your piece – at least four or five full rehearsals before you perform. Also remember to include time for any technical rehearsal that you will need.

How many performers will there be?

This is quite a difficult question to answer. In some units, the exam board states exactly what the minimum and maximum group sizes should be. Here, however, the choice is yours. This may sound great if your class is a reasonably small size, but what happens if there are 15 people in your class? If you all work in the same group, it will be quite difficult for everyone to be fully involved, and – since the performance itself isn't being assessed – it doesn't seem quite fair that some people should have an easy ride and still be able to get the same (or better) marks at the end of the unit.

Our advice is to keep the groups fairly small. We recommend that you use the same group sizes as for the practical units – between three and seven people in each group. This may not work exactly for your class but it's a good guideline. That way, it should be possible for everyone to have a chance to take part, and everyone will feel that their decisions count in the final piece.

Finally, if you do have more than one group in your class, you don't all have to work on the same style, genre or content. If you do all do the same thing, check that your library has enough books for everyone to do the necessary reading. Most importantly, check that the venue is happy for more than one group to perform. If you're putting on a street performance, having different groups performing after one another can be a very good way of keeping an audience interested.

Assessment

You will be assessed on four elements when you come to submit your written commentary:

> **Knowledge and understanding of performance theory** (20%).
> Do you understand the style in which you were working?

> **Evaluation of the success of the performance process** (40%).
> Are you able to evaluate the performance process?

> **Evaluation of the success of the performance** (20%).
> Are you able to evaluate whether the final performance was faithful to the chosen style, and how effectively you used performance skills to convey it?

> **Quality of language** (20%).
> Do you express yourself in good written English?

Performance style and theory

Looking at the assessment headings, you'll see at once how important it is that you understand the style in which you're working – you need to be clear about this from the very start.

The performance process

Further reading

Look back at pages 14–17 of the *OCR AS Guide* if you need to refresh your memory of the performance process.

Remember: your tutor will make the final decision about which style you will work in, and it may be one not listed by the exam board.

Although only 20 per cent of the marks are for the discussion of style, if you're not clear about this, it will be very difficult to evaluate whether what you're doing is right or not. So let's look at the eight suggestions listed by the exam board.

We'll go through each of these options in turn, but remember that you only have to choose one of them, unless your piece is eclectic. For each style or genre, you'll need to consider a number of things:

> What is the **historical and social context** of this style?
> What are the **main features** of this style or genre?
> What are the **performance conventions** associated with it?
> What **opportunities** are there to work in this style?
> How could we **adapt** this style when we have chosen our content?

Obviously, there isn't space here for a lot of detail about these styles. Whichever style you choose, your tutors will give some taught sessions on it, and you will also need to read around and do some research to make sure you really understand what the style is all about.

Cabaret

Historical and social context

The setting of the show became as important as the context.

The origins of cabaret can be traced to 1878 when Emile Goudeau founded a club at *Le Sherry Cobbler* in Paris for a select group known as the Hydropathes. This involved small-scale entertainment, originally to an invited audience in an intimate setting. The name itself derives from the Spanish *caba retta*, which means merry bowl, and the French *cabaret*, which is a name for a tavern. The first 'public' cabaret was Le Chat Noir in Montmartre – an area of Paris associated with culture and entertainment – in November 1881. The style also developed in other European countries during the early 20th century, most notably in Germany in the 1920s and 1930s.

Main features

The style is a hybrid, bringing together both satirical and serious elements of performance. There are some similarities with the earlier styles of music hall and revue, both of which brought together song, dance, mime and comedy sketches, often within an overall subject or theme. The subject matter of individual numbers may be bawdy or irreverent. The music is an essential aspect of the style and is invariably supplied by a solo pianist or a small ensemble.

Performance conventions

The most distinctive aspect of a cabaret performance is the space in which it is performed, the number of people in the audience and the arrangement of this audience in relation to the performers. The setting for the performance is a social club of some description, often with a small stage for the performers, with a small audience seated at round tables scattered around the club. The performers may move between the audience or involve them as part of individual numbers within the show.

Opportunities to work in the style

There are lots of opportunities to work in this style. If you have a number of group members who are adept at writing songs, or devising popular dance, mime or satire, then this could be for you.

One of the strengths of cabaret is that it can bring together quite diverse styles within the overall context of entertainment. The theme could be adapted for local use. For example, a performance at a working men's club could be structured around a theme of 'work' or 'pensions' or a particular industry. Think creatively – it doesn't have to be heavy to make an impact. The real power of cabaret is the ability to entertain and make the audience think at the same time.

Adapting the style

If you have access to a community venue where you could invite a small audience of about 50 people, this could be ideal for you. The theme is less important than having a suitable venue for cabaret. Once you've read around the performance conventions, all you need to do is to see whether the subject matter you were thinking of would work in this style. Most political themes can work as pieces of satire within a cabaret setting. It's also possible that you plan an evening of cabaret where there is no overall theme, but simply a list of related entertainment (some serious, some slapstick), along the lines of the original French approach.

Commedia dell' Arte

Historical and social context

This genre originated in the northern part of Italy in the first half of the 16th century, and was very popular for about 200 years until the mid 18th century. Commedia dell' Arte literally means 'comedy of the professions' and was originally performed by the (then) new acting companies. It was hugely influential across Europe and was one of the direct predecessors of pantomime.

Main features

Commedia is an improvised style with wandering players performing comical and witty plays around a basic plot. The people in the plays were stock characters and the plots were also predetermined. Stock characters included Arlecchino, Colombina and Pantalone. A classic storyline involved a hero and heroine getting together to pledge undying love to each other. All of the tales involved farcical approaches to sex, greed or status. The originality of the performance depended on the way in which the players took on the stock characters and worked within the set storyline. The modern-day Punch and Judy show is effectively a derivation of the same style.

Performance conventions

The performances rely on physical presence, particularly the use of acrobatics and slapstick. Leather masks were generally used to convey expressions that could be easily seen by the audience. Commedia was originally performed on a portable stage or in the open air. One of its main strengths was the way it could be easily adapted to virtually any performance space.

Opportunities to work in the style

This style works extremely well outdoors, as it involves physical gesture, use of space and a strong visual element as well as dialogue. It allows serious subjects to be presented in a comic or satirical manner, and it would be easy to adapt the stock characters to fit the people in a completely different story.

Adapting the style

If you were thinking of an outdoor performance, Commedia is an ideal vehicle. The subject matter is easily adaptable if you want the audience to respond to the visual and the physical rather than to dialogue and characterisation. Some of the stock scenarios would probably fit some true stories of intrigue, lust or murder, and it would be straightforward to adapt a historical story to a Commedia performance. If you are trying to offer a serious, naturalistic interpretation of a scenario, Commedia is *not* the best choice.

Folk music and dance

Historical and social context

A specific historical or social context can't really be pinned down, as all countries have folk traditions. You could take a folk story as the basis of the content of your performance and create relevant music and dance in an appropriate folk style.

Main features

Features vary enormously from tradition to tradition. The main feature of folk art is that it is specific to a local community and passed on from person to person rather than written down. This obviously presents you with something of a challenge, since you will need to be able to find folk music or folk stories that have been collected and written down by someone, or dances that have been filmed and performed by someone. There are specific British folk genres such as mummers' plays or morris dancing that could provide you with something specific to imitate.

For more on mummers' or mumming plays, see pages 27–28.

Performance conventions

Folk material is generated by a local community and normally performed in that community. This might involve village halls, parish halls, public houses, inns and taverns. In Britain, the material often dates back to before the industrial revolution and comes from a society that is both rural and very local. Standards of performance are 'down to earth' – often raw or raucous. This style is a good way for a local community to express its common heritage.

Opportunities to work in the style

If you are looking for a genuine community piece, this style has all of the elements you could wish for, as long as you are able to identify a local story (either something historical, or a folk story or legend) and work equally well with both folk music and folk dance. There is flexibility here as the folk traditions could be drawn from other parts of the UK. Given that you will be devising the dance and/or music to fit the story, you should try to identify generic features of both, based on a study of several examples.

Adapting the style

If your piece is to be performed in a community venue where there is likely to be a genuinely local audience, this could be an ideal approach. It is likely that the audience will be well informed of the content of your piece and you will thus have to ensure that it is authentic, as well as taking a consistent approach to the style of dance, drama and music.

Pantomime

Historical and social context

Although it is generally thought of as an English art form, pantomime is a direct descendant of the Italian Commedia dell' Arte with its stock characters and situations. It is possible to trace the development of the characters from Commedia into pantomime characters – in particular Harlequin, Pantaloon and Colombine. It was not originally the family entertainment it has become today.

Nineteenth-century English pantomime developed a number of traditions: performances tended to be at Christmas or Easter; the dame role emerged; gradually stock dialogue between audience and performers became commonplace ('Oh no you didn't', 'He's behind you', and so on). The essential style involves slapstick comedy, exaggeration of gesture and dialogue, and overly extravagant make-up, costume and sets.

Main features

The central story tends to be a fairy tale such as *Cinderella*, *Puss-in-Boots* or *Little Red Riding Hood*. Within the story, there is ample opportunity for singing, dancing, comedy and audience interaction. Performances are normally given on a proscenium-arch stage with a strong element of projection and exaggeration.

Performance conventions

There are plenty of opportunities, especially if your performance is likely to be around Christmas or Easter. You can still put on a pantomime, however, even if this is not the case. A summer pantomime would be acceptable as long as you demonstrated your awareness of how this differed from the usual conventions of the genre.

Opportunities to work in the style

You could take a story or situation from your local community and set it as a pantomime. Remember that, as with Commedia dell' Arte, you could use the style to satirise a political or social situation. You could also consider doing an adult pantomime – the genre wasn't originally intended to be just for children.

Adapting the style

A successful pantomime is entertaining for all the family. The challenge in scriptwriting is making jokes that will work on at least two levels – for children and adults. You can have a lot of fun writing such a script.

Pageant

Pageants are essentially processions organised to demonstrate a community coming together for a particular occasion. Examples include celebrations that are religious or military, carnivals, or an anniversary of a particular event. The tradition of pageantry itself is ancient and dates back to Roman times. These pageants were sometimes adapted for use by the Roman Catholic church: for example, the carnival in Nice in southern France precedes the start of Lent but can be traced back to pagan feasts such as the Saturnalia, the Lupercalia and the Bacchanalia.

Historical and social context

In Britain, elements of pageantry have waned in the 20th century, but have included Sunday school anniversaries, churches celebrating the feast day of their patron saint, carnival processions with floats and marching bands, political and protest marches, and state occasions (including state weddings).

Main features

The Notting Hill carnival in London is a good example.

A pageant is normally associated with celebrations, using the arts in procession, and as a public proclamation of the cause behind the procession. The pageant is not static – it involves moving the procession between two given points with an audience of bystanders who will only see a few moments of each of the aspects of the procession. The performance itself may involve music, dance, circus arts and spectacle.

Performance conventions

You may be able to find a community group which celebrates an anniversary with some sort of street procession. This might be a church, the Women's Institute, a group concerned with political campaigning (such as CND or Amnesty International). You would

Opportunities to work in the style

need to be certain that everyone in your group was happy to perform for that particular audience. Closing a street for this sort of event can be complex so your school or college must ensure all the legal requirements are attended to.

Adapting the style

You need to ensure that there is a clear reason for holding the pageant, that it is related to the community in which you wish to perform and that, as a group, you have the necessary skills to perform in a procession. You could, for example, organise a pageant for St George's Day (with a ritual slaying of the dragon) or for St Andrew's, St David's or St Patrick's day.

Performance art

Historical and social context

Performance art is a more recent style that developed in the USA in the 1960s, and is associated with the work of such practitioners as Laurie Anderson, George Brecht and Meredith Monk, the 7:84 Theatre Company, and – to some extent – composers such as Philip Glass.

Main features

The style is difficult to define, as it is basically postmodern and therefore eclectic. The Tate Gallery website defines performance art as: 'Art in which the medium is the artist's own body and the artwork takes the form of actions performed by the artist. Performance art has origins in Futurism and Dada, but became a major phenomenon in the 1960s and 1970s and can be seen as a branch of Conceptual art.'

Performance conventions

The conventions may be seen in installations that involve static exhibitions incorporating live elements. The 1960s saw an outbreak of 'Happenings' in which local community arts were very informal and improvised. These would involve a range of avant-garde and experimental artists.

Opportunities to work in the style

If you have an art gallery in your area with a collection of modern art, there may be scope to organise performance work in the gallery, particularly its public areas.

Adapting the style

The style would work extremely well for an abstract piece or for one interpreting a painting or a sculpture.

Melodrama

Historical and social context

Melodrama can be traced back to France in the 1760s. Thomas Holcroft established the new genre in England in the early 1800s.

Main features

Melodrama is a sentimental genre that plays on stock characters and stereotypical situations. The plots are generally far fetched and centre on the changing fortunes of the hero or heroine normally at the hands of a villain. As with other styles, there are certain stock characters. These include the hero, the selfless heroine and the ruthless villain. There is invariably a sentimental tugging of the heartstrings for the heroine, but usually with a happy ending, the villain getting his comeuppance and virtue triumphing.

Performance conventions

The focus of the style is on exaggeration. There is little character development and the focus is on astounding events and stunning staging.

A community show could recreate a melodrama in the style of *Murder in the Red Barn* or *London by Night*. There is considerable potential for retelling a local gruesome story in the style of a melodrama.

Opportunities to work in the style

The style depends on one-dimensional characters and you need to make sure that there is sufficient scope for a balance between art forms in the piece you devise. Choice of music (or composition of new music) is an important part of the devising process.

Adapting the style

Street theatre

Street theatre can be traced back to medieval Europe and may be seen in organised events such as mystery plays and local church celebrations. It is a popular form, in the sense of being 'of the people', and was a way in which communities could be brought together. The modern equivalent is the community play.

Historical and social context

There are a number of potential hazards in working outdoors. It can be difficult to get an audience to stand and watch, the weather in the UK is unpredictable and often inclement, and the human voice does not project well in the open air. Techniques of street theatre, therefore – like Commedia dell' Arte – depend on physical and visual aspects of performance rather than dialogue.

Main features

Street theatre generally depends on short, powerful scenes in which an audience is constantly kept watching. The episodes have considerable physical movement and interaction between performers. There is also an emphasis on physical gestures and loud vocal projection.

Performance conventions

Virtually every town, city or village has a public space near the shopping centre that could be used for a piece of street theatre. Remember though that you will need an entertainment licence to perform in public. It can be obtained from the local council and costs money. Plan well ahead and do your research or you might find yourself with nowhere to perform.

Opportunities to work in the style

You'll need to make sure that you have a good story that will mean something to local people. You must keep it moving, action-packed and entertaining. This is no place for the meaningful stares of television drama.

Adapting the style

Eclectic pieces

You'll have gathered from this that it is best if your piece is conceived within a defined genre, but it may be that it has some diversity in terms of style. In this case, you must ensure that you are able to identify coherent elements of style and the aspects that contribute to this diversity. You must be very careful indeed when you write up your written commentary that the reader is not left with the impression that you had little idea about the style(s) in which you were working. This will almost certainly mean that you will not be able to evaluate effectively whether or not you were successful in achieving your stylistic goals.

Choosing a stimulus

The choice of what the piece is to be 'about' is almost as important as the style in which you work. Remember that the piece has to be performed within your local community and there will be differing opinions within your performance group as to where or what your community actually is. For example, if you live within 30 miles of London, how do you decide that one part of London is your community while another isn't? If you live in the West Midlands, do you have to make an effort to perform in the centre of Birmingham?

The answer to questions like this is: **keep the performance as local as you can**. There is no shortage of material in your area, as we shall see. Your community is the place where people will understand what you are trying to do and recognise you as fellow locals. There is no point in travelling huge distances to perform the piece, especially as this almost certainly means that you will not have access to the performance space to rehearse. Consequently, you should choose stimulus material that is genuinely local, even if the material itself doesn't seem particularly earth-shattering.

 The exam board gives some examples of the type of things you might look at. In summary, these are:

➢ Historical situations or events
➢ Legends and myths
➢ Site-specific performances
➢ The life and work of a local figure.

You'll see that some of these (the first, second and last) rely on stories of some description and one of them (the third) is more concerned with performances that are closely related to the nature of the performance venue. In reality, there is likely to be some overlap between these four categories. For example, you might choose a local figure but decide to perform the piece in a venue where they lived or worked. Or you might take a local event as your subject and decide to perform it in the area where it took place. A performance in an art gallery might centre on one or more of the pictures in the collection. We suggest that you think about the performance space at the same time as you decide on the content, as the two could well be related.

As we have already said, the content of the piece is entirely up to you. Beware of going for the obvious – if you live in Nottingham, for example, doing a piece about Robin Hood might be seen as a safe option and your potential audience might have seen other pieces on the same theme before.

Before you make any final decisions, think through these questions about your local community:

➢ What potential performance places are there, either open-air (market place, park, playground, pedestrianised street, town square) or indoors (village hall, art gallery, museum, church, castle, monument, places where famous people lived, shopping centres, town hall, stately home)?

Actually, style and content go hand in hand, but we've focused on the style first to help you get the content in perspective. Otherwise you might find that you simply do a piece about someone or something without being really sure in which style you are trying to work.

Tip
Consider the locality of your school or college rather than your own home.

The categories here are optional. You're welcome to do something different if you have an exciting new idea.

Remember that there are no marks for the content of the piece: it's what you do with the content that matters.

Thinking through the options

➢ What geographical definition will you give to your community (village, town, suburb, city, region)?

➢ What do you know about the history of your community?

➢ What significant events have taken place there over the years?

➢ Are any local myths or legends associated with your area?

As we have said, the suggestions from the exam board are not compulsory, but they are fairly wide-ranging and most students decide to do one of them. Let's think about the possibilities of each of the suggestions. Even if you don't like them, it might set you thinking about something else that you *are* inspired by.

Historical situations or events

Historical situations are the most popular option with candidates for this unit. The reasons for this are fairly obvious: they can provide you with a ready-made story, with characters, plot and situation all in place. There will almost certainly be something that has happened in your area that can become the basis of a performance piece.

Most of us don't actually know very much about our local area. Perhaps one or two famous people have lived in your area; perhaps there's a beautiful building nearby that has an interesting history. There might even be a few houses in the area that have blue circular plaques showing that someone important was born there. The sort of history we're talking about is local history, not the history of Britain. It may well be that something of national importance *has* happened in your area. But wherever you live, you can find an example of something that has made an impact locally. Remember that people are already likely to be familiar with a local event or place that has national significance, and you may find that a lesser-known event attracts greater audience interest. Avoid the temptation to give some sort of national significance to a local event: this risks seeming ridiculous and is unnecessary. It is the connection to the local community that is important.

Once you've decided on an appropriate event, you need to know the details of it. You don't need to use all of these details in your final performance, however. You can also take some liberties with the storyline. You'll find that most local historians and museums are concerned with complete historical accuracy in their work. You can be flexible with some of the details to make it suit your performance. Your piece needs to be **authentic** (recognisable by a local audience) but not necessarily entirely factually **accurate**. You can omit sections of the story, expand the number of characters, create dialogue and choose an appropriate setting.

Most importantly, you need to work in **at least two art forms**. This can be difficult with a historical piece as you might end up just creating a piece of drama. Simply inserting a song or a dance into that sort of piece can look very strange and might even appear comical to your audience. We recommend that you start with either dance or music when you begin working on your piece. That way you can avoid the temptation simply to produce a piece of narrative drama.

Tip

Make sure that you keep detailed notes about your discussions so that you have some record on which to base your written commentary. Don't assume that you'll remember something and later find that the memory has faded.

If you happen to live in Hastings (the Battle of Hastings), Canterbury (the murder of Thomas à Beckett), Plymouth (Drake and the Armada) or other ancient cities of Britain, you can probably find examples of historical events that changed the course of the nation's history. A historical situation doesn't have to be of national importance. The local market square that was once notorious for cock fighting before its prohibition could be the basis of a good piece.

Further study

There are lots of local history societies scattered across the UK. Most museums have education officers or departments. Why not contact them to discuss the options available to you? They might also allow you to perform in a venue they own.

Tip

Don't twist the story out of recognition. You can adapt some of the minor details to fit your resources and performance intention, but don't force it simply in order to make it fit a specific style.

Legends and myths

While there are some similarities between these and historical situations, you may find that legends and myths offer you more flexibility because they are not historically true. You could base your piece on aspects of the myth and adapt other features of the performance to fit in with this. You will almost certainly find different versions of the story around, and some of these versions may contradict one another – that doesn't matter. All you have to do as a group is agree on a version of the legend or myth that suits your purposes: decide which details you want to keep and which to omit as you bring the different versions together.

Of course, if there is only one version, you can still make these sorts of decisions about the performance.

One real advantage of legends and myths is that they lend themselves to using all of the art forms imaginatively. Because there is often an element of the mysterious to the storyline, you can heighten this by the creative use of dance and music.

You'll also find that many myths or legends are associated with particular places, so it could be that in identifying the story, you have also identified the performance venue.

The life and work of a local figure

It's unlikely you'll have much difficulty identifying a local figure on whom you could base your piece. It's better if there is some historical perspective to what you are doing – it's best to avoid media stars, singers or TV personalities who come from your area. We talked about accuracy and authenticity in the section above on historical situations and events. The same issues apply if you decide to produce a piece about a local figure. Your piece needs to be authentic enough to be recognised by an audience, but you don't need to get bogged down in every detail of historical accuracy.

You also need to make sure that you don't create a piece whereby one person has a leading role while everyone else has a walk-on part. This is a real danger if your group is predominantly female and the historical character you choose is male, or vice versa.

Finally, we've already made the point about balancing the art forms. Don't start by creating a historical narrative. Think about episodes in the life of this person that lend themselves to dance or music and **start with these first**. Construct the drama around these episodes rather than trying to insert dance and music afterwards.

Site-specific performances

Community performances are likely to be site-specific if you decide to perform at a venue related to the content of the piece. However, if your performance is in a village or church hall in your local community, there may not be an exact correlation between the content and style of the piece, and where it is performed.

Think about...

You've already thought carefully about the performance style. Is there a place that particularly suits that style? What content could it be applied to?

In some performances, there is a direct relationship between the performance style, the performance content and the performance space. If you can bring these together, you will have the best chance of producing an excellent piece of performance work, and – more importantly – a very good written commentary.

 What sort of examples are there of this type of piece? The exam board gives two examples:

➤ A performance in a local building that explores its development through the ages

➤ A performance in an art gallery that interprets a collection of paintings.

You could also consider a piece of street performance in a place relevant to the content of the piece. For example, an ancient tavern used by smugglers with lots of nooks and crannies and different levels could become an excellent venue for a physical performance piece. Why not see if the landlord of the pub would be interested in a themed night in which your group performs?

You may find that the local council will allow you to perform in civic buildings to celebrate the achievements of a local politician. You could use the features of the building to accentuate the style of the piece and perhaps also involve the audience. You might even get permission to use the council chamber itself.

As with the other examples, you need to make sure that your piece does not turn into narrative drama or a soap opera. Everyone in the group should perform in at least two art forms, and, as you're not being assessed on your skills, it would be best if everyone performed in all three. The performing arts work best when they are all brought together, so don't ignore one of the art forms, even if you're not feeling too confident about your ability in it.

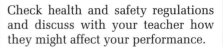

Tip
Check health and safety regulations and discuss with your teacher how they might affect your performance.

Tip
Don't fall into the trap of thinking that using pre-existing songs counts for the music element. Creating dance moves to existing music counts as devising in a single art form, not two. Also remember that lyrics do not count as music unless you are discussing how they affect the melodic line, influence the choice of harmony or affect the composition of a song.

Choosing a community venue

You will have given some thought to venue while you have been considering the style and content of the piece, since the three often tie together; you now need to finalise where you intend to perform your piece. One of the most important decisions you need to make early on is whether you intend to perform indoors or outdoors.

Indoor performances	**Outdoor performances**
(Art gallery, museum, church, castle, monument, places where famous people lived, public house, shopping centres, town hall, stately home, swimming baths, village hall, and so on)	(Airport, beach, botanical gardens, car park, market place, park, pier, playground, pedestrianised street, precinct, railway station, town square, zoo, and so on)
Defined performance space	Flexible performance space
Audience remains in defined area in relation to performers	Audience may move around
Audience stays for the whole performance	Audience is likely to walk off after a very short time and therefore piece needs interest, variety and spectacle to be able to retain interest
Audience is generally seated and comfortable	Audience is likely to be naturally restless
Performance space helps performers to project sound	Sound travels poorly in the open air, especially in windy conditions
Performance space has electricity and props may be available	Performance cannot rely on props or lighting
The performers and audience are protected from the weather	In the UK, there is a constant risk of bad weather affecting the performance

You need to be absolutely clear why you are making certain choices – there's no point doing something just for novelty value. Make sure it's got a clear relationship to the style and content of the piece.

The content of the piece

Relationship to style of piece

You'll see from the list of examples that there are almost endless possibilities in terms of performance spaces, many of which you might never have thought of. The more creative you can be, the more potential there is for a really exciting piece. Think about the following aspects of the performance and how they relate to your choice.

If you've chosen to base your piece on a historical event or a local historical figure, it is possible that the location of the event (or where the person lived) is quite near to your school or college. In that case, you should certainly consider that place as a suitable performance venue. For example, if the birthplace of the person you have chosen has an accessible space, you may wish to consider performing there. Similarly, if you were performing a piece about a plague that swept your town, you might want to perform near the town walls as a symbol of keeping the plague out.

It's quite possible that you might want to incorporate things from the performance space into the performance. The best example of this would be if you wanted to use a collection of paintings by a local artist (displayed in your local gallery) as the basis of an abstract piece of performance art. You could seek the gallery's permission to hold the performance in that space and incorporate one or more of the pictures within the performance area. Obviously you would need to take maximum care to ensure that nothing was damaged.

If you live in a seaside town where there is a pier, there is enormous scope for performance on the pier itself – the pier's distinctive layout, with lots of long open space, could lend itself to an interesting piece.

Another possibility is that you use a display or exhibit in your local museum as part of the performance. For example, you might wish to take an aspect of the industrial heritage of your area and create a piece based on it. There might be artefacts or exhibits within the museum that you could gain permission to use. Often, museum exhibits are less fragile than works of art and may be easier to incorporate into a piece.

Natural properties of the space

All performance styles make physical demands on performers and you need to make sure that the space you are considering has enough space for you to perform it successfully. If your piece is likely to involve considerable amounts of dance (and remember what we have said about including all the art forms) you may need to avoid restricted spaces. Holding a performance in the small cottage where someone famous was born may be less suitable than performing in the round outside. You also need to consider the audience's sight lines – if most people cannot see what is going on, they will quickly lose interest and, in the case of an outdoor performance, will be likely to wander off.

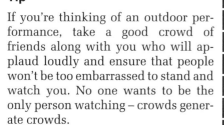

Tip

If you're thinking of an outdoor performance, take a good crowd of friends along with you who will applaud loudly and ensure that people won't be too embarrassed to stand and watch you. No one wants to be the only person watching – crowds generate crowds.

Many possible performance venues have interesting levels – balconies, galleries, staircases, cellars, crypts – that could allow you to create some very effective contrasts. You don't have to use the same space for the whole of the performance. An outdoor performance particularly will benefit from plenty of movement and varied use of space to keep the audience's interest.

Most community venues that we have identified will have fairly limited support available for your performance. In the case of an outdoor performance, you need to devise the performance assuming that almost nothing is available. If there is to be dialogue in your piece, make sure that you are disciplined and keep it powerful – everyone in the group will certainly need to practise their projection, as voices do not carry well in the open air.

In the case of a Commedia dell' Arte performance, you may need to obtain or make appropriate masks, and remember that the nature of the performance relies heavily on physical, slapstick performance. Make sure there is plenty of music and dance in all outdoor performances – audiences are more attracted by a spectacle than by watching a narrative drama.

Whatever your ideas, don't choose a space that has no relationship to the style and content of your piece. Make sure that your ideas are joined up. Don't choose to perform at an art gallery simply because there is a brand-new one in the centre of your town – make sure there is a valid reason for deciding to perform there.

Don't forget to make a video recording of the performance. If you're performing outside you need to be careful about including the audience, as it's illegal to film people without their being aware of it.

When it comes to devising the piece, you will be drawing on all the skills you picked up during the AS course, especially in the Language of Performing Arts unit. Read the chapter on that unit in the AS companion to this guide to refresh your memory on how to approach devising in the three art forms.

Over the following pages, we are going to look at three separate case studies that are intended to give you some ideas about the variety of approaches that can be taken to this unit, and how other groups have developed a piece from their original stimulus. These case studies are all based around venues in the south of England, but there are plenty of similar places elsewhere in the UK: use these as inspiration and find out what's in your local area.

Projection and impact

> **Tip**
>
> In an outdoor performance, keep the dialogue punchy and short. People may not hear lengthy speeches. Also make sure you have a contingency plan in case of bad weather. Will you carry on performing regardless? Will you be able to move under cover?

Finally ...

In these case studies, our intention is to illustrate clearly to you what each group did and consequently we have included a lot of descriptive narrative that would not be appropriate in an actual written commentary. The exam board warns that you should avoid adopting a narrative style in your written work. See the sample written commentary on pages 43–49.

Case study one: Hampton Court Palace

The teachers at the school in question had experience of devising mummers' plays and felt that this would be an ideal folk tradition that might be performed at an open-air venue. This fitted in neatly with a nearby potential performance venue: Hampton Court Palace and grounds on the outskirts of London, which offered a wide variety of possibilities for performance-based work.

All the groups looked at mumming and decided to carry out more research. They discovered the following facts on internet sites:

➢ Mumming is a tradition within England that identifies a particular community.

➢ Mumming asks whether we belong to the same community – are we inside or outside the community?

Style

➢ Traditionally a mumming troupe was all-male, comprising local men who blackened their faces with soot. They would rehearse in secret and pass on stories orally.

➢ Many of the feast days associated with the presentation of mumming plays were celebrated by the Christian church. There would be an elaborate service and the scriptures would be acted out so that the congregation could understand.

➢ The acting would use stylised gestures in short mimes.

➢ The plays seemed to have evolved from a ceremony connected with the spring festivals, which celebrated the passing of winter and the birth of spring. They are also associated with Christmas and other Christian and pagan festivals.

➢ The mummers would stage a perambulatory piece that provided a prologue explaining what was to come and helped clear the performance space, so that the audience was prepared for some entertainment. There would also have been an epilogue in which the group collected a reward for their efforts. Traditionally, in small villages, the mummers would be dressed as strangers, but the audience would know them as part of the village community.

➢ There would be a functional storyteller who transported the audience to a time, location or event, and therefore set the scene. Mumming plays aimed to address the emotional, social or political needs of the community. They were often staged in order to make something happen in the short term and has a moral message.

The group began to see how a piece based on Hampton Court could fit in with this style. There were plenty of important national events associated with the palace, but the group had read in the local paper about the increased entrance fees and the introduction of a charge to look round the gardens. They felt too that the charges for the carpark, and for music, dance and drama events were rather high. The prices might be acceptable to tourists, but they felt that for the local community, who bore the brunt of the increased traffic, there was little benefit. The group decided to raise this issue on behalf of the local community, who until the summer of 2004, had been able to walk in the gardens for free – something which many did on a weekly or even daily basis. The mummers' play would thus have a political message, but would use gentle entertainment and comedy to make its point. They decided to weave this message into the play.

Stimulus   Although the mummers' play style had been chosen, there was plenty of potential for groups to adapt the content to fit the style and the venue. For example, students interested in politics might choose to look at the relationship between the cardinals. The life and times of the monarch might appeal to those interested in history, and there are many aspects of Henry VIII's life that could be incorporated, such as his six marriages, or his relationship with the Catholic Church and consequent founding of the Church of England. The palace itself has a varied history with a variety of people living there. The extensive gardens with their riverside location and maze could also be used within the performance.

The group started by visiting the palace and looking at the interior and exterior aspects of the site. They discovered the main drawback of the palace as a venue very early on: entrance prices are high, security is very tight and the chance of performing within the palace grounds seemed small. However, photographs could be taken in the gardens and these could be used as a backdrop for a performance. The group discovered that they could buy a licence to perform in the field opposite the palace for £100.

The group decided to carry out more research into the palace and its history in order to find an aspect that could provide the basis for a piece. Hampton Court shop had a few helpful books. One of them was entitled *Strange Tales of Hampton Court* and contained a few unusual stories about the palace. The group therefore decided to use some of these in their piece, such as the bed-making ritual, the Cardinal Spider and the 'crestfallen A entwined with H symbols'.

The storyteller would be a character who had worked at the palace all his life and witnessed the changes there. The group decided that this would be the head gardener. He could be dressed in a modern-day outfit, holding a garden fork in one hand, and wearing a gardening apron with various plants sticking out of the pockets. He would deliver the prologue and epilogue, and would start the proceedings by narrating the first scene, entitled 'Bedmaking for Kings'. This was designed to grab the attention of passers-by and make them laugh.

Cardinal Wolsey, Archbishop of York and Lord Chancellor of England, who owned Hampton Court before giving it to Henry VIII, drew up regulations for the royal household in 1525, which included the strict rules for the making of the king's bed. It was an elaborate ritual, as Sheila Dunn explains in *Strange Tales of Hampton Court*:

> It began with a groom summoning four Yeomen of the Wardrobe. They brought in the bedclothes, four Yeomen of the Bedchamber and a Gentleman Usher. Four of the Yeomen stood on one side of the royal bed and four on the other. The Groom stood at the foot holding a lighted torch. In charge of the proceedings was the Gentleman Usher, who stood apart from the others and shouted commands. One Yeoman prodded the straw with a dagger to determine that 'there was no untruth therein' – anything live and dangerous. Next, the feather bed was placed in position and another Yeoman tumbled over it 'for the search thereof' – in case there was an object concealed there. On the word of command, the sheets and blankets were solemnly laid one by one by all eight Yeomen, taking care that all points touched at the same time. At the end of the ritual each made the sign of the cross and kissed the places he had touched. The Groom remained 'until the King felt disposed to go to bed'.

The group used this excerpt as stage directions. They cast the characters and began improvising the movements while the head gardener told the tale and the gentleman usher yelled out instructions. It was decided that this ritual could be repeated in an edited form as a leitmotif throughout the play each time Henry VIII remarried and had another wife to take to bed. This way, the groom would never leave the bedchamber and this could be turned into a running gag.

Venue

Posters could be put in shop windows to advertise the performance, raising awareness locally and bringing an audience. Performing on a day when there was an event on at the palace would also guarantee passers-by who might stop to watch the entertainment.

Researching the content

Further reading

Strange Tales of Hampton Court by Sheila Dunn and Ken Wilson (Lanthorn 1985).

Structuring the content

Tip

Don't assume that storytelling is the same as drama – you can tell stories or narrate through song and dance as well.

The scene gave rise to much physical theatre as the performers exaggerated their movements and at times got carried away – for example, in the kissing section lewd thoughts came into the mind of one yeoman and he began to imagine he was with a young lady, only to be stopped by another yeoman just before the gentleman usher saw him. The head gardener named all the characters by their function, which also increased the sense of merriment, as the passers-by found the entire ceremony completely ridiculous but very much in keeping with the character of the king.

Using all the art forms

The song *Greensleeves* has a simple modal structure and this was used as the basis for the melody that the group composed.

Eventually the narration by the head gardener and the yelling of instructions by the gentleman usher were turned into lyrics for the basis of a song accompanied by an acoustic guitar. As the song *Greensleeves* is heavily associated with Henry VIII, the group decided it would be a good piece to take as inspiration. The musicians in the group played around with the basic melody and added their own sections, while still returning to the melody at various points in the song so that the audience could recognise it. To make it more humorous, Henry wore a green-sleeved gown each time he returned to the bedchamber with yet another new wife.

Another story that intrigued the group was that of the Cardinal Spider, which was named after Cardinal Wolsey. They decided to insert this story in to the re-enactment of a Tudor banquet, which included a jester, lots of acrobatics and Tudor dancing. They took the following lines from the book and used them as a refrain in a song: 'If you wish to live and thrive/ let the spider run alive.'

All kinds of special powers were attributed to spiders at that time. They were thought to be wise and be able to heal. To see a spider was a good omen, so if one turned up at a banquet given by Cardinal Wolsey, it would have been welcomed as a guest.

The group used the Cardinal Spider to make the point that if the spider was allowed to run free in the halls and gardens, then why should the local people have to pay to walk around the gardens, which for years had been shared between the residents of the palace and the local community during daylight hours. Since mummers' plays were often used to make a political point, it was felt by the group that this was an excellent opportunity – especially as the group had to find a venue they could afford to use. The group had studied ground bass in the Language of Performing Arts unit at AS, and they used this to start their composition. They looked at the work of Henry Purcell, such as *Dido and Aeneas*, and were able to use the idea of a ground bass as a recurring structure in their music. This helped to reinforce the idea of people walking around the gardens. It also reinforced the perambulatory nature of a mummers' play.

The banquet/spider scene gave the dancers in the group a chance to experiment with choreography for a courtly dance based on the research they had undertaken. The group watched the 1968 film *Romeo and Juliet* directed by Franco Zeffirelli, taking particular notice of the dance scenes. Intimate relationships between characters are shown through proxemics – physical contact through the touching and cupping of hands, the constant eye contact, moving closer towards each other and the linking of arms. These gestures and movements combine to give the impression of two bodies intertwining and becoming one. Several couples perform the dance while music is played on the guitar.

Another feature of the palace that tourists often find interesting is the Royal Tennis Court and the rules of the game played here. Henry VIII built the first indoor tennis court in England and the group made an allusion to this by having Henry enter stage sporting a racquet. This was performed in the style of mime with some exaggerated gestures mimicking the playing of tennis. In same way, the maze was referred to when a character was noted absent and another replied that he was lost in the maze again.

The group performed well with few problems. Many aspects of the mummers' style were evident in the piece, including the storyteller, stylised gesture, mime, the inclusion of a prologue and an epilogue, and the holding of the performance on a religious festival (the Whitsuntide bank holiday in May). The group all included these aspects in their documentation to indicate the importance of the style of their piece and how effectively they had incorporated it.

The weather was warm and there was no wind, which made vocal delivery easier for the performers. The stage was set clearly – although in a large car park on a field, the group had picked their spot carefully. They observed where the visitors to the palace walked once they had parked their cars and realised that they all converged on a path opposite a zebra crossing. There was enough space just before the field met the road, and the group set up there. The stage was marked out by a few bales of hay set out in a circular pattern.

The group gave three performances of the piece at scheduled times throughout the afternoon, in the hope of catching more audience. A few blankets were placed on the ground for people to sit on, and this encouraged others to stop and watch. Invited guests watched the whole performance while passers-by mostly stopped and watched scenes. A few people came for the entire production as they had seen the posters in the local shops. Others had read the board placed near the edge of the set stating the performance times.

'Royal' or 'real' tennis has different rules from lawn tennis.

The performance

> **Tip**
> Don't be taken in by the fact that we haven't mentioned rehearsal techniques. They are just as important here as they are in any other piece.

Case study two: Life in Art

Style

The staff at the college had close links with the Riverhouse in Walton-on-Thames, Surrey. They had decided before the unit began that this would be a suitable venue for a community performance and considered carefully the style that they wanted their groups to work in.

The teachers decided that the most useful approach for the students was to base the whole piece on episodic structure. It was agreed at the outset that the final piece should consist of six contrasting episodes.

The groups had all studied Brecht at AS, and some had worked on Bruce. The idea of creative episodic work seemed perfectly suited to work in a gallery containing a collection of pictures. At the same time, the students were told about the stimulus, and their teacher spent some lessons looking at episodic structures and how they might be used in the piece. They did some further work on plays they hadn't studied at AS, and made lots of notes about ways of creating episodic pieces. There was a long discussion about epic theatre in one early lesson, but the teacher and the group decided to keep the focus entirely on episodic structures, rather than a broader focus on epic theatre. They looked back over the reviews that they had written of live performance work and discussed which styles might be appropriate to incorporate, bearing in mind that their piece had to integrate the three art forms.

Stimulus

Web link

www.riverhousebarn.co.uk

The stimulus for this piece was an exhibition entitled 'Life in Art' by Steve Pyke, held at the Robert Phillips Gallery, part of the Riverhouse in Walton-on-Thames, Surrey. Life in Art consisted of a series of 60 photographs and showed artists over the age of 50 working in the southeast of England. The photographs showed a portrait of each artist, their art and their place of work, whether it be a painter's studio or an ironmonger's workshop.

There was a useful book accompanying the exhibition that included interviews with each of the artists. Each interview was like a mini-narrative, giving clues about the artist and their life. The group realised that there was a wealth of material in the exhibition, and that one of the problems for them would be scaling it down. There were around 27 artists involved and each had several photographs of their diverse work. It was difficult at first to take in all the detail of each photograph and the group had to spend a long time at the exhibition just looking at the photographs and absorbing what they could. The more the group looked at the exhibition, the more they could see possibilities for developing different 'episodes' for each piece. They felt that trying to cover all the artists would result in a piece that had little depth, so they began to think about which artists seemed to offer the most potential.

Venue

The Riverhouse was built as a barn in the 18th century, but by the 1980s it was simply being used to house lawnmowers belonging to the local council. When the building was no longer needed, a group of local people took on the job of turning it into a theatre space. There is now a small theatre on the ground floor that can seat a maximum of 60 people, as well as a restaurant and bar open to the public. Outside there is a courtyard with statues, sculptures and other art works on exhibition, and there is a newly built craft studio attached to the barn. Riverhouse has hosted a variety of events over the years, including pieces by Matthew Bourne's Adventures in Motion Pictures.

The Robert Phillips Gallery has exhibitions throughout the year, and it seemed like an ideal starting point for the group. The group would perform their piece in the theatre area in October. Riverhouse has an established database of people who visit exhibitions and attend events such as plays and jazz concerts. There is also a brochure that goes out regularly to those on the mailing list, as well as local libraries, schools and colleges. This would help to publicise the production and provide an audience. Selling tickets through the Riverhouse box office would make the production seem more professional and help raise enough money to cover the cost of hiring the theatre for a day.

Back at college, using the catalogue of the exhibition and the Internet, members of the group researched two or three artists each and then presented their findings to the group as a whole. This helped to share the workload, get everyone engaged in the project and promoted a discussion concerning the rejection and selection of material.

There were five artists on whom they decided to focus: Harold Chapman, whose work includes a number of clocks; Hamish Black, whose photographs recorded walks that he had designed, including a long walk that had to be executed walking backwards; Angela Braven, whose work was exceptionally colourful and included a photograph of her wearing a feather mask; Richard Quinnell, who made metal sculptures; Ralph Steadman for his clock with the words 'never mind it's late' on it and his statement 'To me, in life – difference is a virtue'; and Laetitia Yhap, who was fascinated by graffiti. Although this selection of artists was wide-ranging, the group had many ideas about how to proceed.

The group had spent a great deal of time deciding how to use the stimulus of the photographic exhibition within their chosen episodic style. However, because they had arrived at their final focus unanimously, the feeling of engagement with the task was strong, and the desire to collaborate to make an interesting piece that truly did justice to the chosen artists was mutual.

The group eventually decided that the audience might gain a clearer insight into the exhibition if only one artist was the focus, and they chose Ralph Steadman for a number of reasons. Not only is he a well-known illustrator, but he has also produced a large number of visual books in his own right. He also designs vivid set and costume for dance pieces. The group used some of the lines from his interview as a basis for the script and the lyrics. This proved to be a good structuring device. Although the piece seemed quite abstract, there was a montage structure underpinning it that was based on Brecht's idea of episodic structure, where each scene can stand on its own and make sense but is also linked into the overall structure. There were to be four episodes in all.

For the first episode, the group used the line 'creatures of the mind never sleep'. They created a monologue around the idea that there are creatures playing games in your head and causing chaos, but that without such creatures, there would be no imagination, which is a basic necessity for artists. This became the opening scene and showed the artist at work in his studio. A dance was devised using gymnastics to accompany the monologue and highlight the random nature of the creatures that plagued the artist's mind. The dancer was one of the creatures and invaded the intimate space around the speaker, who represented the artist. Floor work and jumps were used to increase the number of levels used, and to indicate that the creatures were everywhere and could not be avoided. It produced a lively opening and hooked the audience.

They wrote two monologues around the lines from Steadman's interview. These monologues were then changed into songs or delivered with music underscoring them to evoke atmosphere. A

Researching the content

" We constantly referred back to their interviews with Andy Gill and to what Steve Pyke said in the introduction to the book: "the images are essentially a celebration, both acknowledging and powerfully illustrating the fact that restless imagination and creative vigour continue to flourish on to maturity". We realised that the idea of time passing was a key to many of the artists' work and intentions and we narrowed the focus of our piece down to this common theme. "

Structuring the content

Web link
www.ralphsteadman.com

duologue was performed with a dancer illustrating the words of one speaker and highlighting the emotions felt. This device was inspired by the physical theatre style of DV8 and their choreographer Lloyd Newson, who is known for breaking boundaries and has often used speech within his work. The group had looked at a video of *Strange Fish*, where Nigel Charnock uses speech in a very dramatic way to expose his loneliness. Wendy Houston, who has worked as a member of DV8, was also an influence since she has independently fused poetry with dance to produce pieces in which each art form supports the other and strengthens the overall impact on the audience.

The group varied the pace by writing a poem based on the line 'never mind it's late', which simultaneously represented Steadman working to a deadline and tied in with the theme of time passing. Choral speaking was used to emphasise the key words and this led into a song based on the line 'the only thing that my father noticed about growing older was the fact that the undertaker raised his hat to him'. They used minor chords to indicate the unnerving idea of death approaching, as well as a dancer performing a slow tap routine in the style of a vaudeville number to mimic the tragicomic aspect of the line. They researched clowns, their deadpan faces, and their sad and otherworldly natures. One example of a clown in dance is *Pierrot Lunaire*, a piece danced by Bruce. The group had access only to snippets of this work, along with photographs of the set and dancer in costume, and articles written about it, which helped explain the plight of the clown. This helped with the dance style, which became a mixture of slow tap and contemporary dance. It supported the song without drowning it out and created a very sombre mood.

Between the scenes, instrumental music was played on the piano to make the transitions smoother. This idea came from seeing *Blue/Orange* by Joe Penhall, where jazz music is played in between acts. In some ways, this reflected the nature of the oldest character in the piece and also linked the acts together to make a fluid play. The tension was kept high and the music reminded the audience of where they had left off before the interval.

In the dance section of 'Never mind it's late', clockwork movements were used to refer to the theme of time passing. In order to depict the theme clearly and to show that the piece was based on Steadman's work, the group decided to copy one of his clocks onto a large canvas at the back of the stage. This was achieved gradually throughout the performance until at the end the entire clock had been drawn. The piece finished with the group walking away from the canvas and kneeling on stage so that they faced the clock and the audience could also see it. A camera flash ends the piece to represent Pyke photographing Steadman's work.

Although the group was not trying to produce a piece of epic theatre, they used a number of techniques that were typical of that style – direct address to the audience, minimal props and costumes – to signify character and changes on stage without using naturalistic costume. The members of the group decided to link themselves visually by wearing t-shirts, each displaying a different

Yolande Snaith, who uses multimedia to good effect in her pieces, also inspired the group, who studied her use of installations to create sets. They liked the way she fused storytelling and poetry with dance to create a postmodern narrative.

Another play that uses this device successfully is *Closer* by Patrick Marber. Again, it has a fast pace, and the music between scenes is fast and loud, keeping the dramatic tension high.

work by Ralph Steadman. The programme featured a clock on the front cover, and ticking was used in the gaps between pieces of music to enhance the theme.

Rehearsals

During technical rehearsals, the group experimented with effects that enhanced the piece, such as red lighting to show anger and blue to convey emotional distance. The piece needed careful technical and dress rehearsals, which took place on the day of the performance. Dress rehearsals also took place at college in order for the group to feel comfortable when performing in costume. The stage area was small and had the large canvas upstage centre and a piano centrestage right. There was a special board placed on top of a rubber mat where the tap dancing took place, as the theatre did not allow tapping on their floor.

The performance

The final performance was successful and the audience responded well. The programme helped clarify the intentions of the piece and the link to the stimulus. The episodic structure was especially effective and the group was able to use this as a structural device when it came to writing up their commentary. Several members of the audience had seen the exhibition and stayed behind to discuss elements of the piece with the cast.

The group successfully fulfilled their intention. Their performance and devising skills were used collaboratively to produce a fully integrated piece based on an eclectic mix of styles. The group of seven managed to produce a piece with strong dynamics and a good variety of skills in a very small performance space with limited staging potential. They realised by the end of the task that the audience were interested in the project and did not necessarily expect to see a straightforward plot with a clear storyline. They showed that they understood the relationship between the performing and visual arts and how the two worlds are not so far apart. The mix of styles was used effectively and created a pleasing piece of integrated work, which reflected the snapshot of Ralph Steadman that Steve Pyke had created.

Case study three: Rape of the Sabine women

Style

The teachers at this college had decided that the groups should all take part in an outdoor piece that brought together many different stylistic elements and was therefore eclectic. It was decided to allow some freedom within this, so long as everything was clearly related to techniques of communication with an audience through an open-air performance. It was intended that the students should read widely about techniques of performing outdoors.

Students had seen a performance by the group Stomp, and decided to include a rhythm section in their piece in which they could use elements of tap along with clapping to make an interesting contrast with other, more melodic pieces of music. They had watched some work by DV8 and were impressed by the shock tactics used to make the audience think seriously about taboo subjects. They had studied Christopher Bruce's fusion of classical and contemporary styles, as well as mixing dance and drama together in the style of several dance companies seen at the Dance Umbrella festival.

Web link

www.stomp.co.uk

Venue

> The design of the park ensures that the visitor is constantly surprised at each turn of a corner, finding a vineyard on one bank of the lake and sheep on another, an alpine walk up a steep hill, a Gothic ruin, a grotto made out of crystal or a statue by an amphitheatre.

The venue for this group was Painshill Park in Cobham, Surrey. The group visited the park and spent half a day there walking around and looking at the landscape of the park and the artworks within it. The members of the group were immediately struck by the park's historic beauty, the calming atmosphere of the gentle sloping hills and the large expanses of water.

The group considered all the possibilities of the park and its attractions but centred on a statue that provided a heavy contrast with the calming nature of much of what had already been seen. The group bought a pamphlet containing useful information and read that the statue was called 'The Rape of the Sabine Women'. This relates to a legend of ancient Rome, in which Romulus, a legendary king of ancient Rome, was concerned that his men lacked wives and that the population was therefore in danger of diminishing. He is said to have invited neighbouring peoples, including the Sabines to a festival. At a pre-arranged signal, his men abducted the women, and later forcibly married them.

The group asked the education department at Painshill Park if they had any more information on the statue, and discovered that it was by an Italian artist named Giovanni Bologna. After closer analysis of photographs of the statue, the group became fascinated by the plight of the women. The statue has three figures: a Sabine man, a Sabine woman and a Roman man. The female is held tightly by the Roman male as he restrains her. She appears to show great emotion in her body posture and facial expression. Her mouth is open in fear. The image's shocking and disturbing nature had a powerful effect on the members of the group. The group decided that this statue in its unique setting in the park created a stark juxtaposition of horror and beauty that would complement their interest in the style of DV8 perfectly.

Change of venue

The project was started in June, when the weather was warm, so the group thought it would be ideal to perform in the amphitheatre. However, there were disadvantages to this. Firstly, they would be performing in October and the weather was very likely to be inclement. It would be difficult to have the sound and lighting that they required without enormous expense. Had the group performed in the summer term, or even late spring, and had live musicians, then the outdoor space would have been beneficial to the piece. Luckily the group was then offered the Barn Theatre at no hire cost. Since this was not too far away in Molesey, the group decided that it would be a preferential venue.

Researching the content

The main advantage to the idea of using the statue as inspiration was that all members of the group found it highly motivating. The group took photographs of the statue and the surrounding landscape that could then be used to make a PowerPoint slide show to create the look and atmosphere of the statue in its historic landscape. In order to make the images seem more authentic and to invite the audience in to the group's own experience of visiting the park, a soundscape was made using natural sounds like leaves rustling in the wind and birds singing. These were recorded at the park over several days and then mixed at college. The audiovisual display created the right atmosphere and set the scene. It lulled the audience into a false sense of security at the beginning of the piece, echoing the visitor's experience of walking in the park before coming across this disturbing image. The group were inspired by the style of musique concrète, a type of music originated by Pierre Schaeffer in 1948. They wrote about this in their commentaries.

As the piece was serious in content, the group spent considerable time looking at appropriate dance styles. They watched *Dead Dreams of Monochrome Men* by Lloyd Newson and DV8, as it dealt with a very serious issue, that of a serial killer who invited men back to his house and then killed them. In the piece, the killer seems lonely, as he keeps the corpses for a certain amount of time before disposing of them. The piece was shocking and the group decided to use some aspects of the style for their own piece in order to depict the rape of the women. The group were not prepared to go as far as Newson, but they still wanted to show the injustice of the brutal treatment of the women and decided that it would be appropriate to incorporate statistics and facts into the piece.

These were delivered in a variety of ways. For example, in the style of Brecht, they were displayed on the slide show and projected on to the white cyclorama while the performers danced on a lower level. At the beginning of the piece, following the slide show of the park and the statue, the performers walked on stage with cue cards, and in a didactic manner read out some of the facts about the statue and the story behind it. After the performance, members of the audience said that this gave a marked change of tone to the piece and that they became gradually aware that the theme was going to be a very serious one.

The group also used a poem written by a rape victim. It had been posted on the Internet and began with the words: 'The hardest to bear isn't the slap or the shove, it's the sting of the words, like a black velvet glove.' Choral speech was chosen for the delivery of these words, using the overlapping of words while the performers danced slowly on the stage and took up positions that depicted the harshness of rape. Repetition of dance motif and spoken line helped to create the tension to the first climax of the piece. The lighting was also successful in highlighting various parts of the dancers' bodies as they became the victims of rape.

Another emotion the group discovered is commonly experienced by a rape victim is anger, and this is where the group felt that the style of Stomp would be ideal for expressing that emotion. They wanted to use a range of stamping, clapping and tapping, to be performed by the group as a whole, but built up gradually to mirror the rising anger. As in Christopher Bruce's work, the group used the device of posing questions and answers through the use of tap. The syncopated rhythms increased in tempo and symbolised the build-up of tension, as if ready to explode. Using different parts of the bodies at different times, the performers layered conflicting rhythms to create a more complex texture. The group decided that a calming, slower section should follow, creating a stark and powerful contrast. The quieter section would also give the audience some respite, as well as adding dynamic to the structure. This section took the group the most rehearsal time, because the

> Musique concrète refers to electronic music composed of instrumental and natural sounds, often altered or distorted in the recording process.

Further study

Dead Dreams of Monochrome Men (PAL video 2680-VI) is available to order from www.dancebooks.co.uk.

Brecht

Anger

complicated and difficult rhythms required an enormous amount of concentration and focus to be performed successfully. The group began the devising process for this section by improvising noise patterns. In the final dress and technical rehearsals they were amazed at how strong and loud the tapping, stamping and shuffling of rhythms sounded on the wooden floor.

Creating tension

After some discussion and several rehearsals of the opening section, some changes were made to heighten the dramatic tension of the piece. Music from the BBC's natural history series *Blue Planet* was used to produce a hollow and empty feel for the dance. There was a gradual build-up of instruments in the middle, bringing the melody back round to the beginning. This was reflected in the dance by using slow and sustained movement. There followed a silence, in order to build tension. After this, the sound of heavy breathing was heard. At this point the performers had left the stage. They appeared again after the breathing, speaking the lines of the poem. Entrances were used to good effect here as they entered from three places. The audience was seated on the three sides of a thrust in front of a raised stage. The atmosphere was one of uneasiness. The voices in the choral section were used at different volume levels, and the whispers were particularly chilling. The whispering continued to create a smooth transition into the next section, which began with instrumental music.

Fusion of styles

A fusion of classical and contemporary styles was used to show the victim's isolation. They looked again at Christopher Bruce's *Swansong*, and the three victims' solos that they had studied at AS, in order to see how a choreographer creates motifs to reflect emotion. They also looked at other Bruce pieces to reinforce this.

The performers each worked in a series of solos and duets before working together as an ensemble. Floor work was used to represent downtrodden women, and intense suffering and anguish. At the end of the section, a heartbeat and blue lighting were introduced to show the cold, emotionless state of the victim. The five performers stood on the raised stage in front of the cyclorama with hands held up to signify surrender and helplessness.

> " Without constant change, a work becomes dead for an audience. "
>
> Lloyd Newson

With another change in the music, the performers danced in unison, with arms outstretched to the audience as if in a cry for help. They turned away from the audience and walked behind the cyclorama, where they very slowly scraped their fingernails down the white material. The group felt that they had to use a change of location on the stage area to keep the audience's interest.

The group researched how women felt after being subjected to rape and found that many could not sleep. They used a track entitled *Insomnia* in a short dance section to depict the victim's whirlwind of emotions and sleepless nights. A stark, white light helped to emphasise the lack of sleep. Slowly the performers walked up on to the raised stage and used their bodies to form the statue. This tableau was held until the lights faded to black, leaving an eerie atmosphere and a chilling silence in the theatre.

Audience response

The group received a great deal of praise from the audience, many of whom had visited the park and seen the statue but had not paid much heed to it. The audience commented on how the lighting, soundscape, music, choral elements and Stomp section worked well to create an effective and powerful texture. The dance and drama were perfectly interwoven, and the piece took the audience through highs and lows and moments of extreme tension.

The theatre was ideal for the performance of the piece as it created an intimate atmosphere. The group felt that they had benefited greatly from the all-day rehearsals that they had held there. They were indebted to the technical crew who helped them, and they felt that the project had been worthwhile. They performed an edited version of the piece for a different audience at college in a much bigger venue, which was end-staged, but they felt that the smaller theatre with audience on three sides had been a far more effective venue. They credited the success of the performance to the strong commitment of the members of the group and the initial impression that the statue had made on them. The Barn Theatre had been extremely helpful and supportive of their intention and efforts, and fully backed the project, which had made the group more confident when publicising the event.

> As the third performance was indoors, the group was able to hold a post-show discussion with the audience.

The venue

The written commentary

As we said earlier, your assessment for the Community Performance Project is based on your written commentary only. So, how can you ensure that your commentary is the best you are capable of? So far in your course, you have only produced one extended piece of coursework (for The Language of Performing Arts). If you think back to that work, you faced exactly the same issues as you do now: how do you show the examiner that you have taken part fully in the performance pieces for the unit and also understood what you were doing? You need to be sure that what you write addresses the assessment criteria – after all, there's no point in writing about things that won't get you any marks. Let's identify what the assessment criteria are looking for.

> For a breakdown of these criteria, see page 15.

You can get good marks for **knowledge and understanding of performance theory** if you can show that you thoroughly understand the theoretical dimensions of the piece. In other words, you need to show that you are completely familiar with the style in which you were working, including quotations from books and other sources that back up your points. You should explain what you learned from these resources and how this helped your understanding, rather than giving a narrative of how you got hold of the books or found the websites. Don't just write a diary of what you did: show that you know what you were trying to achieve.

Knowledge and understanding

> Performance theory is really a way of referring to the style, historical context and performance conventions in which you were working.

You'll notice that in this A2 unit, most of the marks are for evaluation rather than knowledge. It is hard to evaluate – to look at something, know whether it's working or not, and understand what to do to make it work. That's what you're going to be assessed on: did you understand the style, historical context and performance conventions well enough that you knew what to do as you devised the piece? Again, it's no use simply writing a diary about what you did – that won't get very high marks. You need to

Evaluating

show that you had insight into how the process was developing and what needed to be done in order to take it forward.

Evaluating the success of the actual performance is a little like evaluating the performance process. Bear in mind that the sets of assessment criteria build on each other, so, obviously, if you didn't know what style you were working in (in the first set of criteria) you'll be hard pressed to say whether it was successful or not here.

Quality of language

Most A levels test your ability to write to a high standard, and performance studies is no exception. It's not just about being a good performer: you need to show that you have the ability to express yourself in written English. That means that you can:

➢ Structure your commentary in a way that is efficient and uses the word limit effectively

➢ Write in an interesting and engaging manner

➢ Move easily from one idea to another, making proper use of paragraphs

➢ Express complex ideas in a way that opens them up to the reader

➢ Handle specialist language properly, correctly spelling technical performance terms.

☑ Checklist

The exam board gives a checklist of the things that should be covered in your written commentary. We've reproduced these here to remind you what you're trying to achieve. You don't necessarily have to deal with these as separate paragraphs but you could start by using them as headings and writing a section on each.

☐ The style of the piece, and the significant aspects of that style that you chose to use.

☐ The performance issues that grew from the content of the piece.

☐ Researching the content of the piece.

☐ Improvising with performance ideas.

☐ Structuring the piece.

☐ Relationship between the art forms used.

☐ The rehearsal process: refinements and performance issues.

☐ The performance: putting on the final event, the audience's response.

☐ Final evaluation of the group's success in achieving their performance intentions.

You'll see that there are nine different headings here. The overall word limit for your written commentary is only 3,000 words, so you need to keep your points concise.

Ask your tutor to show you the unit content that they will send with your work so that you can see what the moderator will know before they read your work. Avoid duplicating this information in your written commentary.

To help you keep within the word limit, your tutor will submit a **unit content** to the examiner. This will contain details of which performance style you were working in, the performance venue and the content of the piece.

If you wrote an equal amount on all of the nine points, you would have only 300–350 words available for each one. You'll find that if you start by writing mini-essays about each of the points, you'll end up with considerably more words than you need. That doesn't matter to start with: you can always slim your commentary down later. You will probably find that some of the points you make for one of the headings will also apply to another. Once you have tried to answer them all separately, you can start to trim back what you've written and become efficient in your points. Let's look at what you might cover for each of the bullet points.

Style of the piece

Make sure that **style comes first** in your commentary. It sets the scene and tells the reader that you understand what you were trying to do. You need to introduce the style or genre, identify which aspects of it you were trying to incorporate and what your overall aims were. It doesn't matter that you haven't mentioned the actual content of the piece at this stage. You need to show that you can evaluate the success of your piece, and you won't be able to do that if the examiner thinks you don't understand the style.

> In reality, you may have made decisions about the content at the same time as you worked on the style, but for the time being, simply introduce the style.

Performance potential

You need to show that when you had your ideas for the content of the piece, you were quickly able to see the performance potential of your material. For example, if you decided to do a pantomime about a political issue, you must show that you were able to identify how you might use stock characters and stereotypical scenarios. If you had decided to work on a piece of performance art in response to a set of paintings, you must indicate how you could see the performance potential in a set of inanimate images.

> Don't spend time discussing other possible approaches that you rejected: the focus should be what you actually did and why.

Researching the content

A lot of students instinctively start here because it's easier to write about the content of the piece than the style in which you were working. You will need to be very well informed about the content of the piece. If you rejected certain aspects of the stimulus material, you need to say why you did it. That's what evaluation is all about.

> 'Research' is a word that has become devalued: it doesn't mean just printing out sheets from the Internet – go to the library and use a variety of sources.

Improvising with performance ideas

If you think back to the Language of Performing Arts unit at AS, you'll remember learning about the performance process of improvising–rehearsing–performing. That is still just as important in this unit as it was then. Whenever you create an original piece of performance work, there needs to be a structured process. You need to show that you were able to create performance motifs, ideas, and short sections from aspects of the content. The examiner will not want to read a diary of every single idea, however. Select a few of the most important ones, making sure that you give examples from across the art forms. You should be able to find about ten examples from your work. Include one or two still images here if it helps to show what you are talking about.

Structuring the piece

As you'll know by now, structuring a 30-minute piece is challenging. Take an honest look at what you did. Watch the video. Do the sections seem the right length? Is the piece well balanced? Are there points of contrast or does the whole thing move along at the same tempo with hardly any variation? What could be done differently, looking back? In any case, why did you choose to structure the piece as you did? What was there in the performance style that led you to think this was the best way to do it?

Relationship between art forms

As we have said, you only have to perform in two of the art forms, but we want to encourage you to perform in all three. You're not being assessed on your performance work, so there is nothing to lose by taking a risk – your skills will almost certainly improve and this will probably help your mark in the Student Devised Performance later on in the course. You need to show that you were aware of how the art forms relate to each other in your piece. Hopefully you'll have followed the advice from before and not started with drama, as this can make it difficult to include dance and music in the piece.

The rehearsal process

Rehearsal is tough and it can be boring: there's no point trying to pretend otherwise. However, that doesn't mean that you should avoid doing it – you need to show that you got to a stage where the piece was in draft form and that you then started to rehearse it. We suggest that you have at least five complete rehearsals. In those rehearsals, you may have decided to make some minor changes because the piece wasn't faithful to the style, the content wasn't clear or the piece didn't fit the performance space very well. Whatever decisions you made as a group, give plenty of examples and say why you made them and how effective they were.

The performance

Don't spend too long here talking about the details of the event – these will probably be in the unit content that your tutor has produced. Concentrate instead on how effective the final performance was, and offer a detailed evaluation of specific performance points that you were trying to achieve.

Final evaluation

This effectively brings you back to where you started. Having said what you were trying to achieve in your piece, you now need to sum up the extent to which you were successful. In this conclusion, you need to identify the aspects of the performance that were a good example of the performance style, made full use of the performance space and communicated the content well.

You also need to be honest and identify those aspects of the performance that were not in line with the performance conventions of your chosen genre, did not work so well in the performance space or hindered (rather than helped) the communication of the content of your piece.

Finally...

When you've written all of these short sections, do a word count and work towards integrating the short sections into one complete piece of work. Once you have a final draft, your tutor will look at it and offer advice. After that, however, it is up to you to refine and rework the material to achieve the best marks you can.

Tip

Remember that even if your performance did not go as you intended, you can still get credit if you can evaluate what could have been done.

Sample written commentary

On the following pages, we've set out a sample written commentary for you to see how a former student has approached writing up their work. We've included comments on what they've written so you can see the strengths and weaknesses of this piece. You shouldn't see this as a rigid model, but rather use it to get more ideas about your own work. The candidate received a low B grade (71%) for this piece.

Community Performance Project. Midsummer in Sunbury: A Pageant

In this unit, our group of seven students produced an integrated piece of performance work combining dance, drama and music. We were told at the start of the unit that there were four aspects of the work that we had to produce and that each of them needed to be brought together as we devised the piece. These were the style of the piece, the content of the piece, the place where we intended to perform it and the audience for whom it was intended. Obviously all these things were linked and when we started we seemed to be trying to juggle them.

We were told that our piece should build on the work that we did for the Language of Performing Arts at AS. The best piece that we worked on in that unit was our integrated piece, in which we worked on an interpretation of Van Eyck's painting *Marriage of the Arnolfini*. We enjoyed the historical subject and thought that this would give us a lot of opportunities to perform in our local community. It was less clear to us what the style of our piece would be because we lacked experience in working on style.

> This is a vague comment about style.

Our teachers encouraged us to try to establish style and content at the same time, which helped us, as the two were obviously linked and we had been finding it difficult to think of them in isolation. They introduced us to the content and simultaneously told us about the style that they wanted us to work in to interpret the piece.

As we had previously done well on a piece based on a work of art, it was decided that the content of our community piece would be based on a piece of embroidery in Sunbury that had been designed to celebrate the millennium. The embroidery is a large piece of work with an intricate design made up of over 130 separate pieces. The relevance of the panel to the local community is shown by the reproduction of buildings, churches and public houses, which are examples of Sunbury's fine domestic architecture.

It was vital that the style was appropriate to the piece, and the various scenes in the tapestry seemed ideally suited to a pageant as this would allow us to perform at some of the places represented in the tapestry. We would have to adapt the pageant style, though, so that the focus was not simply on a street procession or a celebration. Pageant seemed to be a very flexible style but we wanted our piece to be more than a type of street carnival or celebration. There would be a promenade aspect to our piece but we also wanted to incorporate some other specific stylistic aspects within the pageant. I will discuss these as appropriate.

We used the structure of the embroidery to guide us in the structure of piece. Looking at the embroidery, every detail could be observed, including the River Thames, which occupies a central position on the panel, with many river activities incorporated. Towards the top of the panel are a number of scenes depicting open spaces, such as Sunbury Park and the Walled Garden. The parkland, open spaces and riverside location of Sunbury provide a rich and varied environment for animals and plant life, and this is reflected in the colourful stitch work.

> Evidence of research into the stimulus. However, this section should be far more concise, given that it is the chosen style that is the significant element to this unit.

We considered how these places could act as points in the pageant where we could perform. We also decided at this stage that our group of seven might look a bit lost trying to move in pageant through the streets as there were not enough of us to create a sense of celebration. As there were 21 students on our course, it was decided that the other two groups would also take part in the pageant but with different groups performing different 'episodes' at different points in Sunbury.

> A good evaluation of the visit to see the stimulus and of the way in which all groups were involved in the pageant.

It was also decided that there would be potential shelter at each performance point in case of bad weather. Even though we chose to perform on midsummer's day, there was no guarantee of fine weather and we wanted to make sure that our outdoor performance was not a washout – although in the event it turned out to be one of the hottest and sunniest days of the summer.

Pauline Tredigo, who had worked on the embroidery, gave a talk to all 21 students. She described the Sunbury Millennium Embroidery as 'a permanent, commemorative record that celebrates the ancient riverside village of Sunbury-on-Thames and its community in the year 2000'. The design was by John Stamp from an original idea by David Brown. The embroidery involved over 140 local embroiderers who created the village panel and the eight supporting side panels. It took two and a half years of people working in their own homes to produce the individual subjects (slips), and a further 15 to 18 months to put the whole embroidery together. The final work is a result of over one hundred thousand hours of careful and dedicated effort from all levels and ages across the community.

> Concise and detailed introduction to the project, outlining the relevance of the embroidery to the local community.

This is an image of the central village panel.

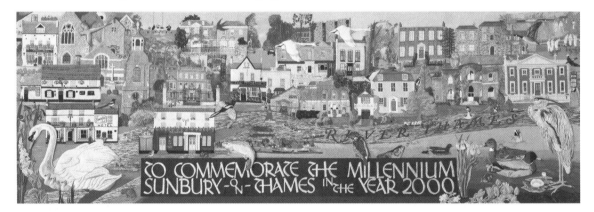

Our teachers identified places for the groups to perform: the Walled Garden at Sunbury which the Queen had previously visited to observe the work; local pubs that were featured in the embroidery, such as The Phoenix, The Magpie and the Flower Pot Hotel; and a theatre called the Vera Fletcher Hall. The other groups were to perform their sections in one of the local pubs and in the walled garden. Our piece was to be the finale of the pageant and would be performed in the Vera Fletcher Hall.

> Reproduced by kind permission of Sunbury Millennium Embroidery. The full embroidery can be seen at www.sunburyembroidery.co.uk.

Our performance at the Vera Fletcher Hall was the only part of the pageant to take place indoors and we realised that people who had followed the pageant would have been standing up for over an hour by the time they arrived at our piece. We looked carefully at the stage space and decided to have the audience sitting down for our section. We knew this probably gave us an advantage as we could be sure there would be some people who would stay for the whole piece rather than wandering off in the middle of an episode.

Having determined the venue for our specific performance, we set to work on creating a scenario from the tapestry. We learned about the choreographer Lea Anderson and looked at her collage method in a piece entitled *Flesh and Blood*. We noticed that she juxtaposed sections in her work that contrasted with each other but fitted together to produce a theme. We also noted that she used lots of pedestrian movement, as does Matthew Bourne, another choreographer we learned about. Our teachers encouraged us in the movement-based approach to fit in with the movement of the pageant of which it was the culmination.

> Specific detail of how style was used to create their known episode.

Contrasting the two choreographers, we saw that while Anderson might take a very small detail such as the moving of an eye or a toe and then work on this to produce a choreographed section of a dance, Bourne takes a simple move such as the royal wave and makes this into a lengthy scene with comic effect and the whole ensemble involved. Audiences react well to this type of mockery of the royal family and they perceive the joke immediately, whereas with Anderson's work the meaning is not always clear or straightforward.

In the 'Joan' section of *Flesh and Blood*, for example, the dancers perform small movements using the tip of the nose to draw the letters of the word 'Joan' in the air. The audience does not necessarily know this but it gives the dancers motivation and an intriguing sequence is produced with head and shoulder shots. We also looked at the way Alan Ayckbourne creates comedy through domestic dramas and attempted to incorporate some aspects of the farcical in our piece so that the light-hearted nature of the pageant was not lost and to give our performance a 'feel-good factor'.

> Good selection of styles in different art forms that complement each other.

This was easier said than done although the comic and farcical elements did finally act as light-hearted sections. Many of the images in the tapestry were serious, though, and to represent some of these, we took the ideas of using pedestrian movement and focusing on very small movements and incorporated them to reflect the sewing of the needlework and the minute detail included in the work. This basic idea of reflecting the work of all the participants meant that we could have a large range of characters rather than trying to single out specific roles. We could touch on their lives to direct the narrative further and create a multi-stranded structure for the piece to make it different and unique. We aimed to show everyone working individually but with a common goal, and we felt that collage was a perfect way of showing this. We did not therefore take only one episode, but incorporated a number of images and strands from the embroidery.

> Very good use of appropriate theory.

This was similar to Brecht's montage structure whereby each individual scene could stand on its own. We thought we could then incorporate placards briefly setting the scene for the area, including scene titles. We also liked the idea of using an episodic structure within our piece to present a detailed narrative produced in a much shorter period of time. We knew that the embroidery had taken over one hundred thousand hours to put together so we wanted to show the time span and effort involved, although we chose to develop a non-linear narrative. As Colin Counsell said about Brecht's work:

"Montage was a key concept in many areas of early twentieth century art e.g. film and entails juxtaposing disparate images so that each informs the other."

We structured the drama aspects of the piece as monologues and duologues so that it was easier to produce work more promptly with minimal difficulties and obstructions as time was of the essence. Another idea we wanted to incorporate was integrating the art forms together rather than having separate music, dance and drama scenes. We carried this out by combining the dance routines and music compositions with monologues or duologues.

More detail needed here on how integration was achieved.

To commence the piece, we had a prologue showing the audience that the embroidery is still on display and is waiting to be housed in a permanent building in the Walled Garden. We devised a train scene in which four characters are on their way to Sunbury to see the work and, in epic style, state facts about the tapestry. The temporal setting is the present day but the time line is fractured to show David Brown first coming up with the idea of the embroidery.

We frequently addressed the audience, as the Vera Fletcher Hall is quite small and the raked stage has a high ceiling where voices can be lost. The atmosphere between performers and audience was quite intimate and we felt that direct address would be effective at this point. One performer then delivered a short speech in the character of David Brown voicing his thoughts on producing such an enormous piece of work. This use of short episodic scenes prevented the audience from accepting the familiar on stage and perceiving it as an illusion. To understand this concept better, we read more about Piscator with whom Brecht had worked. Piscator thought that 'theatre must reflect the age and transform drama of the period'. We tried to reflect David Brown's state of mind when he came up with the initial idea of the embroidery through the use of direct address. We wanted the audience to engage with his concept, but not necessarily with him.

Makes it clear why direct address was used.

To add variation in the drama, we created a musical telephone conversation in this scene between Brown and John Stamp. This was one of the lighthearted aspects of the piece and was based on a song we had studied from the musical *Guys and Dolls* called 'Fugue for Tin Horns' in which overlapping dialogue and witty lyrics are interwoven. This turned out to be an excellent idea and we used a simple tune which our teachers helped us to weave together in the style of the 'Fugue for Tin Horns'. We increased the pace of the movement for this section and moved purposefully around the stage in the song. At the climax of the song, all seven members of the group were fully involved and this turned out to be a showstopper for the audience. This was not exactly what we intended but it was gratifying to us to receive such warm applause.

The next scene was to show the sewing of the embroidery and the weaving of the pieces together using the medium of dance with musical accompaniment. We used a style based on Anderson's work to express the flowing action of the thread moving through the material. The group formed a line and then each broke off, showing the needle taking the thread through to form the stitches. The dancer then joined the line again at a different point on the stage to denote the movement of the needle. We weaved in and out of each other to show a circle, and then split into smaller groups of two or three to show different series of motifs including leg kicks for high-level actions and floor work as low-level. This was important because weaving consists of the thread going under and over so our levels tried to convey this. Each small group performed their section while the other groups remained frozen on the floor. The freeze frame represented the time passing in sewing each individual panel of the embroidery.

Shows how the stylistic features of a studied practitioner can be used to help the devising process.

There were many images of birds in the embroidery so we could invent motifs to symbolise birds standing, swimming and in flight. We looked carefully at the low body positions and bent arms that Christopher Bruce had used in *Swansong*, though we could use only very short references to Bruce, as we had studied him at AS. We devised a Bruce-inspired motif to show the actions of birds, and found this useful in devising our movements.

One episode was about Kempton Park race course and was based on the Ascot scene from *My Fair Lady*. This seemed to reflect the spirit of the pageant that we had held. One member of the group recorded a short piano piece and we all wrote a two-verse song to relate to the racing scene. Short phrases were delivered by singers in turn and then the singers stood in a freeze frame while someone else delivered their line. The simplicity of the music meant that the lyrics were not

Gives details on how the musical piece was composed and then integrated with other art forms. Clear on style.

lost in the notes and we could direct our exaggerated upper class accents at the audience as we uttered lines such as 'it's a lovely day' and 'bubbly champagne' to create the spirit of the day.

We added hand and arm gestures to imitate the drinking of champagne. Gradually the ensemble formed a line and looked stage left to watch the beginning of the race. We all followed the imaginary horses with strong eye focus to create the scene in the audience's minds. To create tension and excitement as the race progressed, we included cheers and shouts. This followed on well from the previous song inspired by *Guys and Dolls*.

In the last scene, the elements of weaving and threading were used to bring in the idea of the embroidery being finished. Inspired by Martha Graham and her use of material in dance pieces, we used cashmere scarves in different colours to represent the threads that were used to sew the panels together. We came in one at a time and performed a set of eight dance motifs with varied dynamics. The actions were again repeats of the turning and leg kicks that represented all the individual pieces coming together to form the whole. We improvised the dance a few times until we found a way to knot ourselves with the scarves to complete the embroidered picture in an effective way with the entire group present on stage.

We had been rehearsing the individual episodes as we devised them and we noticed that we were able to move through the performance process of improvising–rehearsing–performing much faster than in our AS work. In fact, a lot of the rehearsal for the individual episodes happened as we worked on them. Once we had the final structure, we rehearsed intensively and one of our main aims was to reduce the piece to 20 minutes since it took 40 on the first complete run-through. We achieved this by having individual members of the group 'on the clock' each week, encouraging us to keep the pacing slick and snappy. The final time of the piece was 26 minutes although we were sure that we could probably cut this by another two minutes in the final piece.

When it came to the week before the performance, we videoed a dress rehearsal at the theatre and this was useful when working on transitions between scenes because we had the audience's perspective to work from. We checked that we could change costume in time and that our minimal props were in the correct places when we needed them. We had to ensure that we could move properly in costume and that our hats did not obscure our faces when singing.

Clear on the purpose of the technical and dress rehearsals.

The day of the pageant went extremely smoothly and while there are not too many skills involved in creating a procession around the streets of Sunbury, we worked hard on creating audience interest and maintaining a good level of interest and commitment. To help us, the GCSE drama and dance groups dressed up in costume and acted as runners with the procession. The school's African percussion group also led the procession and this was an excellent way of bringing the medieval form of pageant into 21st-century Britain.

When it came to our performance we managed to retain an audience of about 50 people which we thought was very good for 1.00pm. We had timed the end of the pageant to coincide with lunchtime so that some people who had not been part of the procession would be able to come into the theatre for the final performance. One of the things that pleased us most as a group was the way in which the audience moved from stillness in the dance sections to uncontrollable laughter in the comic songs and farcical sections. We were glad that we had used a physical style of performance that almost seemed like slapstick at points. Our teacher pointed out to us that a traditional pageant would probably have incorporated clowns and slapstick elements so this was very suitable.

It is hard to evaluate a performance that you are in yourself so we watched a video of the final performance afterwards. Although the audience seemed to have been very responsive we wondered whether that was because most of them knew us rather than because the piece was genuinely engaging. We became quite critical of the video and we could see that several changes could have been made to produce a more coherent piece.

David Brown's monologue lacked detail and did not fully explain his plans for the project. Gestures and diction were not always clear. Some unintentional overlapping of lines meant that the audience could not always follow the dialogue. Vocal delivery seemed to lack energy and volume, whereas the dance sections were strong and purposeful. Transitions were quite smooth and props were used effectively and without mishap. The weaving of the scarves worked well to represent the colourful weaving of the panels together. The staging of the train scene on the floor area in front of the stage was placed unfortunately as two of the lights for this area failed to work during the final performance and we were mostly in semi-darkness. However we spoke our lines clearly and carried on despite this early setback.

In spite of these problems, we felt our performance had been a success and we enjoyed working on this project. We felt that we had managed to weave elements of performing arts into the style of a pageant, just as the scenes from Sunbury had been woven into the millennium tapestry.

A detailed evaluation of the final performance and the audience reaction. The conclusion refers back to the initial intention of the group and states that they have achieved their aim. The candidate evaluates process throughout the essay although more attention could be given to this as it is worth 40% of the overall mark.

Overall, this is a strong piece of work, although it is about 400 words over the limit of 3,000 words. The candidate should have slimmed down some of the description of the scenes, as this could have been included in the unit content.

Contextual Studies

What do I have to do?

If you think back to your AS performance studies course, you'll remember the Contextual Studies unit, for which you studied two practitioners and one work by each of those practitioners. The purpose of the examination was to test whether you had studied those works in depth and to what extent that study had opened your eyes to the type of things that practitioner did when he devised other pieces. The whole point of the assessment was to see whether you understood the significance of what you had studied: in other words, whether you could discern that practitioner's stylistic trends.

As you might expect, Contextual Studies 2 builds on the skills you developed in Contextual Studies 1. There is one essential difference, however, which you will spot almost as soon as you begin work on the unit: rather than focusing on individual practitioners, you will now study a single topic.

Whichever topic you study, you'll be expected to know a considerable amount about it, and to be able to write about it with a good deal of authority. Once again, you will be assessed in a two-hour written examination, but now you will have to write about the same question for two hours – we'll talk more about examination technique later.

The other major difference now from AS is the way in which the art forms come together within the topics on this paper. You will not be asked separate questions on dance, drama and music. In the AS unit, you were asked to answer only two questions and this meant that there was one art form on which you were not tested. That's all changed now. The questions set on each topic at A2 will require you to have studied pieces in all three art forms and to use examples from each of them systematically.

In your AS work, you will have learned about the 'fingerprints' of a practitioner. You will now be looking for the fingerprints of the style as a whole. This will require quite a lot of discernment, as the topics themselves cover broad periods – you'll need to be able to spot what is essential to a genre and what is simply the pet interest of one person who works in that style.

What are the topics?

You may be aware that the style of the paper for Contextual Studies has changed for examinations in June 2006 onwards. The topics set on the written paper from June 2006 are listed below.

➢ Postmodern approaches to the performing arts since 1960

➢ Politics and performance since 1914

➢ The 20th-century American musical.

In the AS course, you also had to produce some practical work based on what you had studied in the Performance Realisation unit. Note that for A2, there is **no related practical work** – the works that you study for the written paper do **not** form the basis of any of the practical work.

It's easier to study a single work than a whole topic. That's why topics are set for A2 – to see whether you can gain an overview of several works rather than just one at a time.

Tip

If you miss out one of the art forms, you cannot expect to get the highest marks for your answer, no matter how well you discuss the other two.

The paper that OCR set for June 2006 will be the first one that tests the new topics. You can find an example of a specimen paper on the OCR website at www.ocr.org.uk.

All three topics are designed to let you take a broad overview of a historical period, so that you can try to make sense of how things have developed during that time. None of the topics is easier or harder than the others, although it may be that you recognise some of the practitioners in one topic more than another.

In reality, it is likely to be the teaching staff at your school or college who will make the decision as to which topic you will be taught.

What do I have to study?

As we have said, you will need to choose just **one** of the topics listed above. You will look at **three** practitioners in that topic (one in dance, one in drama and one in music), and you will look at **three** contrasting extracts by **each** of these practitioners.

As you can see, this makes a total of **nine** pieces of repertoire in all.

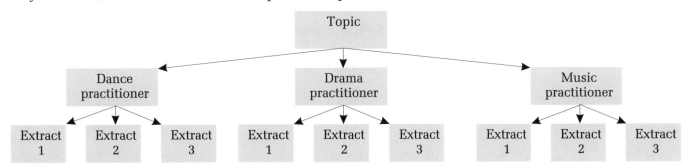

The extracts that you study will be chosen by your teachers and will all come from different works. When you study an extract, you'll to have a **contextual understanding** – of when it was created, where it was first performed and what was happening at the time. You won't be tested directly on this but it's important that you can appreciate the significance of the extract rather than studying it in isolation.

The nine extracts that you study will give you good coverage of the topic. You'll find that the questions that are set are very broad, because they will be written in a manner that allows you to draw on the broad range of examples that you have studied. We'll come to some specimens of questions later on. The important thing to remember at this point is that the examples you study must be capable of giving you that breadth of insight into the topic.

The exam board states that together the extracts must amount to between four and six hours in performance. That means, literally, that if you were to perform them one after the other without a break, the total length of time this would take would be between four and six hours.

You can work out from this that the average amount of time for each extract is between 27 and 40 minutes, but don't worry if you don't have extracts for each art form that fit this time guide. If you're taking your musical examples from a songwriter, for example, you could choose collections of songs on an album, as this would give you about 45 minutes of material for one album. Or you could choose a combination of albums or a collection of individual songs.

You are advised to use only original albums rather than 'best of...' collections.

The important thing is that you have enough material to understand the topic. You may have noticed that each of the topics has a date in the title. Postmodern approaches starts in 1960;

Remember that you will not be allowed to take copies of the extracts into the exam so you will need to memorise the significant elements of whatever extracts you have studied.

Tip

It's essential that you spend some time mapping what you've got. You need to know the exact date of each extract you study. Make a time line of the practitioners and extracts that form the basis of your study. Include significant historical events that happened at that time.

Political performance starts in 1914. Neither of these topics has an end date and therefore you could choose to study one practitioner whose work is brand new. The 20th-century American musical has a start date and an end date: 1900–1999. This is the broadest of the topics in terms of dates, and you need therefore to be absolutely certain that you are covering the whole period.

Make sure that you are able to get hold of copies of each extract. In the case of dance, this means a video recording of a professional performance; in drama, this means a printed version of the play script; in music, this means a copy of the music notation or a professionally recorded performance (which may be a studio performance).

Covering the historical spread of the topic

As the topics themselves are very large, you will need to make absolutely sure that you and your teachers map the extracts against the time span of the project before you begin work on the individual extracts. This will probably be slightly different for each topic.

If you are studying postmodern approaches since 1960, it is quite likely that many of the practitioners will have been born in a fairly narrow span of time. In any case, the very nature of postmodernism separates it from the other topics since it is *ahistorical* – postmodernism refers to conflicting styles existing alongside one another, being used by practitioners in a new context. Trying to find a spread of historical practitioners is therefore less important than identifying differing approaches to handling stylistic difference.

If you are studying political performance since 1914, the period covers the best part of 100 years and there have been a number of significant political upheavals in that time. The start date of 1914 coincides with the outbreak of the First World War and it would be helpful to find one practitioner working in that period. A second practitioner might have been working around the time of the Second World War and could provide contrasting or complementary approaches. It would be possible for a third practitioner to be a contemporary figure – perhaps someone whose work includes reaction to a recent conflict (the war in Iraq or the Falklands conflict, for example).

If you are studying the 20th-century American musical, check that your extracts cover the emergence of the style in the early part of the century (around the time of *Show Boat*), the development in the mid century and more recent developments of the book musical towards the end of the century.

Choice of practitioners and extracts

You'll see from this that it's vital to get good coverage of the topic. Beware of relying on a practitioner who is very recent or whose work is relatively unknown. You are trying to make sense of a broad topic that unfolds over time. The work of a practitioner born very recently may not have had the opportunity to be evaluated and compared with the broad sweep of the topic. It also means that the historical coverage you can get through studying that person would have to be balanced against a number of more established figures. Check with your teachers why they have chosen the practitioners and extracts that they have.

For each topic, the exam board has suggested three practitioners. These are not compulsory and you will find that the exam questions do not mention specific practitioners by name. It doesn't matter whether you end up studying the suggested practitioners in the specification or not. The important thing is that the three practitioners you study give good coverage of the topic. The final choice of practitioners will probably be made by your tutors and will be based on their interests and expertise.

However, note that you may **not** choose any of the practitioners available for study in the Contextual Studies 1 unit at AS, **whether you studied them at AS or not**. This is important because in the actual exam, you will not get credit for talking about works by these practitioners – it's fine to mention them in passing where it is relevant to your point, but do not talk about them in detail.

> Your teachers may simply decide to teach the three practitioners suggested by the exam board. However, it may be that the resources and/or expertise of your tutors would be better served by changing one or two of the practitioners. Your teachers may even choose all three practitioners themselves if they have the resources to do so.

> The practitioners in Contextual Studies 1 are Christopher Bruce, Lloyd Newson and DV8, Bertolt Brecht, John Godber, George Gershwin and Steve Reich.

What do I need to know for the exam?

As we've already said, you are **not** studying set works and you're **not** being asked to answer separate questions on all nine extracts that you have studied. The point of the exercise is to show that you understand the *topic*, and your examples are your means to illustrate your understanding of the topic. So:

➢ You will be expected to write for two hours about a **single question**.

➢ There will be a **choice of two questions** for each topic.

➢ You will need to **decide** which of these two broad questions you feel most equipped to answer.

➢ It's also important to **map out how the examples** you have might be used to address each of the questions set – it may be that your examples are more suited to answer one question than another, depending on what aspects of the topic you have covered, and this should affect which question you choose.

➢ Plan out your answer for at least 15 minutes before you start writing.

➢ If you write at average speed and in average size handwriting (about nine words per line) you will probably write about eight sides during the examination. This gives you ample opportunity to cover all of the examples.

➢ Don't simply write about the examples one after the other – make creative links as you go through.

 So what are the questions likely to be about? The exam board says that the questions will test six different aspects of the topic:

➢ Development of the style

➢ Significant stylistic features of the genre

➢ Techniques used by practitioners within the genre

Tip
Remember that the questions will not treat these six aspects separately. You will find that they are interlinked and it may not be immediately obvious which aspects are being addressed.

> Links between the art forms

> Relationship between works in the genre

> Cultural, historical and social context.

Let's go through these in detail and demystify what the exam is all about. Remember that when you answer the question you are trying to show that you understand the broad trends within each genre and how individual works are either typical of these or differ.

Development of the style

Chronological framework

We've already discussed the historical dimension of studying each topic, and the way in which a genre changes and adapts over time. The first and most important aspect here is showing that you understand the historical dimension of the topic. This involves understanding how the examples fit into the overall timeline and also what was happening socially, culturally and historically at that time.

See below for more on social, cultural and historical context.

Sometimes students find it difficult to make historical references in answering questions, or spend far too much time explaining them. For example, if you are writing about the significance of the Second World War in relation to the establishment of a certain sort of political theatre in the 1950s, you need to make precise, short references to certain aspects of the war rather than spending a long time explaining what the war was all about. In other words, assume that you are writing for the well-informed reader and don't waste time explaining the obvious – you can assume that the examiner will know the basic facts about the period. Your job is to draw attention to the links within the topic you're discussing.

You also need to demonstrate that you understand the **significance** of the chronology rather than simply reciting dates. For example, in the case of the American musical, the significance of studying *Show Boat* is more to do with the way in which the songs move the action along rather than the fact that it was written in 1928, but linking the two points is vital to set it historically.

Practitioners within a framework

You need to know some contextual information to help make sense of the work of your chosen practitioners. For example, to understand why Philip Glass' music is a good example of postmodern approaches in music, you would need to have understood the significance of Terry Riley's *In C* with its return to a strong tonal centre for the music. You wouldn't be expected to quote from *In C* but mentioning it as a passing reference could be a very helpful way of showing that you understand how tonality works in some postmodern music. Similarly, referencing Matthew Bourne's approach to ballet would enable you to talk extensively about the manner in which established work can be interpreted, recontextualised and remade for a contemporary audience.

Significance of individual works

In all genres there are significant works that you can study and recognise as essential in enabling the genre to move forward. We've already mentioned *In C*. Brecht's political plays made a major impact in the development of political performance – although remember that you shouldn't mention these in detail because Brecht was set as a practitioner for Contextual Studies 1. The same would apply to the importance of the choreography of Christopher Bruce in engaging with political issues in his work; you wouldn't be credited for making extensive reference since he is set for Contextual Studies 1, but it would be helpful for you to know of pieces such as *Ghost Dances* in embracing a political standpoint against a corrupt government in South America. The songs of Bob Dylan were fundamental in capturing a political mood in 1960s America, and even if you haven't studied them as one of your extracts, it would be advisable to know a little about the significance of them.

As well as individual practitioners, you also need to be aware of major artistic developments during the period of the topic. Sometimes, you'll have to read slightly outside the period as well. You will not be able to understand the significance of postmodernism, for example, unless you know about how modernism developed in the first half of the 20th century.

Significant stylistic features of the genre

When you were studying individual works at AS for Contextual Studies 1, you may have found it difficult to identify trends because you were focusing on one work. At A2, you are looking for trends as seen through the extracts that you have studied, and your tutors will be helping you to understand these stylistic trends in the lessons.

You'll find that at this level of study you will come across some debate about style and the significance of trends within the genre. It's easy to be panicked by this because it might look as if no one can agree about the style. The important thing is to understand what the **generally accepted** view of the style is. You need to be able to distinguish a minority view from the majority view. If, for example, most books or websites that you come across suggest that the purpose of political performance is primarily to persuade its audience (which is a generally accepted view), it would be strange to come across a view of political performance that suggested its main purpose was to make the audience laugh. However, it is certainly true that some political pieces (such as the plays of Dario Fo) have the intention of making the audience laugh at a given political situation in order to lampoon it and so strip it of its power. You need to be able to interpret individual views of a genre in the light of what you know about the mainstream views.

Each of the three genres set on this paper contains great diversity and you need to be able to interpret how this affects the trends in the genre as a whole. To take the previous example a little further, the use of comedy in political performance would be an ideal topic if your drama examples were drawn from the work of Dario Fo, but there is nothing especially comic about the work of Pina Bausch or Bob Dylan. Given the working definition of political performance as that which intends to persuade or rouse its audience to action, comedy is simply one means of achieving that.

Beware of making exaggerated claims when you are writing about the genre. Don't take isolated examples and try to grow major points from them – use examples to reinforce your point rather

Tip

Practitioners do not work in a vacuum. They are influenced not only by what came before but by what was going on at the time. You'll learn a lot about the practitioner you're studying if you read around your topic to understand what other practitioners (who you haven't studied) were doing at the time.

Major artistic developments

Tip

A reminder: as soon as you know what the extracts are, start to locate them within the overall chronological framework of the topic.

Accepted views of the style

Diversity within a genre

Tip

If your extracts are all very similar, you probably need to look at some others to help you appreciate the diversity of the genre you're studying.

Making claims for the genre

than simply quoting an example and then trying to think of a reason for using it. For example, if you're writing about the American musical, do not get too focused on individual songs or you may miss the point of the genre as a whole. It is true that some songs use interesting harmonies, but it would be difficult to make a claim that the harmonies always became more complex as the period progressed. Some of George Gershwin's harmonies, for example, are far more complex than those of Richard Rodgers, although Gershwin's work came first.

Techniques used by practitioners in the genre

How practitioners establish style

One of the challenges in this study is being able to understand the distinctive contribution of each practitioner to the genre as a whole. It's quite likely that each practitioner that you study will have made a distinctive contribution within their own art form. Yet the way practitioners work within the individual art forms may seem very different in some of the topics. Of the three, there is probably the most commonality of approach in the American musical option, because teams of choreographers, composers and playwrights work together on pieces within the genre. On the other hand, if you look at political performance, there are plenty of examples of practitioners working in quite different ways to produce pieces within each art form. Similarly, within postmodern performance, there is plenty of diversity in the way that practitioners in different art forms work with their materials.

You need to be very sure about the way in which each practitioner uses distinctive techniques, irrespective of what contribution this makes to the topic as a whole. There are two quite distinct tasks here: you need to be absolutely clear about the style of the individual practitioner concerned and then you need to be sure about what kind of contribution that person's work makes to the topic as a whole.

Conventions of the genre

In order to understand the extent of an individual's distinctive contribution to the topic you are studying, you need to understand the **conventions** of the genre – the things that most people do when they are producing works in this genre. For example, in political performance, the majority of practitioners would seek to engage with an issue and attempt to persuade their audience of a particular standpoint or view. There would normally be some attempt to change the thoughts, motivations and actions of the person watching the final piece in order to make some change to their behaviour subsequent to the performance. Yet not all pieces adopt all of these conventions. You need to make sure you list all of the conventions commonly used by the majority of practitioners. When you were studying individual practitioners for Contextual Studies 1, you made a list of 'fingerprints' for each of the two practitioners you studied. You need to do the same thing for each practitioner for this A2 unit.

However, you will also need to make a list of 'fingerprints' for the genre as whole. Then you can compare your practitioner fingerprints to the genre overall, thus seeing the extent to which each practitioner follows the conventions of the genre. Do not be tempted to think that all practitioners follow these conventions closely. You need to ask yourself whether any of the practitioners that you have studied is a maverick – someone who does not always obey all of the 'rules'.

The exam board makes it clear that you need to avoid setting up unfair comparisons. If you are studying political performance, but choose to study Alan Ayckbourn, there is a good chance that because his domestic dramas generally focus on human relationships and the way in which families relate to each other, this will be at variance with the type of gritty, persuasive material produced by the dance and music practitioners you may have studied.

Links between the art forms

Performance studies as a course of study exists mainly because of the opportunity it gives for considering the art forms of dance, drama and music together. In the case of the American musical, the art forms were deliberately intended to complement one another (at least in most cases). This gives something of an advantage (but only in this aspect) for those studying musicals, but it does not necessarily make the study any easier. You still have to be able to demonstrate the way in which the art forms work together in this genre. In the case of postmodern performance or political performance, the links are not always that obvious, because the practitioners you study did not always intend their work to link the art forms.

It's quite reasonable for you to draw attention to any differences between practitioners. No one is expecting you to pretend that they did exactly the same thing. In fact, one of the features of a weak answer is where the candidate tries to pretend that all of the practitioners they have studied did exactly the same thing.

The whole reason that the performing arts work together effectively is because of the real contrasts and differences that exist between them. Some of the people that you will study have worked with other practitioners; others have worked primarily as choreographers, composers or playwrights. Perhaps they never expected their work to be considered alongside that of practitioners in other art forms. Yet that is precisely what you are required to do.

Relationship between works in the genre

We have already mentioned the need for you to understand the significance of the individual works that you've studied. This is to some extent a reiteration of a point that we started to make earlier about the **inter-dependence** of repertoire. In other words, no piece of repertoire exists in a vacuum. Someone writing a piece of music in 2005 is bound to be influenced by other pieces produced in that year or recent years, even if they are not conscious of this. So whether intended or not, there will be some ways in which other pieces have made their mark on a piece, simply because the practitioner would be familiar with other things written at about the same time.

> **Tip**
> To appreciate the links between the art forms, you will need to be aware of similarities and contrasts. In some cases the links will be obvious; in other cases you may be more aware of contrasts than similarities. The important thing is that you are able to make a fair comparison between the three art forms.

How many similarities really exist between the three practitioners in the topic you have studied? You can get credit for identifying differences too.

Tip

We've already mentioned the need to produce a 'map' showing the chronology of the main works produced during the timeline of the topic that you're studying. You'll need to do some research – through books as well as the Internet – to ascertain what the most important works are and how the extracts you study might have been influenced by them.

You need to be sure what was happening in the world at the time that your set of extracts was written. Don't try to gloss over these – world events can be absolutely vital to understanding the influences on performing arts works.

It is notoriously difficult, however, to prove the influence of one piece on another, and you need to avoid trying to show a cause-and-effect relationship between individual works. It would be better for you to think back to the list of fingerprints of the topic as whole so that you can make some reasoned judgements about the extent to which an individual work reflects the commonly accepted trends within a genre.

Cultural, historical and social context

The most difficult thing here is to interpret the extra-artistic influences on a practitioner or on a style. For example, how can you prove that the Second World War had any effect at all on political pieces written immediately after. How can it be possible to prove that the Wall Street financial crash had any influence on the American musicals written immediately before or after it? How can you prove that the 1960s were the most important decade for establishing the rise of postmodernism?

Ultimately, all you can do is to make reference to the factors that are commonly held to be influential in the development of the genre and refer to external factors that could be seen as being of direct relevance. For example, most social historians would see the 1960s as being of major significance in the thought-world of artistic products, because a new spirit of acceptance for works – regardless of their style or background – ushered in a new age of tolerance and cultural democracy. On the other hand, some commentators will dissent from that view to say that there is simply no clear link between the two things, and claim that the reason for the whole postmodern condition is just that the 1960s were a reaction to the 1950s. They may feel that in due course there will be a radical re-assessment of the social outlook embodied in the 1960s, as has become increasingly common in the political world of the first decade of the 21st century. Remember also that works in a particular style may well critique rather than reinforce the culture that gave rise to them.

In summary, you'll need to be very familiar with these six aspects so that the questions on the paper don't take you by surprise. It's rare to be told what the questions on an examination paper will be about – so make the most of this opportunity.

Postmodern approaches to the performing arts since 1960

Looking for a definition

Postmodernism has been discussed and defined by various theorists and written about in numerous books and articles in recent years, but it still tends to elude quick and easy definition. A web search produces the following definition:

> **postmodernism**: genre of art and literature and especially architecture in reaction against principles and practices of established modernism.

Obviously, this is not particularly helpful if you're not sure what modernism itself is, so it's important to look at a definition of this too:

> **modernism**: the deliberate departure from tradition and the use of innovative forms of expression that distinguish many styles in the arts and literature of the twentieth century.

From looking at these two definitions, you might conclude that modernism broke away from traditional forms and structures, and that postmodernism in some way moved back toward them – and to some extent, this would be true. In the postmodern era, styles can be mixed within works, and earlier styles and conventions can be used freely without reference to their original context. One way of explaining this more clearly is to use the example of dance:

➤ **Classical ballet** is considered to be a traditional art form that follows a set of very strict rules. These rules apply not only to the movement vocabulary but also to the way the ballet company consists of a hierarchy of dancers from chorus to prima ballerina.

➤ **Modern ballet** breaks away from some of these set rules. Different types of music are used, and the ballet might appear more experimental and abstract while still using a high degree of technique.

➤ **Postmodern dance**, on the other hand, can use whatever style it likes or invent a new vocabulary for each piece as and when required. There can be a fusion of styles, or styles can exist alongside one another in the piece. There are no rules that govern what the piece should be about, nor what structure it should have or where it should be performed. It can be theatrical if it wants to be, it can have extravagant costumes and sets, and it can be performed in a proscenium arch theatre or in a warehouse or both. It uses what has been set up in the past – traditional art forms – and mixes them up, or simply takes what it needs from each art form or style. Non-dancers can be used in pieces, and all body shapes and sizes are included. Able-bodied and disabled dancers may be used side by side. Each dancer has an equal status and elitism is avoided.

Don't worry if you are still finding the concept of postmodernism difficult. Read through the following definitions offered by theorists and discuss them with other students on your course.

66 Postmodernism tries to come to terms with and understand a media-saturated society. The mass media, for example, were once thought of as holding up a mirror to, and thereby reflecting, a wider social reality. Now that reality is only definable in terms of surface reflection of the mirror. 99 Dominic Strinati

Consider the difference between a reflection of reality and a surface reflection of reality. What does the word 'surface' imply?

66 Postmodernism is sceptical of any absolute, universal and all-embracing claim to knowledge and argues that theories or doctrines which make such claims are increasingly open to criticism, contestation and doubt. 99 Dominic Strinati

Consider whether people believe what their governments tell them, or what a certain religion says about the creation of the world.

Further reading

If you studied Christopher Bruce at AS, you should already be familiar with eclecticism and the use of ballet with contemporary dance. See pages 55–64 of the *OCR AS Guide* for more on Bruce. Eclecticism can be defined as the process of making decisions simply on the basis of what seems best, rather than following a single doctrine or style.

What others say

Mass media refers to public communication that reaches a large audience.

Further reading

Come on Down? Popular Media Culture in Post-War Britain by D.Strinati and S.Wagg (eds) (Routledge 1992).

Scepticism: a doubting or questioning attitude or state of mind (compare 'uncertainty'); **or** the doctrine that absolute knowledge is impossible either in a particular domain or in general.

Further reading

The Postmodern Condition: A Report on Knowledge by Jean-Francois Lyotard (Manchester University Press 1984).

Further reading

Jean Baudrillard wrote an essay entitled *Simulations* (Semiotext(e) 1983), in which he tried to explain the differences between reality as portrayed by the media and reality as experienced by individuals in their everyday lives. This quote is from *Jean Baudrillard, Selected Writings*, ed. Mark Poster (Stanford University Press 2001).

> 66 Eclecticism is the degree of contemporary general culture; one listens to reggae, watches Westerns, eats MacDonald's for lunch and local cuisine for dinner, wears Paris perfume in Tokyo and retro clothing in Hong Kong; knowledge is a matter for TV games. 99 Jean-Francois Lyotard

Consider what kinds of food you eat and where it comes from. Do you ever eat food from restaurants? Is each cuisine from a different country? Think about the clothes you buy, the music you listen to and the films you watch. Do they all reflect one type of culture – for example, French – or are they from a mixture of different countries and cultures?

> 66 Disneyland is there to conceal the fact that it is the 'real' country, all of 'real' America, which is Disneyland... Disneyland is presented as imaginary, in order to make us believe that the rest is 'real', when in fact all of Los Angeles and the America surrounding it are no longer real, but of the order of the hyper-real and of simulation. It is no longer a question of questioning a false representation of reality...but of concealing the fact that the real is no longer real, and thus of saving the reality principle. 99 Jean Baudrillard

Baudrillard discussed the idea that **simulations** or copies of things are taking the place of real artifacts in postmodern society. For example, when we visit a theme park that has a cowboy ranch, we think that this represents a real ranch, even though it is probably little like the real thing. We are more familiar with the imitation than with a genuine cowboy ranch. Consider the slogan for Coca Cola: 'the real thing'. What exactly is this saying about the drink? What does the word 'real' refer to? Is there a difference between your experience of drinking Coca Cola and the experience offered by the advertisements? Can you tell the difference between reality and illusion?

Technological developments

Over the last 25 years, there have been enormous developments in technology and communications. Some of the technological developments of the late 20th and the early 21st centuries have made the following possible:

➤ We have access to news from around the world at any time of day. We have access to live events in other countries and no longer have to wait to see recorded versions of them.

➤ We can communicate via email, Internet and mobile phone on a global level. We can jump straight from one Internet site to another and flick through a myriad of channels on television.

➤ We can travel quickly from one country to another and think nothing of a weekend away in a foreign capital.

➤ We have experience of many different cultures around the world and these have influenced our lifestyles and our identity.

➤ We buy more commodities and enjoy owning gadgets such as the latest mobile phone, DVD player, digital camera, iPod or fashion accessory.

➤ We can create our own social identities and change them at will.

Think back to the Lyotard quote above about eclecticism: in today's society, we're surrounded by cultural elements from around the

Further study

Look at pop icons such as Madonna and David Bowie, and trace how their public identity has changed over the years. Do you dress in the same way now as you did when you were 14?

world on a daily basis. Everything is mixed together in a way that was not possible prior to these technological advances.

Collaboration is a significant part of postmodernism; it recognises the value of art forms working together. There is mutual respect among all theatrical art forms (lighting, sound, costume and set design) and developing art forms such as the use of digital media in performance. In dance, choreographers are constantly trying to find new ways to express meaning through dance and to interplay with other art forms.

Intertextuality is a term that you will frequently encounter when reading about postmodernism. It means that in one text, such as a film, you can see references to other texts. When the viewer detects these references, it adds to their sense of engagement with the film.

How is your identity constructed? Who are you? Consider the society in which we live today. How are different cultures portrayed? What have you seen in terms of live performance that has taught you something new about a culture with which you had previously had little contact? On what is your identity based? Is it your family background? The social class your parents belong to? The school you went to? The clothes you wear? Which group of friends you have and the music they like? When considering the following practitioners and the extracts from their body of work, try to think about how identity is portrayed.

Now look at the extracts that we discuss below (pages 63–79) and familiarise yourself with the three practitioners and their work. Consider the features of postmodernism and the fingerprints of each of the practitioners' work. Try to make links between them and keep in mind that you are studying postmodern approaches to performance from 1960 to the present day. You will not have to give definitions of postmodernism in your essay but you will need to know about how the extracts that you study reflect the practitioners' postmodern approaches to performance.

Fingerprints of postmodernism

The distinction between 'high art' and popular culture is now blurred, and in performance work the two are often mixed. High art refers to forms such as opera or classical ballet, or a well-known and respected painter's work hanging in a national art museum. Popular culture includes such art forms as pop music, football and *Big Brother*.

When considering form and style, it used to be possible to find a progression from one historical period to another. Artistic techniques, styles and genres from one style or period evolved into others. In the postmodern age, the proliferation of a broad range of artistic styles at the same time has made it increasingly difficult to speak of what is mainstream or to see any obvious direction for future developments. Practitioners now borrow elements from a variety of historical periods and mix them up.

Simple stories are told with a clear beginning, middle and end; the events are presented in the order in which they happened. But is this a reasonable way to present information to the listener or

Integration of art forms

Web link

Wayne MacGregor's *Nemesis* is a good example of this. See his dance company's site at: www.randomdance.org.

Looking for an identity

One term to consider in relation to identity is **multiculturalism**, which can refer to a social or educational theory that encourages interest in many cultures within a society, rather than one mainstream culture. It can also refer to a condition whereby many cultures exist within a society and maintain their cultural differences.

High art and popular culture

Anderson uses the work of Bosch alongside that of Escher. Glass is inspired by opera as well as pop music.

The end of history

In *Top Girls* Churchill puts female characters from different historical contexts in a dinner party scene where they sit at the same table and converse. Glass draws on styles from different periods and traditions.

Lack of a linear narrative

viewer? Consider everyday conversations that you have with your friends. If you're telling them about what happened at the weekend, you don't necessarily go through the events in the order in which they took place. In real life, we interrupt each other and fill in details that we may have forgotten to give before, thus jumping around on the timeline.

In performance terms, this jumping backwards and forwards constitutes flashbacks and flashforwards. The end of the event may be presented halfway through the play or even at the beginning; the rest of the play could be one long flashback, bringing us back to the present day or going beyond it. The events could be presented in the wrong order or from multiple perspectives. You might see the same event over and over again, but each time from a slightly different angle. The structure and form of a postmodern piece – whether it is dance, drama or music – is not dependent on the linear presentation of a story.

Indeed, there may be no storyline. The piece may look at themes or aspects of something that has caught the practitioner's eye (or ear). The piece may be a type of study in relationships, but these need not be between defined characters. The characters might not have names. They might represent groups of people. There might be groups of performers representing certain groups of people, as Anderson has in *Cross Channel*, to create juxtaposition between different gender groups. The structure might be that of collage or montage, where there is no intention to tell a story. The practitioner wants to present ideas and allow an audience to interpret them in different ways.

No sense of closure

If there is no story to tell, there need be no ending. Audiences sometimes criticise pieces that appear to have no discernable ending with no sense of completion or a character coming to a definitive realisation about something. Many pieces are left open so that the audience feels they might continue or go around in a circle. If the events are presented in what might be considered the 'wrong order', how can the audience know where they end? The events are presented by different characters or performers, encouraging the idea of multiple perspectives. The audience is as valuable as the performers in adding their perspective on the work. Akram Khan in *Ma* seems to offer a certain type of circularity to his piece, even when talking about stories. Wayne MacGregor's *Nemesis* appears to offer a narrative thread as creatures mutate on stage. However, the audience is never really sure of what is happening in narrative terms or whether they should even be looking for a story.

Mixing styles

Postmodernist practitioners have broken through a barrier as far as style is concerned. Rather than keeping to one style – for example, classical ballet, where one must adhere to a set of strict rules and a set vocabulary of movement – they reject such codes and conventions, and take from different styles what they will. It is not unusual to see ballet, tap and contemporary in one piece. Some practitioners invent a completely new dance vocabulary and even develop new vocabularies of movement for each piece that they make. Some practitioners admit to fusing different styles together, but others talk of one style existing alongside another without the two being mixed.

In this chapter, we are going to consider Lea Anderson, Caryl Churchill and Philip Glass as postmodern practitioners. Even if you are not studying these practitioners, you should be able to draw a lot of valuable information and tips about postmodernism and how different practitioners have approached it from the material presented here.

In the course of this chapter, we've given you a fair amount of biographical detail about each of the practitioners discussed. However, remember that while you should have some idea of the background of your practitioners, you are advised not to spend time relating biographical information in your exam essay unless it is directly related to a point you are making about the genre.

Lea Anderson

Postmodern dance

As we've said, a postmodern art form challenges pre-existing codes and conventions to offer something new. This does not mean to say that previous forms cannot be used – indeed, the past is often revisited and reworked to produce a new perspective.

In postmodern dance, strict techniques such as classical ballet do not need to be followed but aspects of these techniques such as a straight back or a pointed foot can be employed. Any technique from martial arts to pedestrian movement can be employed and new ones invented. The hierarchy of the ballet company need no longer exist as all dancers have equal status on stage – there is no longer a prima ballerina and a chorus. Instead, there are different relationships between dancers from solos to duets through trios and other formations to ensemble work where the whole company performs together on stage at the same time. It is no longer just the men who lift and support the women. A dancer can lift dancers of the opposite or same gender. The emphasis on the perfect body has also disappeared. Dancers can be of any height and size: everyone is entitled to dance. Several companies have been created that employ both able-bodied and disabled-bodied dancers who then work together to create pieces.

Further study

For example, StopGAP have worked with different choreographers to create new works, and run workshops in schools and colleges encouraging participants to find their own strengths within the domain of dance. The emphasis is finding an appropriate dance vocabulary to express intention. www.stopgap.uk.com

Background

This art background explains her concern with visual impact in the décor, colours, textures and other details of materials and costume in her pieces.

Lea Anderson was born in 1959 and attended ballet classes as a child. She did a foundation course at St Martin's School of Art, but abandoned art to complete a dance degree at the Laban Centre. In her final year at Laban, she choreographed *The Cholmondeley Sisters* (1984), inspired by a painting of the same name in the Tate Gallery. It was performed at the Edinburgh Fringe Festival with Teresa Barker and Gaynor Coward and thus The Cholmondeleys (pronounced 'Chumlies') company was born. The company performed at one-off gigs, cabarets and small arts venues, and eventually was invited to perform at The Place, London. The company grew in number and the all-male Featherstonehaughs (pronounced 'Fanshaws') were created. Sometimes the two companies dance separately, and sometimes together, for example for *Flag* (1989), *Birthday* (1992) and *Precious* (1993).

Anderson has collaborated over a long period of time with musical composers Steve Blake and Drostan Madden, and designer Sandy Powell (Oscar winner for costume designs in *The Aviator*).

How is Anderson postmodern?

Anderson recycles images from art, and reassembles texts and images from popular culture to create new meaning through collage and juxtaposition. Anderson usually keeps a working notebook, and places in it ideas, images and text that she later shares with those working on the project. Movement material can be taken from an image or perhaps an observed movement. The pedestrian movement and gesture in her pieces also introduces everyday elements, and she incorporates an eclectic range of styles.

She uses unconventional venues and locations for her pieces, and mixes historical and contemporary styles in her costumes. Unison work is an important part of her choreography, and she rejects any hierarchy of dancers or any prejudice regarding certain body types. Her work shows a keen awareness of gender issues.

The three pieces that we have chosen to look at here are *Flesh and Blood* (1989), *Cross Channel* (1991) and *Car* (1996). Other works that would be suitable to study are *Jesus Baby Heater* (1992), *Lost Dances of Egon Schiele* (2001) and *Speed Ramp* (2002). All of these are all available on video from admin@thecholmondeleys.org or 020 7378 8800.

Extract 1: Flesh and Blood

We noted above that one of the postmodern features of Anderson's work is her use of unusual sets and locations for her pieces. *Flesh and Blood* demonstrates this from its opening, with a duet that takes place on a derelict wharfside. There is no eye contact between the dancers, and the dancer at the back seems to be controlling and manipulating the dancer in the front, who tries to escape. The duet is static, but eventually the front dancer steps sideways with her hands clasped in front of her body as if genuflecting (bending the knee as if in prayer) and runs away.

In complete contrast, the second section is located in a black studio and consists of five dancers doing floor work, including crawling, rolling and stretching. There is a strong element of unison work, and a sharp contrast between the staccato movement at the beginning of the section and the more lyrical sequence where the dancers touch the floor around them with their fingertips. Anderson is well known for her use of gesture and small movements. Later in the section, with performers in the reptile position, the floor becomes a sea of bodies wriggling and undulating, creating a powerful visual image.

This section is an excellent example of how Anderson uses other art forms, and images from elsewhere in particular, as a starting point for her work. Here her inspiration was the 20th-century graphic artist Escher, who produced a body of work depicting flat, interlocking shapes, often in the form of animals. His *Reptiles* (1943) is a portrayal of lizards seen from an overhead perspective as they appear to be crawling out of a book. The flatness of Escher's imagery can also be seen in the positions of the dancers and the use of flat palms held out with arms at the aide of the body. The 15th-century Dutch artist Hieronymus Bosch was another source of inspiration. His work depicted scenes of monsters and devils and lowly creatures, which can be seen in the floor work of *Flesh and Blood*.

The third section takes place in two locations – a cathedral and the black studio. There are three dancers standing and four lying down. The section is tranquil and the pace slower, enhanced by the gentle sounds on the keyboards. The dancers use their heads, eyes,

---

Flesh and Blood was choreographed as a live stage performance for the Cholmondeleys in 1989 and was adapted for television as part of the series *Tights, Camera, Action*. It consists of five sections and has seven performers. There is a distinct piece of music, composed by Steve Blake, and a change of location for each section.

Further study

To mark the 20th anniversary of the Cholmondeleys in 2004, the two gendered companies swapped roles, and the Featherstonehaughs performed *Flesh and Blood*. A video of this performance will be available from autumn 2005. A useful resource pack on *Flesh and Blood* can be obtained from National Resource Centre for Dance (NRCD), University of Surrey: www.surrey.ac.uk/NRCD, 01483 879316.

Web link

Many Escher and Bosch images can be found online. See, for example, www.mcescher.com and www.ibiblio.org/wm/paint/auth/bosch.

> " While the upright movement has associations with heavenly aspirations and virtuousness, the floor work is symbolic of lowliness, death and being cast down to hell. "
>
> Sherril Dodds.

fingers and thumbs to present images connected to a religious theme. The short haircuts and the eyes raised up to heaven are reminiscent of Carl Dreyer's film *Joan of Arc*.

The dancers lying down perform slow movements with a gentle, flowing dynamic, rocking and knocking the ground. There is a religious significance in the use of vertical and horizontal positions. The vertical dancers look almost angelic as they are well lit and wearing shimmering dresses. Section four takes place in the cathedral, with two pairs of dancers performing duets and facing to the front. Again the duets are mostly static but do involve lifts and falls and support work. There are also religious gestures such as kneeling.

In section five, all seven dancers are present, and the location is the black studio mixed in with shots of the crypt's blue ceiling. Motifs are used from previous sections and there is a lot of unison work with sometimes a duet or a trio performing. The imagery of the cross can be detected in the positions and gestures used by the dancers. More space is used in this section and there is a greater variety of movement. The ending of the piece shows three dancers curled up on the floor and four looking upwards, one hand pointing up to the ceiling and the other pointing down.

Anderson offers multiple perspectives on the representation of the female gender and of religion in *Flesh and Blood*. The women can be seen as supportive carers in the contact duets and then as obedient servants when kneeling. Then, as if out of character, the women can be seen writhing on the floor and using violent gestures, their faces looking transfixed and perhaps possessed. Anderson chooses a non-linear, non-narrative form and prefers to put the five sections together in a type of collage. The piece is left open to the audience to interpret.

Extract 2: Cross Channel

The piece lasts about 30 minutes and takes place in various locations as it shows a journey across the Channel from Dover to Calais. Both companies are in the piece and behave as distinct gender groups through much of it. The journey starts at Victoria train station and moves through the countryside, showing a pub, a green and the inside of the train carriage. The dancers move on to a ferry, and later we see them on a beach, in a hotel, inside a tent and in a beach hut. The changing locations had implications for the choreography because, although some of it was created in rehearsal, some was made or adapted on site. The variety of locations, the showing of the film on television and the quirky humour of the piece make it more accessible to a wider audience.

As we said earlier, Anderson often takes movement material from an image or perhaps an observed movement. For *Cross Channel*, she used photographs by Hoyningen Huene (1900–1968) who produced images of the 1920s leisured classes. Jacques Tati's film *Monsieur Hulot's Holiday* (1953) was another source of inspiration as it was based on visual comedy.

> " Flesh and Blood...is a particularly expert mix of contradictions. Gestures of fervent piety and penance become riffs of edgy, mechanistic dance, and religious ardour is mixed with images from hell: figures sprawled, clawing. "
>
> Judith Mackrell, *The Guardian*, 25 May 2004.

This recalls the condemnation as witches of women who were different from the majority, an aspect of women's history that we will look at in Churchill's *Vinegar Tom* below. Both Anderson and Churchill offer different representations of women and raise questions of sexuality and behaviour.

Cross Channel, directed by Margaret Williams and shot on 16mm film, was shown on BBC2 in 1992 and 1994. Steve Blake composed the music which Anderson wanted 'to contrast with the images that we were working with' and 'to be contemporary and supportive'. (Cross Channel Resource Pack).

Further study

As well as the video of *Cross Channel*, there is an accompanying resource pack available from admin@thecholmondeleys.org or 020 7378 8800.

> ❝ Anderson's work may be said to reflect postmodern society in that, although she draws upon recognisable elements from the real world, she assembles them in a fragmented form…her movement vocabulary is made up of pedestrian movement, gesture, popular dance forms, tableaux imagery from high art and elements of contemporary dance. ❞
>
> Sherril Dodds in her analysis of
> *Flesh and Blood* (NRCD, *see below*)

In other words, we behave and dress in a way that we have learned from watching films, reading magazines and looking at representations of our gender in the media.

Intertextuality is an important part in Anderson's work – for example, there are references to Fred Astaire films and to icons such as Marilyn Monroe. This allows for many different interpretations of the text and multi-layered meanings – different audience members will see different things in it.

The movement in *Cross Channel* is characterised by pedestrian movement such as the men cycling, the women putting on suntan cream or make-up. The lighting is used to highlight the naturalistic setting. This is very different from staging a dance piece in a theatre or staying in one specific site where the site becomes like a stage and can therefore be lit accordingly. Some of the dance takes place on sand or pebbles or in a corridor so the surface with which the dancers are in contact changes the dynamic of the movement and gives rise to different interpretations from the audience. Unison and repetition are used to give clear images of the two genders and how they behave when they are together.

The costumes (designed by Sandy Powell) help to distinguish the Cholmondeleys from the Featherstonehaughs. There is a typically postmodern mixture of eras present in the costume from 1950s white dresses trimmed with black, straw hats and gloves for the women to 1990s lycra cycling outfits for the men. There are also orange boiler suits, French-looking blue-and-white-striped tops with navy shorts and shoes, bathing suits (rubber for the men), suits, smart waiter costumes for those tending the bar and Hawaiian shirts for the customers.

Also in postmodern fashion, there is a mixture of historical styles. This borrowing of images from other eras is characteristic of the postmodern idea of the end of history, whereby images and texts are available simultaneously from different periods, leading us to lose any sense of history.

The costumes are juxtaposed against one another in the various sections of the dance and add to the humour and lightheartedness of the holiday atmosphere. The use of props develops the humour further. For example, the bicycles, used by the men as a means of transport, provide an amusing contrast of energy with the women travelling on the train in more sedate fashion.

Gender is presented in unexpected ways so you need to be aware of the representation of groups of men and women throughout the piece. Consider how the two genders behave when there is a mixed-gender group and when they are presented as a single-gender group. When doing this, consider the postmodern idea of the death of the subject – it is believed that we are no longer independent, freethinking and unique, but rather the result of social constructions.

Anderson is well known for her use of unison work. In *Cross Channel*, look for unison work that reinforces the idea of one gender operating in a certain way. It may go with or be contrary to your expectations. Ask yourself whether we behave in a certain way because we have been born male or female, or whether we have learned to behave like that because society and the media have constructed our gender behaviour. Look at the dancers and decide whether they have specific fully rounded characters or whether they flit from one image to another. Do they have any sense of depth as people? Can you see any evidence of the influence of snapshots? Look for the use of two dimensions rather than three.

Extract 3: Car

In *Car*, Lea Anderson makes use of non-theatrical spaces, as the Cholmondeleys dance in and around a shining silver car in a variety of unusual venues, including a warehouse and outdoor carparks. One of the interesting aspects of this unusual piece of site-specific work (or perhaps one should say set-specific or even prop-specific) is the way the light changes throughout the day to bring different moods and atmospheres to the choreography. In one section, filmed outdoors, the sun is setting and gives a romantic orange wash to the action.

Anderson explores many possible scenarios that might take place in a car, including some very well known scenes such as the assassination of John F. Kennedy. All the dancers wear pink suits and sunglasses in the style of Jackie Kennedy. They start in the car, and are just getting out as they perform a sequence of waves at the crowd, which reminds us immediately of the iconic status of the late president's wife. The music jars and the dancers' bodies move as if violently shaken by the gunshots that in real life killed President Kennedy. This is typical of Anderson's use of references to popular culture and her fusion of styles

Anderson goes on to show scenes of abduction, joy-riding and sexual action in the back of the car, exploring all the car has to offer. Each part of the car is used as a surface, including the boot, which opens as if in time to the music to reveal two dancers lying on their backs, performing leg kicks as in some bizarre warm-up class. In one section, a dancer walks along the side of the car with body horizontal, aided by another dancer.

The costumes give an immediate interpretation of character – their personality and status – whether it be Jackie Kennedy or a ninja warrior. However, the idea of character is not straightforward, because where you might expect to see one Jackie Kennedy, you see six, offering multiple interpretations. This follows on throughout the piece with six ninjas.

Look carefully at how Anderson manages to turn a dull and traditionally non-theatrical space into a theatrical one.

Car (1996) was directed and choreographed by Anderson. The music is by Drostan Madden and Sandy Powell designed the costumes.

Further reading
It would be worth researching New Dance in Britain, which began in the 1980s, as this is the period when Anderson evolved as a choreographer. Read *Out of Line: The Story of British New Dance* by Judith Mackrell (Dance Books 1992).

Caryl Churchill

In much postmodern drama, the plot of a piece is less important than its content. Thus plays have a non-linear structure that does not simply show the journey of one character. At AS, you may have come across the dramatic unities of time, place and action – whereby the action takes place in real time and in chronological order, in one location with a rational, consequential plot. You may have encountered the concept of the 'well-made play'. The well-made play has a very clear, linear structure that centers

Postmodern drama

Background

around its main character and how they deal with some kind of obstacle or conflict. The action of the play sets out the situation and characters clearly at the beginning, has a clear plot development with suspense building to a clear resolution. In postmodern drama, there is no need to work within such rules – the structure does not need to be linear and it does not need to focus around a single character or any particular conflict. The structure can be episodic, can move backwards and forwards in time and can take place in multiple settings.

As with postmodern dance, there is often a sense of the end of history, with a mixing of periods and styles within a single piece. Other art forms may well play an important part, with music and dance being introduced into a drama. Speech and dialogue forms can be mixed, with songs and everyday language alongside more formal or poetic speech. Modern technology can also be used to create effects that previously would not have been possible.

Caryl Churchill was born in London in 1938, though she spent much of her youth living in Canada. She returned to England to study English language and literature at Oxford, where she began to write plays, including *Downstairs*, which was first produced in 1958. After graduating, Churchill spent ten years writing for BBC radio (1962–1972). The nature of radio drama impacted noticeably on her work – without the visual element of theatre, the spoken word took on extra significance, and the freedom from stage directions afforded her more experimentation with structure, chronology and location.

Churchill's televised work started in 1972 with *The Judge's Wife*, and in 1974 she became resident dramatist at the Royal Court Theatre, London, a venue well known for encouraging new and radical writing. This position allowed her to begin writing specifically for the theatre. During the mid 1970s she collaborated with theatre companies, most significantly Joint Stock and Monstrous Regiment, both of which were dedicated to exploring feminist issues. These collaborations had enormous impact on her writing, as she found herself meeting, thinking, sharing and working with actors, rather than writing in isolation. This collaborative approach to writing supported the character creation so important to the drive of Churchill's plays. The attention to detail in the language used, the feeling of a real history and life for the characters, the emotional depth and poignancy that each character has – all are the product of working directly with actors. The character is not a fiction created on paper, but a tangible person formed in collaboration with an actor.

There is a vast body of work to choose from when looking at Churchill as a postmodern practitioner. If possible, you should look at works from different eras of her life and check that they have been performed live on stage and not just for television or radio. Elaine Aston's book *Caryl Churchill* divides Churchill's work up to 1997 into five different categories, which is useful when trying to give a broad view of Churchill and her development over several decades.

One of Churchill's most well known stylistic features is her approach to speech and dialogue. She makes great use in her plays of overlapping dialogue, whereby characters interrupt and speak over one another. This is a more faithful representation of the way we converse in real life than more formalised dramatic dialogue. She also mixes high-level with everyday language, and introduces song and verse into her plays. This makes the drama less naturalistic.

Churchill's narratives tend to be non-linear, often with a lack of closure, and she adopts an experimental treatment of time and place. All of this moves away from conventional rules about dramatic unities and the well-made play.

Often referred to as a feminist writer, Churchill explores gender issues, often using historical figures and events as parallels for contemporary matters. She is concerned with investigating the changing nature, or even loss, of culture, and again historical parallels enable her to do so. Her plays often use multi-roling, character doubling and cross-gender casting.

As a postmodern playwright, Churchill tends to play with different styles and to collaborate with other art forms such as music and dance, as well as with practitioners from other fields (Ian Spink from Second Stride, for example). Intertextuality is important in many of her plays. Her workshop techniques and collaboration with theatre companies such as Monstrous Regiment, Joint Stock and Out of Joint have a huge impact on her work.

The three extracts chosen for examination here are *Vinegar Tom* (1976), *Top Girls* (1982) and *Ice Cream* (1989). You might choose some later plays from the 1990s such as *Mad Forest*, *The Skriker* or *Blue Heart*, which show further stylistic development and an interesting linguistic fascination on the part of the playwright.

Extract 1: Vinegar Tom

Vinegar Tom takes its name from a cat owned by an old woman in the play who is accused of witchcraft. The play is set in rural 17th-century England, and revolves around a group of women from various backgrounds. Churchill wrote *Vinegar Tom* while working with Monstrous Regiment, who she had met originally on an abortion march.

The play tells the story of each character and asks the audience to consider the position of women in contemporary society through its use of song. As Churchill says in the introduction to the play: 'The women accused of witchcraft were often those on the edge of society, old, poor, single, sexually unconventional; the old herbal medical tradition of the cunning woman was suppressed by the rising professionalism of the male doctor.' The play is not about witches but about persecuted women and about prejudice.

Vinegar Tom has an episodic structure, with its 21 scenes broken up by contemporary songs that are not part of the action and are sung 'in modern dress'. The use of songs allows the characters to show people who are marginalised or absent from the overall picture often painted of a society or a community. They throw up

How is Churchill postmodern?

Tip

With a Churchill text, do not expect to find a straightforward plot and easily recognisable characters. Allow yourself to read through the entire text without understanding all of it. Then reread it while looking up certain words or allusions with which you are unfamiliar. Be aware of your reaction to the text each time and jot down a few notes.

If you can, see a live production or find a video as this should help to make the play clearer.

If you have the opportunity, read the play with a group of friends and follow the casting advice given in the introduction to the play. This will also help you visualise the play on a stage.

Further reading

There are three good collections of Churchill's plays, two by Methuen and one by Nick Hern Books.

Vinegar Tom was first presented at the Humberside Theatre in 1976. It was directed by Pam Brighton and designed by Andrea Montag. For the songs, Churchill wrote the words and Helen Glavin the music.

Monstrous Regiment was formed in the mid-1970s as a response to the male bias in theatre at the time. The Women's Liberation Movement and feminism were important in the 1970s.

A suitable length for an extract from *Vinegar Tom* would be about eight or nine scenes.

issues that are often ignored or taboo subjects that many do not want to tackle. In the production notes, Churchill states 'it is essential that the actors are not in character when they sing the songs'. This creates a modern reference to the period action, alerting the audience to the relevance of various attitudes towards women. They remind the audience that women are still unfairly treated and often persecuted. The song 'Oh Doctor' demonstrates how the female patient is disempowered when looked at by the male doctor, who considers her body in parts rather than as a whole being. The patient is not party to the conversation that the doctor has with the nurse even though the subject of the discussion is the patient's own body.

The 'metal eye' looks into holes in the woman's body and has the effect of dissecting her when she would prefer to be treated as an entirety. This song reveals how men look at women as objects and – worse – as pieces rather than as a whole. This reflects feminist theory of the time and reminds us of the fight against pornography whereby women are shown as sexual objects with the emphasis on their sexual organs.

Many of the scenes are duologues with the sense of one character confiding in another. In this way the characters' stories are exposed to the audience. The form of the play indicates that Churchill and Monstrous Regiment did not want a male character as the central focus, or a linear plot focusing around one character's journey, but rather wanted to show the lives of *several* females to illuminate how women were mistreated.

Churchill includes the characters of Kramer and Sprenger who were the authors of the *Malleus Maleficarum* – a book on the identification of witches highly regarded in the 17th century. They concluded that all witchcraft originated from women's 'insatiable' sexual appetites. These two men are played by women and appear in the final scene in music-hall style with top hat and tails.

The cross-gender casting and introduction of music-hall style makes the audience stand back from the rest of the play and consider the dangerous potential of the words delivered by Kramer and Sprenger. It raises the point that women should not be condemned for their sexual appetite.

Extract 2: Top Girls

The extract we look at here is taken from the opening act of *Top Girls* (about 40 minutes in performance time), takes place in a restaurant on a Saturday night and introduces us to the central character Marlene, a career-minded woman. She has organised a dinner to celebrate her promotion to managing director of an employment agency. What is unusual is her choice of guests: rather than contemporary peers, they are all women from different historical eras: Isabella Bird (1831–1904) was a Victorian traveller from Edinburgh; Lady Nijo (b.1258) was a Japanese courtesan and later a Buddhist nun; Dull Gret is the girl from the Brueghel painting *Dulle Griet*; Pope Joan is said to have been Pope – disguised as a man – between 854 and 856; and Patient Griselda is the obedient wife whose story is told in Chaucer's *The Clerk's Tale*.

> " Tell me what you whisper to nurse,
> Whatever I've got, you're making it worse.
> I'm wide awake, but I still can't shout.
> Why can't I see what you're taking out? "
>
> 'Oh Doctor'

Web link

See www.malleusmaleficarum.org.

Top Girls was first produced in 1982 at the Royal Court Theatre, directed by Max Stafford-Clark. The Methuen edition of this play is strongly recommended.

Immediately we see that Churchill is playing with our notions of time and space and experimenting with the dramatic form. Set apart from the rest of the play, the act serves to introduce certain themes about love, duty, marriage and other relationships with men as well as the position of women in society. Each character tells their story in their own words and the women interrupt each other and overlap their words as they ask questions of each other and pass comment.

JOAN	I dressed as a boy when I left home.*
NIJO	green jacket. Lady Betto had a five layered gown in shades of green and purple.
ISABELLA	*You dressed as a boy?
MARLENE	Of course,/ for safety.
JOAN	No, not alone, I went with my friend./ He was sixteen.
NIJO	Ah. an elopement
JOAN	but I thought I knew more about science than he did and almost as much philosophy.
ISABELLA	Well I always travelled as a lady and I repudiated strongly any suggestion in the press that I was other than feminine.
MARLENE	I don't wear trousers in the office./ I could but I don't.

> * indicates that a speech follows on from an earlier one.

> / marks an overlap: the character starts to speak over the words of the previous character.

The script is very unusual, and at first it is difficult to master the three techniques of overlapping dialogue as explained in the introduction to the play:

➤ One character can start speaking before another has finished

➤ A character sometimes continues speaking right through another's speech

➤ Sometimes a speech follows on from a speech earlier than the one immediately before it.

Although some people have found this confusing and irritating, it is a close representation of the way real-life conversation develops, particularly when each person wants their story heard.

As the evening progresses and the women imbibe more alcohol, the atmosphere turns from order to chaos and the language becomes more fragmentary. Up to this point, the women have spoken articulately and in an educated manner about their past exploits, but now Joan is speaking in Latin and being sick, none of them is listening to the others and the party disintegrates. The character who is different from the others as far as linguistic capability is concerned is Gret. She is crude and to the point, describing the scene from the painting that is her reality. Her language is not grammatically correct. Her lack of manners at the table also distinguishes her from the other women.

Marlene acts like a professional middle-class woman, but we learn later in the play that she is from a working-class background and has given her only child Angie to her sister to bring up. Churchill **questions the role of women in society** and highlights what they have given up along the path to success. Is it possible for a woman to have job fulfilment and a happy family life at the same time?

> " My big son die on a wheel. Birds eat him. My baby, a soldier run her through with a sword. I'd had enough, I was mad, I hate the bastards. "
>
> Gret

In real life, people often tell stories in many different orders, and Churchill reflects this in her structure. Changing the order also helps juxtapose certain events for special effect or to make a point. The placing of Marlene among a group of successful women in Act 1 and then having her story shown through the following two acts shows different perspectives of her character and is akin to real life where a woman may reveal different sides to her personality to work colleagues, family members and new acquaintances.

Ice Cream was first performed at the Royal Court Theatre in 1989, directed by Max Stafford-Clark. The play has 20 short scenes and lasts for 75 minutes. It ran in conjunction with *Hot Fudge*, which played in the RCT Upstairs.

" The first half is exactly like a Hitchcockian movie in which a pair of holidaying Americans turn up in Europe and find themselves in a dizzying whorl of violence. The second half is a truncated road movie that sees rural America as a disquieting place filled with pockets of eccentricity. "

Michael Billington, *The Guardian*, 11 April 1989.

In the remaining two acts of the play, we witness other aspects of Marlene's life. We see her at work, where she is in control and enjoys telling others how to get on in life. Act 3 takes place a year earlier and reveals that Angie is Marlene's child. Through Marlene, *Top Girls* contrasts the type of feminism that simply creates powerful women striving to be like patriarchal men with a more socialist, inclusive feminism.

The **non-linear narrative structure** is a typical postmodernism approach – writers often play around with the presentation of chronological events and put them in a different order with flashbacks and flashforwards.

Extract 3: Ice Cream

In *Ice Cream*, Churchill presents us with two acts, one set in Britain and one in the USA, exploring the cultural identities of these different places. In scenes 1, 2 and 3, an American couple, Lance and Vera, are on holiday in Britain and represent stereotypical American tourists who see Britain as a heritage site and a way of tracing their ancestry. It is comical for a British audience who see their country in a culturally different light. Juxtaposed with the idyll of the English castle, cottage and pub is the east London flat where Lance finds his distant English cousins, Phil and Jaq. Similarly, the English cousins have a skewed vision of America as 'Old Cadillacs. Cactus. Long straight roads'.

The title of the play highlights the fact that although all four characters speak the same language, they do not pronounce the words in the same way and the emphasis is different. The same words can mean different things in each culture and thus lead to confusion as the speakers of the common language assume that they are all using the sign system in the same way.

The superficiality of the heritage culture soon gives way to a sinister side to British life. Examples include when Phil tries to kiss Vera (scene 6) or when a dead body is revealed (scene 7), the result of 'self-defence' according to Phil. The American couple help bury the body in Epping Forest. The macabre is further developed in Act 2 when the British cousins visit America. Phil is knocked down by a car and killed, and later Jaq kills an American professor who tries to assault her.

Critics have commented on the filmic quality of the play, which certainly seems to have been influenced by both American and British films. This intertextuality is a feature of postmodernism and used to good effect in this play with its fast-moving dialogue, overlapping lines and bursts of violence.

Churchill sets a different focus for each of her plays, but remains experimental in her treatment of themes and her fascination for form and structure. In this third extract, her enthusiasm for film is noted and reflects her intention to remain culturally relevant.

Philip Glass

As with dance and drama, postmodern approaches to music demonstrate eclecticism in form and genre. Increased interaction with other cultures and mass production of music has had a huge impact, making a large variety of very diverse music available, with numerous forms and genres co-existing and thus influencing one another.

In the early years of the 20th century, many composers felt that the romantic style of the music of previous years had become exhausted, and they therefore sought entirely new means of expression in what became known as modernist music. For some, this involved abandoning the idea of key and exploring new ways of organising pitch; for others, it meant experimenting with the use of two keys at a time. For many, it meant a much freer use of dissonance and an emphasis on new and exciting rhythms.

In the late 20th century, there was a reaction against the dissonance and preoccupation with technique that characterised much of the modernist music of preceding decades, and postmodern music came to the fore. Composers started to write in ways that seemed much more familiar to audiences than earlier avant-garde music had done. This was partly because they used a number of traditional techniques (such as mainly diatonic harmony) albeit in new and often very sparse ways.

Philip Glass was born in Maryland, Baltimore in 1937, a year after fellow American composer Steve Reich. Glass' music has often been compared to that of Reich and in many ways this is fair, since both grew up in the same musical environment in 1950s and 1960s America.

Glass' father ran a radio repair shop that also sold records. When certain records were not selling well, he would take them home and play them to his children in an attempt to discover what lay behind their poor sales. In this way, Philip Glass was introduced to much music considered unconventional at the time, and only began to discover more standard classics as he moved into his late teens. While growing up, Glass learnt to play the violin and flute, but became frustrated with the limited repertoire available for the flute. After graduating with a degree in mathematics and philosophy, Glass decided he wanted to be a composer and moved to New York to the Juillard School, where, like Reich, he undertook formal study in composition.

The similarities between Glass and Reich are most obvious at the start of their compositional careers. They both, along with Terry Riley and LaMonte Young, adopted an approach to composition that became known as minimalism, although there are quite significant differences in style between these composers and they have all publicly rejected the title minimalist. In Glass' case, the title only applies to music written between about 1964 and 1974.

After studying at the Juilliard School, Glass travelled to France to study with the renowned French teacher Nadia Boulanger. While in Paris, Glass also met Indian sitar player Ravi Shankar who introduced him to the ideas and sounds of Indian music. The way

Postmodern music

Background

Remember that you may make only passing references to Reich. See also pages 95–101 and 133–137 of the *OCR AS Guide*.

Web link

You can find a comprehensive account of Glass' music at his site: www.philipglass.com.

Minimalism

Glass' career as a composer has now lasted over 40 years and it would obviously be wrong to refer to all his music with a title that applies to only a quarter of it. For the three extracts, we have deliberately chosen only one piece that was composed during Glass' minimalist period in order to give you a sense of balance of his style across his output.

Further reading

There are two useful books by Glass himself about his music: *Opera on the Beach* (Faber 1989) and *Music by Philip Glass* (Da Capo Press 1995). You might be able to get these from your local library.

that Indian musicians used rhythms fascinated Glass and in his book, *Opera on the Beach*, he spoke about the way this changed his whole approach to rhythm:

> In Western music we divide time ... and slice it as you slice a loaf of bread. In Indian music you take small units, or 'beats' and string them together to make up larger time values.

From his fascination with Indian music, Glass developed the idea of additive rhythm in his early work. This is a flexible approach to rhythm whereby a small unit is repeated constantly, gradually getting longer or shorter with each repetition. Glass composed his music for his own ensemble. This meant that the incessant, intense rhythmic units in the pieces could be directed by the composer himself. We shall be looking at *Strung Out* (written in 1967) as an example of a minimalist piece from this period.

Theatre, opera, film

Unlike the other so-called minimalists, Glass was interested in theatre from early on in his career, and this led him to attempt the development of a new form of opera. His first three operas form a trilogy, each one concentrating on a different historical figure. The operas are *Einstein on the Beach* (1976), *Satyagraha* (1980) and *Akhnaten* (1983). We will be looking at an extract from *Einstein on the Beach*. The composition of these operas marked a turning point in Glass' output as he moved from the strict minimalist style of his early pieces to compose larger pieces. From the early 1980s, Glass also began to compose film music, his first such work being *Koyaanisqatsi* (1981), which contained images and music but was non-narrative. This collaboration across art forms is, of course, a significant feature of postmodernism, as are non-narrative structures.

Glass' operas and films use non-narrative structures in a similar way to Churchill and Anderson.

Orchestral music

Glass has been the most successful of the minimalist composers at working with the orchestra. Although his early works were composed with his own ensemble in mind, Glass began to write music for orchestra at about the same time as he began composing opera. He has written a large number of orchestral works, but it is the symphonies that we will be discussing here, because his approach to the symphony is an excellent example of postmodernism. The symphony was established in 18th-century Europe and developed enormously in the 19th century. By the 20th century, the form was thought to belong to a past age. Glass, however, has taken the symphony and reinterpreted it for the end of the 20th century. By 2002, the composer had produced six symphonies and we shall be looking at features of his Symphony No. 4 ('Heroes Symphony').

How is Glass postmodern?

Postmodernism in music is just like in the other art forms: it is not simply one more period. It is effectively the end of music history as we know it.

Philip Glass uses a mixture of techniques and demonstrates a range of influences. He brings these together to create his own individual approach to composition.

It is probably easiest to see how this works if we think about the elements of music. At the start of your performance studies course you spent some time exploring five different aspects of music: rhythm, melody, harmony, texture, timbre. What aspects of these elements demonstrate Glass' postmodern approach?

➤ He uses the orchestra and traditional instrumentation, but often in a 'non-symphonic' manner.

➤ He uses long-established classical forms (such as symphony or concerto), but in his own innovative way.

➤ His music demonstrates influences from other cultures, and the incorporation of technological advances and electronic music into his composition.

➤ His music has strong tonal centres, unlike much modernist music.

➤ His approach to harmony is often based on arpeggios and broken chords, sometimes including some light syncopation.

➤ He uses chords but the harmony is not used in the same way as chord progressions. In other words, the harmony is **non-functional** because it does not move the music along.

➤ Use of arpeggios is often linked with a very calm use of instrumentation – woodwind that 'ripples', strings that pulsate.

➤ A lack of tension in the music. It has been said that 'his music does not argue; it exists'.

> " [A] style characterised by exuberant, hypnotic melodic and rhythmic repetitions in which Western musical tradition, rock and pop are fused with elements of African and Indian music. "
>
> Otto Karolyi

Extract 1: Strung Out

Strung Out was written in 1967 and is an excellent example of Glass' fully developed minimalist style. Most books about minimalism concentrate on the repetition of small rhythmic and melodic units and this is certainly the most obvious feature of pieces such as this. While Glass' minimalist period lasted only a short time – about 12 years at the most – its significance, especially in the context of postmodernism, lies in the way the style made use of previous musical features in a new context.

As you can see from the extract below, the actual number of different pitches in the piece is very small – only four in total. You can easily identify each group of notes by the way the stems of the notes are joined together and you can see that each of these units contains some combination of the notes C, D, E and G, although these appear in different octaves as the piece progresses. When you look at these notes more closely, you'll see that if you play them at the same time, they form a triad of C major – C, E and G – which means that the units have a strong harmonic feel to them. It would be easy for a listener to think that the music was firmly in the key of C major since there are no chromatic notes at all.

> You may need to revise your technical knowledge of tonality: 18th-century music was normally in a key and this meant that it was easy to hear where the music was going. Tonality began to break down in the music of composers towards the end of the 19th century.

For most of the 20th century, many notable composers had moved away from this type of clear tonality in favour of music that was atonal.

Because of the repetitious nature of the music, it is difficult to take an *extract* from this piece – there would be no point in jumping in halfway through. The extract above is therefore taken from the opening, but the same techniques continue throughout.

This form of repetition contrasts with the non-linear structures used by Anderson and Churchill. Glass' approach is even more extreme – the music seems stuck in one moment in time.

The music does not 'go' anywhere in the sense that there is no series of chords that lead from start to end – there is no development as such in this style of music. The only change is through adding or subtracting notes from the musical units. Because of the constant repetition, the key centre is firmly established because the ear hears it over and over again. There is a regular flow of notes in these short units and they sound almost like arpeggios. The units get longer and then shorter but they do not develop as such. Although there is incessant movement in the music, the units only change as a result of additive rhythms. For example, the first unit has E, G as the first two notes. The next unit has these two notes twice at the start to add to the rhythm. There is no variation of pulse or rhythm.

Monotimbral means that it is written for only one sound – in this case, an amplified violin.

The piece is monotimbral. This means that the music is effectively static in a number of ways. The harmony does not move anywhere, the notes used in the motifs themselves are very restricted and the ear is bombarded with the sound throughout. This potentially makes the music difficult to listen to as the human ear is always trying to identify contrast and quickly tires of the same sound, the same timbre or the same pulse.

You will see from this that there is nothing especially radical about the elements of music that Glass uses in *Strung Out*. It is the manner in which he uses them that gives the music its radical quality. In fact, the most significant postmodern feature of this music is the way in which Glass takes apparently simple musical material and organises it so that the listener is forced to hear it in a completely new way.

Extract 2: Einstein on the Beach

Philip Glass' austere minimalist compositions occupy the early part of his career and it is probably not accurate to use the term minimalist for his music after 1976. Written in 1975–1976, *Einstein on the Beach* marked a turning point in Glass' compositional career as he came to embrace opera and musical theatre as genres in which he wished to work. *Einstein* became the first opera in a trilogy – the others are *Satyagraha* (1980) and *Akhnaten* (1983), which profile the characters of Gandhi and Akhnaten respectively. The decision to work with opera could be seen as typical of a postmodern composer re-engaging with forms established in the past, re-interpreting them for his own time. Although Glass is often seen as an orchestral composer, he has often cited theatre as his first love – borne out by the number of operas he has written.

Glass' approach to opera in *Einstein* was radical. He collaborated with Robert Wilson, an American stage director who had become known for a radical approach to theatre that was typified by its **non-narrative** nature – an essential feature of *Einstein*. Glass has talked about 'taking the subject out of the narrative'. This may seem peculiar, but the subject is what makes the narrative linear.

One of the challenges of writing opera is how to produce vocal lines that can be sung, and despite his radical approach to structure, Glass has demonstrated something of a gift for melody in his operas. The extracts that we shall concentrate on here is taken from the opening of the work before Act 1 begins and is entitled *Knee 1*.

There are five sections in *Einstein* that have this title. Referred to as *Knee Play 1*, *Knee Play 2* and so on, they appear at the end of each of the four acts. These sections have a major structural function in completing the music of each act. There are strong similarities between *Knee Play 1*, *Knee Play 3 and Knee Play 5* and the comments made here apply to each of them.

The music itself appears extremely simple in relying on only two vocal parts and a sustained organ sound. This later builds up into four vocal parts with the sustained organ sounds. This may not seem radical, but if you compare it with *Strung Out*, where the music was monotimbral, there is clearly some development in style. The opera was written for Glass' own ensemble and the range of instruments used during the opera as a whole is much broader. In total it is written for a selection of woodwind, four voices, two organs and violin and this allows the composer to create some sense of contrasting sections, a feature not present in the minimalist pieces.

In *Knee 1*, Glass uses harmony in a different way from his earlier pieces. The voices sing numbers in a regular and even manner, and the purpose of the chords is not to harmonise the melody but to mirror the movement of the rhythms. However, the fact that numbers are used helps the listener to feel that the music is moving forward, even though in reality the sequence starts again in each new bar. There is a strong sense of the music being static and the harmony barely changes. However, the significance here is that Glass engages with harmony in the same postmodern sense that he did with tonality and melody. This was first established in 1975 with his *Another Look at Harmony* and this interest continues in *Satyagraha* and *Akhnaten*.

While much could be said about Glass' postmodern approach to opera, the essential features are the way in which he takes an existing art form, thought to be dead by the end of the 20th century, and develops a new approach to it. This approach contains some aspects that were always there but the non-narrative nature of the work ensures that the overall effect is quite different.

"It never occurred to us that *Einstein on the Beach* would have a story or contain anything like a plot."

Glass and Wilson

All of the six symphonies Glass has composed to date engage fully with the orchestra. Symphony No. 1, the *Low* Symphony (1992) and Symphony No. 2 (1994) are for full symphony orchestra while symphonies 5 (1999) and 6 (2002) include voices. Symphony No. 3 (1995) is for chamber orchestra.

> ❝ *Heroes*, like the *Low* symphony of several years ago, is based on the work of David Bowie and Brian Eno. Just as composers of the past turned to music of their time to fashion new works, the work of Bowie and Eno became an inspiration and point of departure for a series of symphonies of my own. ❞
>
> www.philipglass.com

Tip

The decision as to how much to study is probably best considered in the light of the overall amount of material your teachers have chosen for you for the topic, bearing in mind the total playing time of between four and six hours.

Extract 3: Symphony No. 4: Heroes

As a form, the symphony had been abandoned by many 20th-century composers. The reasons for this were not hard to find: the original form had been developed in the 18th century at a time when the tonality of pieces was clear and the movement between sections of movements was based on the relationships between key centres. The breakdown in tonality in the 20th century and the way in which the symphony had expanded at the end of the 19th century made it difficult for composers to know how they might approach the form in an original way. Glass' approach to the symphony is another example of his postmodern approach; he takes a form that is clearly associated with the past and reinterprets it for the late 20th century.

Glass' symphonies have been composed so far within a ten-year period between 1992 and 2002, by which date he had written six symphonies; there is a possibility that he may write more. The extract here is taken from his fourth symphony, composed in 1996, and more commonly known as the *Heroes* Symphony.

Glass builds on the approach he had established in the earlier *Low* Symphony. The way in which Glass uses the work of Brian Eno and David Bowie is essentially postmodern as their music is re-contextualised within Glass' work. A casual listener would be unlikely to pick it out with knowing it was there in the first place. The symphony is in six distinct movements, each derived from a different work by Bowie and Eno. These are as follows:

1. Heroes (5:53)

2. Abdulmajid (8:53)

3. Sense of Doubt (7:20)

4. Sons of the Silent Age (8:18)

5. Neuköln (6:41)

6. V2 Schneider (6:48).

As each of the movements are of a similar length, it would be possible to take two contrasting ones because this would provide examples of contrasting tempi, moods and approaches.

Glass' symphonic style is a clear development of the musical language of his earlier pieces. The label 'symphony' refers more to the spirit and intention of the pieces than to their construction. Glass weaves his themes into expanded textures but makes no attempt to relate them in the same way as the classical symphonic writers. The music is tonal and this has clearly developed from the early minimalist pieces, but it does not use chord progressions or other musical structures intended to move the music along in a linear fashion. The musical style is typical of Glass: a reliance on quick repeating arpeggios and patterns that extend in a manner derived from the additive rhythms of the early pieces.

The music of Philip Glass is postmodern in the sense that it uses elements of music associated with the past (such as tonality, melody, harmony and instrumentation) and uses them in a new way, sometimes in musical forms that were also developed in an earlier age. The overall effect is to take apparently historical elements and create a new style by bringing them together.

And finally...

Once you have studied the three extracts from each of the three practitioners, you need to consider the similarities and differences between them.

Have open discussions in class about your experiences of the extracts and your reactions to them. Read reviews of the different works from which they have been taken. This is probably the most exciting part of this unit. Carry out your own research and converse with others in your class as well as the teacher. There are no right and definitive answers.

Look back to the definitions of postmodernism and modernism and be clear about what an approach to post-modern performance means. Consider the genre as a whole and keep an open mind. The following bullet points might give you some starting points to compare and contrast extracts.

➢ Evolution of ideas and the notion of the end of history

➢ Using historical figures or concepts with contemporary ideas

➢ How postmodernism breaks away from modernism

➢ How a variety of contemporary styles are mixed with styles from the past, and how the art of the past is re-used

➢ Juxtaposition of styles to create a specific effect

➢ Eclecticism

➢ Non-linear narratives that fracture the time line and challenge the audience

➢ Collaborative projects between dancers, dramatists and musicians, and the combined use of art forms

➢ Intertextuality

➢ Use of collage

➢ Use of different types of venue

➢ Use of art forms mixing together

➢ Lack of value judgement of the relative worth of works of art

➢ Desire to use what is on offer both artistically and technologically

➢ Mixture of what has been called high and popular art forms

➢ Humour.

The above points are only starters for discussion. You could video your discussion and make notes from it when you play it back. Remember to focus on the extracts you have chosen to study. This discussion could be the basis for an essay written in preparation for the examination.

Allow ten minutes at the end to sum up what has been said and try to group points or put them in a logical order which could be the basis of a coherent argument for an essay. This is an exercise that should be carried out on at least three separate occasions: initially for your first reaction to the extracts: secondly when the extracts have been studied in depth; and finally for revision purposes.

You should always have the nine extracts and your class notes to hand otherwise you will not be able to cite references – this is very important in the written examination.

Politics and performance since 1914

What is political performance?

Consider the word 'politics'. Look at a political system in a specific country – start with Britain – and ask yourself the following questions:

➤ Who is the most powerful person in the country?

➤ Which party is in power? Who is prime minister?

➤ Do you agree with the way they are running the country?

➤ What is wrong with the country and what has the government done to improve these areas?

➤ How is your life affected by the decisions of the government?

Politics is not only about governments. A performance piece might be about injustice or corruption or prejudice. Look at pieces from other countries. What message is the practitioner trying to convey to the audience? Is it about inequality? Is it about oppression? Poverty? Sexuality? Gay rights? The corruption within corporate institutions?

Consider issues that affect you at your school or college. Are you perhaps a member of the school council or the college student union? Why do these bodies exist? Do they have any power in instigating change? Is there any issue that you feel strongly about? Could a performance help raise people's awareness and make them want to take action to improve the situation? If you studied Brecht at AS, you will remember that he radically changed theatre. He did not want the audience to become emotionally involved with the action. He wanted them to remain objective about what was happening on stage, so that they could make decisions and ultimately take action. He used a variety of techniques and devices to achieve this, such as the use of placards and banners to let the audience know what was about to happen, thus removing any suspense.

When you study a play extract, try to read the play in its entirety. This will give you a better idea of the playwright's intention and his political message. Read around the play as well – look at reviews on the Internet, past issues of magazines in your library and books on the playwright's work.

What do I have to know for this topic?

 Here is what the exam board says about what you are expected to study for this topic:

> This topic requires candidates to consider the relationship between performance and politics in works written since the start of World War 1. The connection between the politics and

---

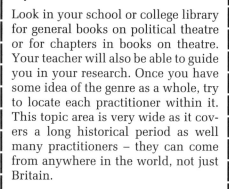

Tip

Look in your school or college library for general books on political theatre or for chapters in books on theatre. Your teacher will also be able to guide you in your research. Once you have some idea of the genre as a whole, try to locate each practitioner within it. This topic area is very wide as it covers a long historical period as well many practitioners – they can come from anywhere in the world, not just Britain.

We're just using Brecht here to make a point. Remember that in the exam you won't get marks for writing about practitioners on the set list for AS.

Collate the three extracts and keep them in a folder for quick and easy reference. Reread them in the light of your research.

---

the performance may be through content, style or structure but in all cases there will be an *intention* on the part of the practitioner to persuade an audience and to convince them of a need for action…Whatever political message is embodied in the extracts studied, candidates should focus primarily on stylistic techniques used by practitioners rather than the political issues themselves.

You'll see that what is important is the relationship between politics and performance – how a practitioner uses their performance art to convey a political message. While you'll need some familiarity with the political issues that concern your practitioners, you need to focus on the techniques that they use to make their point within their works.

Practitioners and their intentions

The intention of the practitioner will depend on their political stance and beliefs and on the era in which they are writing. Political practitioners will use their work in an attempt to alter the audience's expectations, opinions, values and worldview. They challenge 'norms' that are established in their society. Again, their techniques will vary, but many practitioners use structural devices to set up contrasts between traditional ideas and their contemporary ideas.

Even though this topic seems serious, the extracts are not without their amusing side. Comedy is a means frequently used to mock a system with which the practitioner disagrees, often through exaggeration.

To help you understand how political performance operates, we'll use the example of David Hare, a practitioner who writes plays about contemporary issues to make overtly political points. His play *The Permanent Way* (2003) is about railway crashes and the privatisation of the railways. The play covers the Hatfield Crash in 2000 when a train ran over a damaged rail and killed four people; the Southall crash in 1997, which killed seven people; the Ladbroke Grove crash in 1999, which killed 31; and the Potters Bar crash in 2002 which killed seven. By recalling all these deaths in the minds of audience members, Hare makes his feelings very clear regarding the state of the railways in Britain.

To look at *how* Hare put this message and information across to his audience, we turn to the style of theatre he used. In putting together *The Permanent Way*, he worked with the director Max Stafford-Clark, who had given him Ian Jack's essay in the first place. Hare, Stafford-Clark and the actors interviewed those who had been involved in the crashes, from the bereaved and the survivors to the engineers and the civil servants, but *not* the politicians, because Hare thought that they would say little. For example, an actor interviewed the mother of a train crash victim. The actor listened to the mother's painful story, then came back into the theatre studio and retold the story in the first person, as if he were the mother. He tried to use the words and gestures that she had used. From these stories, a script was written. This is known as **verbatim theatre**. This style gave Hare the opportunity to see the situation from different perspectives and led him to the conclusion

Further reading

The Guardian has a series of articles about political theatre: www.guardian.co.uk/arts/politicaltheatre. Try other newspapers as well as magazines such as *Time Out*. Look at regional and local press and contact theatres in your area or in cities near to you. They should have archives where they keep reviews and should be able to direct you in your research.

David Hare

Further reading

The play was based on an essay called *The Crash that Stopped Britain* by Ian Jack (Granta Books 2001).

that his play would be about honour and dishonour. He could not believe how badly the survivors and the bereaved had been treated by the authorities involved, and he wanted to bring this issue to the attention of the general public.

In this topic, we will look at the work of Union Dance, Dario Fo and Bob Dylan. There are many differences in their work, but you'll also find similarities:

➢ They have all taken their work to the general public by touring.

➢ Each of them has a political statement to make, and they make it through performance.

➢ All three practitioners use music, although in different ways. Union Dance uses a good deal of contemporary music that has its roots in street culture and speaks of the people. Fo uses songs to break up the action, much like Brecht did, and to entertain while informing the audience about political situations and to make satirical comments. Dylan makes political protests against issues like the Vietnam War through his songs.

➢ Each practitioner wants to make the audience sense the need for change and therefore take action.

➢ Each uses a variety of styles to communicate their message. For example, Union Dance uses a fusion of dance styles that reflects the cultural background of the dancers. Fo uses Commedia dell' Arte, satire and farce. Dylan uses folk music.

Union Dance Company

Consider the following statement by Corrine Bougaard, the South-African born artistic director of Union Dance, from the programme notes to *dance in house*:

> I created Union Dance Company because I wanted to explore, as a dancer and choreographer, the varied cultural references that make up my background. This need resulted from long-standing questions as to why these important creative traditions have become misunderstood and discriminated against, consequently downgrading them and making them less valuable. It is important to me to create work that communicates the philosophy of cultural diversity. Over the years this feeling has not diminished, but has become more urgent as our children enter a society which needs to come to terms with its multi-racial heritage. Union Dance's repertoire reflects this philosophy.

The statement clearly states the intention of Corrine Bougaard and her dance company. Each piece they have created and their working method clearly reflects their philosophy. The company's work demonstrates their concerns about our society, and the way we value one another and respect one another's cultural heritage.

Union Dance was formed in 1985 by Bougaard and is now well known for its use of a mixture of dance forms including hip hop, capoeira, aikido, street dance and contemporary dance. You will find brief definitions of the main styles of dance they use in the margins of this section. Company members use their own choreographic skills to contribute to the dance as a whole.

In the course of this chapter, we've given you a fair amount of biographical detail about each of the practitioners discussed. Remember, though, that while you should have some idea of the background of your practitioners, you are advised not to spend time relating biographical information in your exam essay unless it is directly related to a point you are making about the genre.

Tip

You will be able to add to this list when you have read about the three practitioners. Remember that you should illustrate your points by reference to specific extracts. Don't write about one practitioner at a time and go through their extracts laboriously.

Further study

The company performs regularly and the best way to understand their approach is to see one of their shows live and take part in their workshops. They have work available on video and resource packs, but taking part either as an audience member or as a workshop member is very helpful in appreciating the company's stylistic techniques. www.uniondance.co.uk.

The company's name indicates the way its members work together on pieces and collaborate with various choreographers on different styles and approaches. Union Dance seeks to use a mixture of styles to express a cultural diversity that reflects British society today. The company has a far-reaching educational programme that brings a rich experience of dance to schools and colleges nationally and internationally. The sharing of different dance styles and cultural knowledge offers enrichment for dancers of all ages.

Extract 1: Dance Tek Warriors

Dance Tek Warriors consists of four pieces linked by the theme of the Quest of the Warrior: *Mass Equilibria in the Sea of Tranquility*; *Three Young Blades*; *Eye Open, Path Chosen*; and *Bright Flames in Dark Waters*. The original idea was conceived by Corrine Bougaard and can be interpreted in many ways. It could be the search of the Holy Grail or the journey made by an individual through life. Ursula Bombshell designed the costumes and the lighting was designed by Lisa Auduoin and Bill Deverson. The use of a variety of music is a characteristic of Union Dance, including classical, hip hop and a commissioned score by Tunde Jegede.

Dance Tek Warriors was premiered at the Queen's Theatre, Hornchurch in 1997. A short film on the making of the first two pieces was produced by London Weekend Television in 1997.

Collaboration between the art forms is a priority for the company and this is evidenced by their live shows, which demonstrate a successful coming together of several theatrical art forms. The audience leaves with the feeling that each person involved in the company's productions has an equal status and that no one part of the show is more important than any other. Indeed, the production is only a success when all the parts combine together in a harmonic way to create a rich audiovisual experience. We have focused here on the opening and ending of the piece.

Mass Equilibria in the Sea of Tranquility. The computer game Tekken is used as a starting point, showing Union Dance's interest in the changing nature of society as well as their awareness of the strong effects of technology on our lives. Those familiar with the game will recognise movements seen in the preparation and combat sequences of the computer game. Two art forms – capoeira and wushu – are used as part of the dance vocabulary. These are appropriate for showing the training necessary for battle of any kind. A warrior must prepare mentally and physically for combat and this is clearly shown in the meditative sections of the piece. Michael Joseph uses yoga during warm-up sessions and as a training method, and this influence can be detected in this section. The dancers take energy from a light source and then the movement starts with an intake of breath. As in the game, the dancers run out of energy and have to be recharged. Another influence on the dance styles are Michael Joseph's background in street dance. The robotic quality of the movements clearly reflects the style of movement in the game. There is a mixture of body waves, contemporary dance, martial arts and sudden mechanical movement. The costumes were inspired by the computer images and are silver and close-fitting. A film is projected in the middle of the piece to connect to the overall theme of falling from grace. It shows bodies falling through space.

Bright Flames in Dark Waters. This piece represents the goal of the quest and shows a celebration following spiritual enlightenment. Several dance forms are used (capoeira, contemporary, classical, hip hop and contact improvisation) as well as Asian and folk dance and references to the styles used in the three other pieces. Look carefully at the sections in this piece and note down the different styles used in each. How and why are the costumes different? What do they represent? How are contrasts set up between the sections? Why is this piece placed in last position? In what way is it a finale? Look carefully at the floor patterns used, particularly in the last section. What do they represent? How does this piece link to the overall theme and the title of the production? What political points are being made? What do you understand by the term the global citizen?

Extract 2: dance in house

According to their mission statement, the company 'exists to explore and express an identity through dance which reflects the growing cultural fusion of contemporary society'. This piece explores directly the identity of the individual in an age when a brand name says more about you than your own personal views.

In *dance in house*, there is a good mixture of serious comment with a sense of playfulness and light-hearted humour. In 'Quintessential Vibes in Music', Garry Benjamin concentrates on the individual movement style of each company member exposing their strengths and unique skills. In 'Zenith and Nadir', Michael Joseph experiments with the highs and lows of movement and shows different stages in life. Aural and visual elements are mixed. You can hear cries and conversations. The relationships explored comprise solos, duets and an ensemble section to finish. In 'Dance Divine Dreams' by Corrine Bougaard, we witness the dream world of a girl whose life is about to end. This section has a stronger narrative than most of Union's work. There are religious and spiritual aspects to explore as well as the philosophical divide between east and west. What is the function of the male mourner at the end? Does he help create an equilibrium? The last section 'Be Cat, See Spot, Run (Tiger's Pursuit)' by Doug Elkins is an amusing reflection on black dance from music hall to dance hall to disco. Using improvisation, his wide dance vocabulary and knowledge of styles, he worked with the dancers, observing them and enhancing their creativity to show and merge a variety of dance styles form different eras.

Extract 3: Permanent Revolution V2R

Permanent Revolution V2R came together as the result of a high degree of collaboration between choreographers and the two media artists Thomas Gray and Derek Richards to explore themes of migration and transition through time, space and virtual reality.

It comprises three pieces: *Fallela* (travelling to) by Vincent Mantsoe explores the spiritual search for a better life and how this can be achieved through teaching others about the diversity of cultures. The second piece *Holla* choreographed by Bawren Tavaziva to music composed by the choreographer displays a

dance in house premiered in 2002 at the Lilian Baylis Theatre, Sadler's Wells. Bill Deverson was the lighting designer. Peter Emina was the video/digital director. Costumes were designed by Abigail Hammond and the photographer was Thomas Gray. The music ranges from Artful Dodger to Bix Beiderbecke to Talvin Singh, reflecting the variety and cultural diversity of the contemporary music scene in Britain.

" The Company is called Union Dance because it has a holistic philosophy, the essence of which is the union of art forms: dance, design, music, lighting, theatrical experience. All created together to convey the union of spirit, mind and body – in movement. "

Programme notes for *dance in house*.

V2R stands for Virtual to Reality.

As you may have realised by now, Union Dance's political views are often about the integration of culture and diversity.

range of styles from British street dance to Caribbean and African forms. The three dancers represent three strangers who become friends and demonstrate their different cultural backgrounds. The emphasis is on bonding rather than fighting. The third piece *Fractured Atlas* by Doug Elkins shows the importance of knowing your history and background, as well as understanding your present relationship to others and to the world. There is an emphasis on what has gone before you and how you connect to it.

Revolution can be considered in at least two ways. Firstly it can be the turn of a circle and secondly a powerful and political change. The word 'permanent' indicates that this revolution is on-going and that society is always in a state of flux. Dance mirrors this because it evolves as we move around the globe and share forms, styles and techniques. These can become mixed together creating a cultural fusion that reflects the cultural make-up of the individual who is constantly encountering new cultures and new ways of thinking and behaving. Union Dance brings a very positive message to their audience: that this exchange is an enriching experience for all who take part.

Derek Richards is a musician who now works with new technology as a multimedia artist, primarily with digital media in live contexts. He sees Union's work as more than a mere fusion of styles and experiences. The training of Union Dance members in contemporary dance and ballet, and their study of non-western forms allows them to understand on an intellectual level what they have lived through on a cultural level. The piece is about migration and has become electronic in the sense that people can travel in a cultural sense by listening to music and samples on a variety of media.

When choosing extracts from Union Dance's repertoire, consider carefully how long each one is. We have cited work from three of their productions – you will only need to discuss a section from each of the productions. Consider how long the sections last and remember that the total performance time of the nine extracts should be between four and six hours. Return to page 51 and look again at the diagram so that you fully understand what to prepare for the exam question.

> " [The piece is] about migration and how transition can affect and has affected cultural change and the individual. As in the title of this new production, everything seems to revolve, to go round in circles. It brings to mind not only the current issues around asylum seekers, but for me how my parents in the late fifties came to the UK and had to leave all family behind in South Africa, unable to return due to apartheid. "
>
> Corrine Bougaard, *Permanent Revolution V2R* programme notes.

> " By the time the piece was being exhibited, 'fusion', 'hybridity' and 'diversity' had become fashionable terms. But the ideas behind the work went deeper, to explain the natural and inevitable dynamic nature of culture powered by migration. "
>
> Derek Richards in the programme notes to *Permanent Revolution.*

Dario Fo

Dario Fo was born on 26 March 1926 in San Giano, a small town on Lake Maggiore in the north of Italy. He is no stranger to political struggle. During the Second World War, Fo helped his father (a member of the resistance) to get escaped British prisoners of war and Jewish scientists across the border to Switzerland. Fo spent his holidays as a child on his grandfather's farm in Lomellina. His grandfather would travel the countryside selling his produce and telling amusing stories to attract customers. He inserted news and anecdotes about local events into the stories and earned himself the name of Bristin (pepper seed). From listening to these stories, Fo learned the art of story telling and how to mix humour with serious comment.

Web link

Fo won the Nobel Prize for literature in 1997, and there is an extensive biography along with a list of all of his works at: www.nobelprize.org/literature/laur eates/1997/fo-bio.html.

Fo went to art school and planned to be an architect, learning skills that later helped him in designing his own sets. His career as a playwright started in small cabarets and theatres. His early works are one-act farces where he mixes Marxist philosophy with Commedia dell' Arte devices. In Fo's work, political statement is often achieved through comedy or satire.

In partnership with his wife Franca Rame, Fo has produced many satirical dramas. The couple performed comic sketches on television and their public profiles are high. In 1968 they founded the acting group Nueva Scena, which had ties with the Italian Communist Party, but when the Communist Press criticised Fo, the couple broke these ties and openly attacked the party's bureaucracy. In 1970, Fo started the Colletivo Teatrale La Comune where plays were constructed quickly in response to specific local, national or international issues. These plays used improvisation and revision as techniques.

Fo is known all over the world for using the role of jester to make people laugh while raising their awareness of injustice and corruption in society and particularly in governments. *Accidental Death of an Anarchist* (1970) is a good example of this. Scripts are adaptable to the moment and can be updated and politicised for the country in which they are performed. Improvisation and comedy help make the harsh messages in the plays more accessible to the audience. Fo uses grammelot, the jesting language that he has based on dialect and onomatopoeia and his inspiration from one of his favourite characters: Arlecchino. Not only does Fo write scripts and act, he also directs, designs the set and the costumes, and sometimes even composes the music for his plays.

The three plays we have chosen to look here at are *Accidental Death of an Anarchist, Can't Pay? Won't Pay!* and *Trumpets and Raspberries*. Another suitable work for study would be *Mistero Buffo* (1969), which consists of a number of monologues taken from medieval religious works which present contemporary issues as well. When *Mistero Buffo* was screened on television, the Vatican described the performance as 'the most blasphemous show in the history of television'.

Extract 1: Accidental Death of an Anarchist

The basis for *Accidental Death of an Anarchist* was a real-life explosion in the Agricultural Bank in Milan on 12 December 1969. More than 16 people were killed and the anarchists were immediately blamed. One of them, Giovanni Pinelli, was taken to be interrogated by police where it was claimed he 'flew out of the window on the fourth floor'. The police said it was suicide. Ten years later at Catanzaro, southern Italy, the trial finally ended and three fascists were found guilty of the bombing. One of them, named Giannettini, turned out to be an agent for the secret Italian police. The incident had been staged to frame the anarchists, whereas all along it had been a right-wing conspiracy. Ministers and generals were brought to court but there was an extensive cover-up.

Further reading

Among these works are *Guerra di popolo in Cile* (1973) about the popular revolt in Chile, *Fedayn* (1971) about the Palestinian question, *The Open Couple* (1983) about the place of women in society and *Zitti! Stiamo Precipitanto* (1980) about AIDS.

The title *Mistero Buffo* (which means 'Comic Mystery') was borrowed from Mayakovsky's *Mystery Bouffle*, a satire written in 1918.

Further study

To read the text in full, try the Methuen edition. There is also a very good production of the play by Belts and Braces which appeared on television. More recently there has been a production at the Donmar Warehouse in London.

The play centres on whether Pinelli jumped or was pushed through the window. Initially, Fo staged the play to make the public aware that the real culprits of the bomb massacre were not the left-wing anarchists but the right-wing fascists who held power at the top of the hierarchy. At the time, people believed what they saw in the media and Fo wanted to intervene with 'an exercise in counterinformation'. He used authentic documents and complete transcripts of the investigations carried out by the various judges as well as police reports to produce what he called a 'farce of power'.

Fo uses satire to attack the police, the legal system, the judges and the church – all those who wield great power in Italy. The effect of the comedy is to make the audience laugh out loud, while leaving a bad taste in their mouths as they realise the grotesque nature and full horror of Pinelli's death, and of those killed in the bank massacre.

In the main character of the play, the Maniac, we witness a man who can don any disguise and fool people. The Maniac runs the show and trips up the police at every turn. He tricks them into confessing their mistakes and in some ways is similar to Shakespeare's Fool or the giullare, in that he is the people's spokesman. He gives a satirical voice to resentments felt by ordinary people against authority. The giullare made his living from travelling from town to town, telling stories, acting, singing, dancing and doing acrobatics. All these skills can be seen in the skills and techniques that the Maniac employs as he runs rings round those in supposed power. Twinned with this is Fo's use of *lazzi* – a large store of stage business which the performers in the Commedia dell' Arte could use at moment's notice to give the impression of on-stage improvisation, much like stand-up comics use prepared jokes and rants today.

> The giullare was a type of minstrel, juggler and busker.

Let us have a look at an example of how Fo uses comedy in the text. In reply to Inspector Bertozzo asking him whether he has ever passed himself off as a judge, the Maniac says:

> No, unfortunately. Chance never arose. I'd love to, though: best job in the world! First of all, they hardly ever retire... In fact, just at the point when your average working man, at the age of 55 or 60, is already ready for the scrapheap because he's slowing down a bit, losing his reflexes, your judge is just coming into his prime... the more ancient and idio... (*he corrects himself*) ...syncratic they are, the higher they get promoted... these characters have the power to wreck a person's life or save it, as and how they want.

Like many of the Maniac's other speeches, this one is long and allows him time and space to attack all the major facets of the Italian establishment.

Extract 2: Can't Pay? Won't Pay!

The political background to *Can't Pay? Won't Pay!* was one of 'widespread discontent among young people' and the policy of *autoriduzione*:

> The adaptation that appears in the Methuen edition was commissioned by Omega Stage and first presented at the Criterion Theatre, London in 1981. There was an earlier production at the Half Moon Theatre in 1978.

> It was developed by workers who of their own accord limited their working hours and output. The tactic was taken up and applied in different ways and contexts by young manual and

Stuart Hood in the introduction to *Dario Fo Plays: 2* (Methuen 1997). In addition to Hood's introduction, the Methuen edition contains another informative piece by Franca Rame.

white-collar workers and students, who refused, for instance, to pay the prices demanded by cinemas or by the organisers of pop concerts. It was also applied in shops and supermarkets where the protestors carried out acts of expropriation by refusing to pay for goods. The established parties of the Left found this development difficult to deal with and the Communist Party disapproved of it.

Fo employs a technique that uses one character to relate what has happened – that she was in the supermarket when the shoppers started to refuse to pay the prices. The story is told by Antonia to her friend Margherita in an anecdotal fashion and using dialect and colloquialisms such as 'scarpered'. Antonia enjoyed making a protest against the 'bosses' and now has to hide the food from her husband Giovanni who arrives home suddenly.

A series of visual jokes follows, in which Giovanni thinks that Margherita is pregnant (Antonia has hung a bag of shopping round her neck and buttoned her coat over it). When the Inspector arrives to search the flat, Margherita cries out as if she is in labour and he insists she goes to hospital. A bag of olives splits and starts to leak so Antonia pretends Margherita's waters have broken. Later, after the women have left and Luigi arrives at the flat, he eats the olive that has come out with all the brine. The joke is extended using Luigi's ignorance of the preceding events and makes the audience laugh, while Fo makes jibes at the Catholic Church and their attititudes towards contraception.

Dramatic irony is used to create more humour as the audience witnesses everything that happens in this farcical situation. The police are made to look like idiots as Fo paints a negative portrait of them using pejorative terms. Giovanni describes the policeman who came to search the flat as: 'The died-in-the-wool, raving, steeped-in-Marxism out-and-out copper! Right in there with the lunatic fascists, psycho bullies and subnormal everyday street coppers.'

Extract 3: Trumpets and Raspberries

The Red Brigades, or Brigate Rosse, is a militant Marxist-Leninist group in Italy that was most active in the 1970s and 1980s. Their aim was to separate Italy from the western alliance.

Trumpets and Raspberries was written in 1981 in response to events that took place in Italy in the 1970s. The Red Brigades made their political protests in a violent manner by kidnapping and murdering people in significant political positions. Aldo Moro, former prime minister and Christian Democrat politician, was murdered in 1978. While the circumstances of his captivity and murder are unknown, some think that during the two months he was held, he appealed to the authorities and his political allies but they did not come to his aid, as the Christian Democrats wanted to show that they were not 'soft on terrorism'.

As with *Accidental Death of an Anarchist*, farce is the style that Fo chooses to make serious political comments on the injustice and hypocrisy of the Italian establishment as the following outline of the plot shows.

Antonio Berardi, a Fiat worker is making love to a female shop steward in his car when he sees Gianni Agnelli, head of the Fiat Motor Corporation, in what appears later to be a terrorist attack.

Antonio pulls Agnelli from the wreckage but the car explodes and Agnelli suffers burns. Antonio wraps him in his own jacket and takes him to a Red Cross ambulance so that he can be taken to hospital. Antonio then takes fright and disappears. As Agnelli is wearing Antonio's jacket, this gives rise to a case of mistaken identity on which much of the subsequent comedy hinges.

Agnelli's face is reconstructed with skin from his buttocks using a photograph of Antonio so there are later two apparent Antonios on stage. They give rise to much confusion in true farcical style when Rosa locks them up and they seem to escape. She feeds the real Antonio with an intricate machine that is so close to an instrument of torture that even the police are envious. The audience witnesses the awful pain and discomfort of Antonio being stuffed full of minced food while he cannot breathe so Rosa gives him a clarinet to blow through. The crude side of life is often the butt of jokes and appeals to the audience's sense of toilet humour. Although the images are grotesquely funny, there is a serious undercurrent concerning police mistreatment of those in custody.

The play is in two acts and either act would serve as a useful extract. Fo played both Antonio and Agnelli and called on his skills in *lazzi* to create highly comical moments when both characters just miss each other on stage. As usual, high energy, comic timing and strong physicality coupled with carefully rehearsed use of facial expression and voice brought out the strong visual comedy in the play. We have chosen the opening of Act 1 here for an extract.

Act 1 starts in the hospital with Antonio's wife Rosa visiting the man she thinks is her husband. Fo employs visual humour by using a dummy instead of an actor to play the patient in the first scene. The dummy is connected to a series of overhead wires and can therefore be moved like a puppet. The dummy's entry is accompanied by a musical interlude which turns the scene into a farce. At one point Rosa pulls on one of the strings by mistake and the dummy leaps off the bed. The use of slapstick is effective in making the audience laugh before they realise the serious nature of the situation.

Fo stops the flow of the scene by having Antonio enter from backstage to interrupt the action. The other actors freeze and then exit as 'a platform is wheeled on. On it are two car seats and assorted scrap parts of motor cars'. This stage direction shows that we are in a breaker's yard. Antonio distances his audience from the action by introducing himself directly to them (direct address) and then explaining what has happened and who is who. Thus the audience knows more than most of the actors on stage, which in turn causes dramatic irony and more comedy.

The script is full of gags, many of which make a comment about the relationship between the workers and the capitalists (in this case Agnelli, the owner of Fiat). For example, when Lucia, Antonio's girlfriend, tells him that it was Agnelli he saved, Antonio realises that his situation is even worse:

> Fo's work is political in the way he uses slapstick comedy and visual humour. Audiences are persuaded of the correctness of his cause as they laugh at the drama.

Mirafiori is one of the main Fiat plants in Turin. The use of onomatopoeia in this context makes the image of Antonio being beaten up like a comic strip and intentionally more funny.

ANTONIO   Agnelli?! I saved Agnelli? I took him in my arms, I wrapped him in my jacket… Me! If my workmates get to hear about this at Mirafiori, they'll line me up and run me over with tractors…! They'll bang me up against a wall and… splosh! splosh! splosh!…

Fo uses language to good effect when the patient is being taught to speak. He is asked to make many strange sounds which are amusing in themselves but when asked to pronounce more complicated words such as 'astronaut' and 'concupiscence', Rosa says that he will never need those words: 'He's a worker… Make him say the words that he is going to use every day: wage packet, lay-offs, redundancies…'

Bob Dylan

Bob Dylan was born Robert Zimmermann in Duluth, Minnesota in 1941; he later adopted the surname Dylan as a sign of respect to the Welsh poet Dylan Thomas. He is one of the most important songwriters of the last third of the 20th century, and his output has been enormous, with his songs covering a range of themes and styles. Indeed, one of the most significant features of Dylan's career has been his ability to reinvent himself, while keeping the essence of his vocal performance the same. It is his distinctive singing voice combined with his poetic lyrics that set him apart from other singer-songwriters of the period. As befits his adoption of the name Dylan, he is better described as a poet-songwriter. Dylan's early determination was to be a folk singer, and his early songs owe a stylistic debt to Woody Guthrie both in the style of composition and in performance.

Musical intentions

Further study

See what you can find out about these events.

Dylan's songs of the early 1960s are strongly linked with two social and cultural phenomena that were sweeping America during the decade: the protest movement that embraced the championing of civil rights for African Americans led by Martin Luther King Jr (1929–1968), and the anti-war sentiment that arose as a result of the Cuban missile crisis of 1962 and the Vietnam war (1964–1973).

Dylan as a political artist

In what sense are Bob Dylan's songs political? The simple answer is that they are not *all* political. In the course of his output, Dylan has worked in many styles. The early songs owe a debt to folk music, with Dylan accompanying himself on acoustic guitar and interspersing his singing with the harmonica. The use of electric guitar in the mid-1960s and the subsequent broadening of the instrumental accompaniments alienated some of his original fans who had been attracted by the gritty determination of the first collections of songs. Furthermore, Dylan's songs have frequently embraced religious themes, both Jewish and Christian, with *Slow Train Comin'* being the first overtly Christian album. Finally, you should be aware that a significant number of his songs are love songs that have little in the way of a political dimension.

The poetic nature of the words of Dylan's songs marks them out as distinctive. In some cases, this can lead to a style of writing in which the meaning is virtually impenetrable; at other times, he is able to use the cadences and rhythms of everyday language, and capture a turn of phrase in a memorable manner. As we have already indicated, however, it is Dylan's style of singing that does most to bring to life the nature of the protest in the songs. There is a directness about the words that is reflected in the simplicity of the melodies, harmonies and instrumentation. But it is the quality of Dylan's singing voice that is most memorable and this explains why cover versions by other artists often lose the essential nature of his songs.

The works by Dylan that we shall be using as examples are all taken from the 1960s, as these give the clearest indication of his style. In the case of a songwriter such as Dylan, we are taking extracts from three different albums rather than three songs from a single album. This is an important distinction because taking only three songs from the same album is unlikely to give a broad enough view of Dylan's output. The three albums are *The Freewheelin Bob Dylan*, *Another Side of Bob Dylan* and *Bringing it all back home*.

The Freewheelin' Bob Dylan

The Freewheelin' Bob Dylan album was produced in 1963 and demonstrates Dylan's early style very well. The album contains 13 songs, and we shall look at four that reflect the singer's range of social concerns. This gives an 'extract' lasting just over 20 minutes.

Blowin' in the wind is probably one of Bob Dylan's best-known songs and is written within an established folk-song pattern. The song consists of three verses, and the music is the same for each verse. Each of the three verses is regular in metre and consists of four sets of two lines. The first three sets of lines each pose a rhetorical question, which is then answered in the final set of lines. The first verse is

> How many roads must a man walk down
> Before you call him a man? **(A)**
> Yes 'n' how many seas must a white dove sail
> Before she sleeps in the sand? **(A)**
> Yes 'n' how many times must the cannon balls fly
> Before they're forever banned? **(A)**
> The answer, my friend, is blowin' in the wind,
> The answer is blowin' in the wind. **(B)**

The rhetorical style, typical of protest songs in asking questions, relies on the repetition of 'how many'. The structure of the music follows the same regular pattern and emphasises this rhetorical style. The first three sets of lines have the same melodic line (although the ending of 'before she sleeps in the sand' has a slightly different ending). The answer in lines 7 and 8 has different music. If you refer to each pair of lines as a section, the musical structure of the sections is therefore AAAB.

Masters of War is much longer and more overtly political. It is a song that Dylan has admitted was motivated by hate. The style of the song is similar to *Blowin' in the wind* in its use of the same music for each verse. The style of the words is aggressive, addressing commands at the 'masters of war'. The song builds up its political message by naming the various things that these people do – build guns, death planes and big bombs. They are compared to Judas in their treachery and the song rises to a climax as the final verse shouts for their imminent death.

Tip

The use of music for political purposes has a strong history but we are looking at the way in which composers make political points through their music. In most cases, it is the titles of pieces, the lyrics of songs or the context in which the music is written that give the strongest indication of its political nature.

Blowin' in the wind

This approach to using the same music for each verse is sometimes referred to as **strophic**.

Masters of War

The anger in the song is captured through the faster tempo and the use of the minor mode for the melodic line. The style of the guitar playing is similarly insistent and maintains the same rhythmic style throughout.

A Hard Rain's A-Gonna Fall

> " Every line in it is actually the start of a whole song. But when I thought about it, I thought I wouldn't have enough time alive to write all those songs so I put all I could into this one. "
>
> Dylan's notes to the record

A Hard Rain's A-Gonna Fall, written during the Cuban Missile Crisis of 1962, maintains the folk-song tradition of being written as if a parent were singing to a son. In the context of the nervousness about imminent nuclear war, the imagery of 'hard rain' becomes a metaphor for a nuclear storm, the fallout from a catastrophe that would be the result of uncontrolled conflict between nations. Here, Dylan encapsulates this in the parent-child relationship.

The song consists of five verses, although these are not all of similar length with the final verse in particular probing at length the harrowing effects of war. In each verse, there is a short refrain in the last two lines based on the model of *Blowin' in the wind*. In this case, this is the statement and restatement (to the same music each time) of 'It's a hard, it's a hard, it's a hard, it's a hard, it's a hard rain's a-gonna fall'.

Talkin' World War III Blues

This obsession with the possibility of nuclear conflict and the potential wiping out of mankind is continued in *Talkin' World War III Blues*. Here the imagery and context is highly explicit and uses images of fallout shelters. The verses are irregular, and the guitar playing is very complex and interspersed with forceful harmonica playing. The style of singing is largely lacking in melody and is much more declamatory, all of which adds to the furious style of the song. The sentiment of the song captures the anger and disillusion of a generation for whom the political process seemed to be irrelevant in establishing peace across the world.

Another Side of Bob Dylan

Another Side of Bob Dylan has been described by critics as an electric album without the electric instruments, as it seems to be a transitional album before Dylan 'went electric'.

Another Side of Bob Dylan was released in 1964 and continues in the same broad musical style. The album contains 11 songs, two of which will be discussed here. The album seems to take a different thematic approach from the overt protest of the previous songs, and there is a much greater focus on personal and emotional expression in the songs. This can be seen, for example, in songs such as *To Ramona* and *All I Really Want To Do*.

Chimes of Freedom

Chimes of Freedom falls clearly within the protest song tradition, although some writers have referred to it as the last of the protest songs. It has a much more developed literary style than the previous songs discussed, and each of the six verses is packed with vivid imagery and a sense of inspiring freedom. The mood is radically different from the anger contained within songs such as *Masters of War*, and it combines protest with a sense of vision of what could be achieved. This more aspirational style of protest returns in our final extract below, *Gates of Eden*.

The song works on a broad canvas and lasts for around seven minutes. Each verse consists of eight lines and the music for each verse is similar. The music is in triple metre, which lends a lilting quality to the music, again a feature that returns in *Gates of Eden*. The format of the words dictates the structure of the music.

Far between sundown's finish an' midnight's broken toil
We ducked inside the doorway, thunder crashing **(A)**
As majestic bells of bolts struck shadows in the sounds
Seeming to be the chimes of freedom flashing **(A)**
Flashing for the warriors whose strength is not to fight
Flashing for the refugees on the unarmed road of flight **(B)**
An' for each an' ev'ry underdog soldier of the night
An' we gazed upon the chimes of freedom flashing. **(B)**

As with *Blowin' in the Wind*, the verse falls neatly into four sets of two lines. These couplets are then treated musically as individual lines so that the melody is composed of four melodic sections. The first two and the fourth of these are broadly similar, with the third one introducing new melodic material. This gives an overall structure to each verse of AABA. Each of the verses concludes with the same final line.

I Shall be Free No. 10 also takes the notion of freedom and protest, and sets it in a personal context. This song is much more in the style of the protesting preacher and the melodic line is highly fluid and shaped entirely by Dylan's talking/singing style. This moves away from the heaviness of some protest songs into a light-hearted approach whereby the lyrics have an almost comic quality at times – 'I'm a poet, and I know it. Hope I don't blow it.'

The song runs to 11 verses and arrives at a point where any sense of protest has effectively fizzled out. The song ends with the statement 'you're probably wondering by now/what this song is all about'. This song is a good example of a transitional piece, as Dylan moves from the overt political protest of some early songs to his engagement with personal spirituality in the later songs.

Bringing It All Back Home

The *Bringing It All Back Home* album was produced in 1965 and develops from Dylan's early style, although there are clear musical differences, the most significant being the use of the electric guitar as the main accompaniment, a feature that outraged the singer's fans at that time.

The album contains 11 songs, and we shall be commenting on three that reflect the singer's concerns. Within this album, there are fewer explicit references to war but many of the songs deal with themes of inclusion and the individual on the outside of society, reflecting the racial struggle taking place in the United States in the mid-1960s. The most well-known song on the album is *Mr Tambourine Man*.

Maggie's Farm has the same declamatory style as the earlier songs and defiantly asserts: 'I ain't gonna work on Maggie's farm no more.' Each of the five verses begins with this statement, borne of slavery, that enough is enough and that Maggie's whole family are nothing but slave drivers. Each member of Maggie's family is caricatured in the successive verses and all fare badly. Even Maggie's Ma who 'talks about man and God and law' is a tyrant just like the rest of them. The melodic line has a melancholy, yearning quality as the same bittersweet style of delivery bewails the fate of the 'slave' who is working for a family of slave drivers. The song

I Shall be Free No. 10

Protest can rely on comedy at times – here it is used in just one line, but compare how Dario Fo extensively makes the audience laugh about the issues he is highlighting.

Tip

Although it would be tempting to look for a later album by Dylan to give broader coverage of the period, it's not necessary. Coverage can be achieved through the skilful choice of the practitioners rather than the extracts. Given the concentration of protest songs at the outset of Dylan's career, it is more appropriate to take the extracts from the early- to mid-1960s rather than looking at albums where overt protest is less apparent.

Maggie's Farm

could be seen as a commentary on the social situation of African Americans in the 1960s.

Outlaw Blues

The same sense of being on the fringe of society is captured in *Outlaw Blues*. Using an accompaniment figure based on a blues chord progression, Dylan adopts a style of singing clearly influenced by the blues. The theme of geographical origin and being an alien in the place where you find yourself recurs throughout the song. In particular, the fifth verse culminates in the revelation that he is in love with an African American in Jackson, and at this, the song fades away, almost as if acknowledging that such a relationship cannot be accepted at that point in America's history.

> The blues is a type of music that was developed by African Americans, as a form of release from the social conditions in which they found themselves. In time, the notion of a blues chord progression became a compositional device used by composers.

Gates of Eden

The title of *Gates of Eden* captures a sense of what the point of protest is – to achieve a better state, in this case indicated by the reference to Eden, the garden of paradise. The pulse of the song is in threes and has a much more lilting quality than the more hostile, declamatory style of the other songs discussed here. The style of the accompaniment has much in common with the style of earlier songs such as *Blowin' in the Wind*, and complements the more optimistic tone of the vocal line. The nine verses of the song have a narrative quality that paints a much more utopian picture of the world. The recurrent theme of the song is the hope for a better existence inside 'the gates of Eden'.

And finally...

Once you have studied the three extracts from each of the three practitioners, you need to consider the similarities and differences between them. Do not worry if you can't find many similarities, as there are many ways of creating political performance. Remember that these practitioners were working at different times and in different art forms. It is likely that there will be many differences and you could draw up a table to list them. However, do look for similarities because you will find some and they might surprise you. It might be that the practitioners come from similar cultural backgrounds or have similar political beliefs and that this consequently inspires their work.

> **Tip**
>
> In order to find similarities, try to think broadly about how to create performance work that persuades an audience.

Have open discussions in class about your experiences of the extracts and your reactions to them. Read reviews of the different works from which they have been taken. This is probably the most exciting part of this unit. Carry out your own research and converse with others in your class as well as the teacher. There are no right and definitive answers.

Consider the genre as a whole and keep an open mind. The following bullet points might give you some starting points to compare and contrast extracts.

> **Tip**
>
> These points are only starters for discussion. You could video your discussion and make notes from it when you play it back. Remember to focus on the extracts you have chosen to study. This discussion could be the basis for an essay written in preparation for the examination.

➤ Which issue or event is the piece based on?

➤ Which topical allusions have been cited?

➤ What was the political climate at the time and who had the power?

➤ How does the extract question or challenge the status quo?

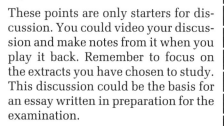

➤ Which techniques are employed by the practitioner to deliver his political message?

➤ Is allegory used to poke fun at political figures?

➤ Why are some extracts more serious than others?

➤ How are other art forms (such as song and dance in a drama piece) used to comment on the political dimensions of a situation?

➤ How is speech used in a dance piece?

➤ Which styles are employed to create the piece and why were they chosen?

➤ What is the structure of the piece?

➤ How important are set, costume, lighting and props?

Allow ten minutes at the end to sum up what has been said and try to group points or put them in a logical order which could be the basis of a coherent argument for an essay. This is an exercise that should be carried out on at least three separate occasions: initially for your first reaction to the extracts: secondly when the extracts have been studied in depth; and finally for revision purposes.

You should always have the nine extracts and your class notes to hand otherwise you will not be able to cite references – this is very important in the written examination.

The 20th-century American musical

The American musical is a distinctive art form because it is one of the few western genres that purposely sets out to bring together dance, drama and music. There are many examples of choreographers, composers and playwrights working together in other styles during the 20th century, but the musical stands alone as being the most thorough in integrating the art forms.

What do I have to know?

 Here's what the exam board says about what you're expected to know in the exam:

> Candidates should demonstrate knowledge of the roots of the musical in operetta and musical comedy (vaudeville and burlesque) and in the spectacular works of the *Ziegfeld Follies*. Candidates should be aware of the how the genre moved towards establishing credible drama rather than being performances that were merely a succession of unrelated songs, comedy routines and dance numbers. Candidates should study the way in which the art forms are integrated within the genre and the ways in which choreographer, composer and lyricist work to produce an integrated work. This will include the dramatic importance of the musical score and the importance of stylistic accessibility for the audience. Individual songs need not be analysed in detail but candidates should be aware of the songwriting styles employed in the extracts studied. The social, cultural and historical context of 20th-century America, the rise and importance of jazz and impact of the two world wars in fostering an escapist genre should be studied.

Note that it's the American musical only. The musical developed during the 20th century on both sides of the Atlantic, and it would be difficult to underestimate the impact of Andrew Lloyd Webber's work on Broadway in the last decade of the century. However, you must study **only American writers** of the musical and **not** writers whose works are simply performed in America.

The history of the 20th-century musical forms a coherent narrative, and our approach with this topic will be to take you through a brief history of the development of the form. This is not exhaustive, though – there are many details that we have omitted in the interests of space. We have selected extracts from practitioners that are intended to give you effective coverage of the 20th century, and to demonstrate how the genre changed.

It is perhaps worth stating at the outset that this history of the musical is centred on the development of the **book musical** – an art form based on a coherent play in which the songs and choreography all serve to move the action along. To understand this genre, though, you need first to look at how the art form developed.

We have selected our extracts from three practitioners whose work covers the majority of the century: Bob Fosse, Oscar Hammerstein II and Leonard Bernstein.

Roots of the musical

The roots of the 20th-century American musical are surprising complex. There are a number of strands that can all be shown to have influenced the way the musical developed, but none of them can be said uniquely to have led directly to its development. We will introduce you to each of these elements and describe the characteristic style of each. You can decide for each of the extracts that you are studying how easily you can spot these influences.

Burlesque-type shows

Burlesque flourished in Europe and the United States for most of the 19th century. An adult entertainment, it was a form of musical extravaganza or variety show that combined singing and dancing. Towards the end of the century, it became increasingly glamorous, and troupes of dancing girls became an important feature of the entertainment. Other related forms of entertainment were revues and vaudeville. In practice, the boundaries between these were sometimes blurred. Revue was a form that had achieved popularity in Paris at the end of the 19th century but contained similar elements of burlesque. Music hall – a popular British entertainment of song, dance, comedy and acrobatics from the same period – was also highly influential, as was pantomime. The term 'vaudeville' introduced by theatre managers to indicate a show that was more suitable for families, unlike the risque leg-kicking routines of the Ziegfeld Follies.

These shows developed into the *Follies* of Florenz Ziegfeld and the *Scandals* of George White. If you studied the songs of George Gershwin for Contextual Studies 1, you'll remember that George Gershwin wrote music for some of the *Scandals*.

Minstrel shows

Variety shows became very popular in America between 1880 and 1900. The form can be traced back to the minstrel shows of the mid 19th century. These were normally performed by white performers who blacked their faces to perform song and dance routines in imitation of how they perceived African American (originally slave) styles and manners as a form of variety entertainment. As the tradition grew, however, some troupes of black performers also began to be established. The songs of Stephen C. Foster (1826–1864) grew from this tradition.

An operetta is essentially a light opera, possibly with a comic theme and with spoken dialogue. There are examples of European operettas that are slightly different from this, but the form that took hold in America was largely influenced by the English operettas of W. S. Gilbert and Arthur Sullivan. Gilbert's satirical lyrics combined with Sullivan's jaunty melodies caught the comic nature of the genre. Operetta was different from other antecedents of the musical in that it had dialogue, plot and characterisation. The singing intentionally moved the plot along, unlike the other types of shows, in which songs were often unrelated to the action.

Operetta

Landmarks in the development of the musical

There are a number of works that are often cited as being direct forerunners of the musical.

You will find that many books refer to *The Black Crook* (1866) as the most important predecessor of the musical. It was something of a historical accident that when ticket sales for the original play were low, a large ballet troupe from France found themselves in New York City with nowhere to perform after their intended theatre space burned down. The two companies combined and the resulting show was a spectacle with lavish costumes and glitzy sets. Bringing together drama, dance and song, the show lasted for five-and-a-half hours and relied on complex scenery using stage machinery for special effects.

The Black Crook

The Brook (1879) introduced elements of music hall, although these may have appeared more akin to vaudeville to American audiences.

The Brook

One of Gilbert and Sullivan's Savoy Operas, *HMS Pinafore* was given its US premiere in Boston in 1878 and proved enormously popular – such that within a year it was the most frequently performed work in America.

HMS Pinafore

Little Johnny Jones (1904) is often referred to as the first American musical. Written by George M. Cohan, it contained two songs that outlined the show: 'Give my regards to Broadway' and 'Yankee Doodle Boy'. Cohan's background was in vaudeville and his achievement was to make the transition from this form to the 'respectable' stage.

Little Johnny Jones

With music and lyrics by the Austrian composer Franz Lehár, *The Merry Widow* (1905) transferred to the USA in 1907 in a revised version that appealed to local tastes. The work was enormously influential in establishing the elements of plot and song in the musical. This built on the tradition of operetta established in America in the performances of Gilbert and Sullivan operas.

The Merry Widow

The 20th-century musical before Show Boat

The early American musicals were essentially variety shows that included elements from all of the sources discussed above. They were characterised by spectacle and showmanship, and these were more important than the development of story or plot. The plots of these shows were often very loosely constructed and the songs themselves were not intended to move the action of the plot along.

The songs in most of Gershwin's shows had little to do with the action of the drama.

Occasionally, there might be a perceived link between the songs and what was happening on stage, but more often than not, the songs dealt with generic emotions that might fit any number of plots. It was not uncommon for songs to be taken from one show and placed in another.

The book musical

The influence of operetta, containing as it did plot, character and dialogue, took the musical in a different direction, towards what would become known as the **book musical**. This is the form that came to dominate the American musical in the 20th century.

When you are looking at the drama practitioner for this topic, you may find that person is the writer of both the book and the lyrics, but that may not always be the case.

You will need to understand what is meant by the 'book': it does **not** mean the original source for the drama (for example, the use of George Bernard Shaw's play *Pygmalion* as the basis of *My Fair Lady*; the book in that case was written by Alan Jay Lerner). The book of a musical refers to the plot, character and dialogue used in the show and how they work together – and this may or may not be written by the person who wrote the lyrics for the songs.

Operetta declined within the first two decades of the 20th century while the musical as we now know it began to take shape. By bringing together plot, characterisation and dialogue within the context of song and dance, the musical had the potential to be a more wide-ranging popular entertainment than operetta could ever be. It was the element of spectacle in particular that transformed the European genre of operetta into the American musical.

Jerome Kern

There are many people associated with the development of the book musical but the most important was Jerome Kern (1885–1945). Kern's songs took the musical in a new direction as he attempted to reveal the thoughts and motivations of characters through the songs he gave them. His songs attempted to move the action of the drama along and also convey the emotion of the characters. They were quite different from the loose collections of songs associated with vaudeville and burlesque.

For more on Hammerstein, see pages 104–109.

Kern collaborated initially with the author P. G. Wodehouse and the lyricist Guy Bolton. Although these collaborations produced some fine songs, Kern's greatest impact came as a result of his collaboration with Oscar Hammerstein II (1895–1960). Hammerstein's work with Jerome Kern in producing *Show Boat* in 1927 was of immense importance. It brought together a variety of strands to present its audience with credible drama in contrast to the succession of songs, comedy routines and dance numbers typical of the predecessors of the musical.

The impact of Rodgers and Hammerstein

Lorenz Hart

Hammerstein went on to work with Richard Rodgers (1902–1979) in a partnership that was one of the most significant in establishing the American musical as a genre in its own right. Rodgers had also had an earlier collaborative partnership, having previously worked with Lorenz Hart (1895–1943). Hart was a skilled wordsmith who could use language creatively to invent witty lyrics. In the 1920s it was not unusual for composers to produce melodies to which lyrics would be added by their collaborator – this is the way in which George and Ira Gershwin worked, for example.

Lorenz Hart was an important lyricist as, like Oscar Hammerstein, he believed that the lyrics of a song should move the drama along and help to reinforce the characterisation of the drama.

Rodgers' partnership with Hart was enduring but Hart's alcohol dependency made collaboration increasingly difficult. Following Hart's death in 1943, Rodgers began serious collaboration with Hammerstein, whom he had known for many years and with whom he had also worked on occasion. Following *Show Boat* in 1927, Hammerstein had been eager to achieve the same success for another show but had produced a series of works that were considered mediocre or even outright flops. Yet the partnership between them seemed destined to succeed, as both men shared the same vision for what a musical should be – a coherent piece for the stage in which the music was a fully integrated part of the drama.

The first collaboration between Rodgers and Hammerstein was *Oklahoma!* which we shall be discussing in more detail later. The piece established once and for all the principle that the purpose of the composer was not simply to produce showstoppers that would detract from the flow of the drama rather than move it along. This principle seemed to be accepted almost immediately by other writers and the formula on which *Oklahoma!* was based was immediately taken up by other musicals, such as Irving Berlin's 1946 musical *Annie Get Your Gun*.

> As well as being the lyricist, Oscar Hammerstein also wrote the book for most of the musicals on which he collaborated. This is the reason that we have chosen him as a practitioner for study, as you will be able to see how he uses his lyrics to move the plot along.

The partnership between Rodgers and Hammerstein lasted until Hammerstein's death in 1960, and during the 18 years they worked together they produced a string of Broadway hits, many of which were also made into Hollywood films. These include *Carousel* (1945), *South Pacific* (1949), *The King and I* (1951) and *The Sound of Music* (1959), most of which have enjoyed revivals in London's West End in recent years.

> Oscar Hammerstein's most famous pupil was Stephen Sondheim who proved to be one of the most significant figures in musical theatre at the end of the 20th century.

Other partnerships: Lerner and Loewe

The other significant partnership of the mid-20th century was that of Alan Jay Lerner (1918–1986) and Frederick (Fritz) Loewe (1901–1988), although both men collaborated with other partners in between working with each other. Loewe was born in Austria – his father had taken part in the original production of Lehár's *The Merry Widow* – and he did not move to the USA until 1924. Lerner was born in New York and was successful in Americanising Loewe's European artistic tendencies to produce something distinctively American.

The musicals follow the same pattern as that established by Rodgers and Hammerstein in terms of integrating the art forms. For their first major collaboration, *Brigadoon*, they worked with the established and successful choreographer Agnes de Mille who had also worked with Rodgers and Hammerstein. The partnership of Lerner and Loewe produced a series of successful musicals, many of which had associations through plot and subject matter with Europe – *Brigadoon* (1947), *Paint Your Wagon* (1951), *My Fair Lady* (1956), *Camelot* (1960) and *Gigi* (1958) which began life as a film and was only adapted for the stage in 1973.

The mature musical

Bernstein

Leonard Bernstein (1918–1990) is best known for his composition of the music for *West Side Story* (1957), but this obscures the huge diversity of his musical talents – conductor, orchestral composer, musicologist and critic. His impact on the musical life of the USA was out of all proportion to any other 20th-century composer of musicals because his compositional activity was spread across a number of genres. Most importantly, he was able to take a symphonic approach to orchestration and offer a more radical and sophisticated take on the musical as an art form.

As a highly accomplished musician, Bernstein's music immediately stood out from the Broadway scores of Richard Rodgers and Fritz Loewe. He was able to approach the rhythms of songs in a creative and complex way that pushed the music far more than the ballads of the earlier musicals. It is for this reason that we have selected Bernstein as a composer for our examples below. It is also because of his collaboration with Stephen Sondheim (a pupil of Oscar Hammerstein II) on *West Side Story*.

The musical at the end of the 20th century

Sondheim

The dominant figure in American musicals in the last quarter of the 20th century was Stephen Sondheim (born 1930). Like Bernstein, he had a formal musical training, which enabled him to adopt a highly sophisticated approach to the musical as an art form. The collaboration with Bernstein on *West Side Story* in 1957 established his career as a lyricist. He also collaborated with Richard Rodgers on the 1965 musical *Do I Hear a Waltz?*

Since the 1962 show *A Funny Thing Happened on the Way to the Forum*, Sondheim has achieved success as both composer and lyricist for his musicals. While it would be fair to say that Sondheim's musicals have not achieved the popular appeal of those of the mid century or of the imported shows of Andrew Lloyd Webber, he has produced a string of frequently performed works. These include *Company* (1970), *A Little Night Music* (1973), *Sweeney Todd* (1979), *Sunday in the Park with George* (1984) and *Into the Woods* (1987). Each of these shows makes intellectual demands on their audiences that elevate the mid-century musical into a distinct art form. The nature of the drama is less stylised and characters are often more rounded and believable.

The three practitioners we have chosen to discuss here are Bob Fosse, Oscar Hammerstein II and Leonard Bernstein.

> Sondheim's musicals are still book musicals but they take the form to a higher level and away from musical comedy – hence the term 'art musical'.

> Sondheim's lyrics show the way in which he is able to exploit fully the rhythmic and emotional properties of text. He is the only recent practitioner to have depended on his own abilities rather than working through collaborators to write shows.

> In the course of this chapter, we've given you a fair amount of biographical detail about each of the practitioners discussed. However, remember that while you should have some idea of the background of your practitioners, you are advised not to spend time relating biographical information in your exam essay unless it is directly related to a point you are making about the genre.

Further reading

There is much to read about Fosse's life, his family, his work and his womanising. An entertaining biography which provides excellent background reading is *All His Jazz: The Life and Death of Bob Fosse* by Martin Gottfried (Da Capo 2003). See also www.fosse.com.

Bob Fosse

Bob Fosse (pronounced *foss-ee*) was born in 1927 on the north side of Chicago to Norwegian parents. He died in 1987 on a street corner in Washington in the arms of Gwen Verdon, the last of his three wives and one of his best dancers.

The son of an insurance salesman who enjoyed ballroom dancing, Bob Fosse attended the Chicago Academy of Theatre Arts at a young age. The managing director of the academy was Fred Weaver with whom Fosse had a longstanding friendship. Weaver ran the academy in the hope of developing child performers whom he might go on to manage. When Fosse's father Cy could no longer afford to pay the dance school fees, Weaver offered Bob a scholarship loan in return for 15 per cent of the boy's earnings until he was 21. Bob Fosse was teamed up with Charles Grass to become the Riff Brothers, a junior version of the Nicholas Brothers. They led a double life, going to school and never admitting to their daily dance rehearsals after school and their vaudeville engagements at the weekends. They performed in a variety of places, some more seedy than others, and their encounters with all types of people – including striptease artists – was to influence Fosse's sexually suggestive choreography.

One of Fosse's early hit routines was 'Steam Heat' in a show entitled *The Pajama Game* (1956), a George Abbott musical. Gottfried describes it as follows:

> As Fosse started them out in the studio, with the dance already completed in his head, they were posed side by side, their backs to where the audience would be, hats held high above their heads in a freeze. Then they turned, edging sideways toward where the footlights would be. With each raising a shoulder, they toss the hats in unison, catching them simultaneously. The rhythms are jazzy and syncopated, the music starts to build, and then it abruptly shuts down as they dance in silence, except for the sound of their scuffling feet. The three skinny clowns elbow and slide and drop down on their knees and stand up again and then edge along with their elbows tucked and their hands spread in the gesture that would soon be known as 'Fosse hands'. They become a little machine, clacketing to the sounds of clucking tongues and knocking mouths, with hissing and finger snapping and counter-rhythms of hand clapping and foot stamping.

This description of this one Fosse dance piece shows most of the fingerprints of his trade: shoulder rolls, splayed hands, snapping fingers and hats, in particular. Influences from choreographers Jack Cole and Fred Astaire are detectable, as is the precison demanded by Fred Weaver in the days of the Riff brothers. The number became a showstopper, which George Abbot did not like because he felt that narrative flow should be more important. He wanted the number taken out as he thought it did not further the plot but as the audience loved it so much, he was forced to keep it in. Fosse had risen to the challenge, worked in an original way with the sounds that come from hissing radiators and knocking pipes, and produced an excellent dance for a trio.

Here we look at *Sweet Charity*, *Chicago* and *Cabaret*, but *All That Jazz* and *Fosse* would be suitable alternatives.

Extract 1: Sweet Charity

Charity Hope Valentine is a dance hall hostess who wants a better life than that in the Fan-Dango Ballroom. Ditched by her fiance, she ends up in the bedroom of Italian film star Vittorio Vidal but is once again unsuccessful in snaring her man. She then meets and dates the shy Oscar, who at first does not seem to mind her profession, but later changes his tune.

Web link

See www.nicholasbrothers.com for more on the Nicholas Brothers.

Martin Gottfried, *All His Jazz: The Life and Death of Bob Fosse.*

Sweet Charity is based on the screenplay *Nights of Cabira* by Frederico Fellini. It was produced by Fryer, Carr and Harris in 1966. The music is by Cy Coleman, the lyrics by Dorothy Fields and the book by Neil Simon. It was conceived, directed and choreographed by Bob Fosse. Gwen Verdon played Charity when the show opened at the Palace Theatre in 1966. Fosse won a Tony Award for *Sweet Charity*.

Many of the numbers danced by Charity would make good extracts for study. There are several different styles used in the production and the following numbers would offer a good range:

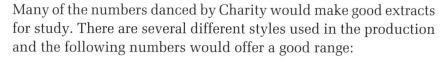

➢ 'If My Friends Could See Me Now'– a solo with hat and cane.

➢ 'There's Gotta Be Something Better Than This' with its flamenco rhythms.

➢ 'The Rich Man's Frug' – a three-part ensemble piece.

➢ 'Rhythm of Life' – a large group piece with plenty of scope for ensemble dance.

➢ 'Big Spender' – with its provocative poses and overt lyrics.

➢ 'I'm a Brass Band' – a military strut with drum majors.

The lyrics of the songs often reflect Charity's hopes in life and the dancing helps to illustrate the character. There is always a pure entertainment factor in the dance numbers.

In 'Big Spender', the Fan-Dango ballroom dance hostesses express their seedy life and dependence on men with money, and their opening poses demonstrate Fosse's excellent eye for group positioning. He uses levels well and gives each girl an independent and unique pose to catch the attention of the audience. There is a sense of a double audience – those watching the show from the stalls as well as the men in the ballroom who are looking for a chance to dance with one of these apparently provocative and confident women. There is also comedy in the way their bodies are used. The knees are often turned in and touching or bowed out with the weight on outer sides of the shoes. There is a paradox in the ungainly image of womanhood thus presented and the beauty of the choreographer's precision and attention to detail when presenting character through dance.

Fosse had strong ideas about physique and costume. For Charity, he told Irene Sharaf, the costume designer: 'I want her in a plain black dress, and she'll wear it the entire time.' He wanted each dancer to cut a sharp image on the stage whereby wrists, elbows, knees and hips played a vital role in developing a jagged impression of a body. The tight-fitting garments and pointed high heels gave an elongated look to the limbs. The heels were dug into the floor and the foot was flexed to the ceiling in Gwen Verdon's opening image of Charity. These precise poses and subsequent sharp movements present the dancers as strong and in control.

Extract 2: Chicago

Roxie Hart shoots her lover dead and ends up in jail where she realises that she could be hanged for the crime. She gets her husband Amos to hire a lawyer called Billy Flynn. Another prisoner, Velma Kelly, is awaiting her own trial for murder. The two women compete for the limelight. Roxie is acquitted thanks to the lawyer and the two murderesses team up in a vaudeville double act.

Some of the chorus work in *Chicago* is renowned for its almost organic quality. Fosse and his assistant Kathy Doby worked with the female dancers by teaching them three movement combinations, each lasting for four measures of music. Two dancers start combination A, two start combination B and the third pair starts combination C. The combinations begin on different measures of the music and create overlaps that, as Kathy Doby said 'made it look like a moving organism'. This is reminiscent of 'Richman's Frug' in *Sweet Charity* where the dancers move as one body demonstrating a certain type of social class. They are stiff and rigid when walking and look like mannequins, cold and aloof. The black-and-white costumes set them apart from the colourful costumes of the rest of the characters as they represent a richer class who are far removed form everyday life and humanity. In contrast to them are the beatniks or hippies who dance to the 'Rhythm of Life', interpreting the lines of the song in a literal fashion, using swimming movements of the arms and legs or flying just as it states in the lyrics. Their movements are more joyful and free as they focus on their idol 'Daddy'.

In 'Chicago', there is a chorus that sings and dances and comments on the action. In 'Razzle-Dazzle', Billy Flynn stands beneath the scales of justice and begins the defence. Flynn is positioned on a flight of steps with the judge at the top and the dancers writhing about the steps as if they are engaged in an orgy. Fosse wanted the dance to demonstrate the corruption of justice. This scene did not go down well with the audience who were not sure where to look, and eventually Fosse was indirectly persuaded to cut the sexual dancing. The show was slick but not well received on Broadway. It had a much better reception in England. Now, of course, as a revival, it has become a hit. The show makes a statement but still has a great entertainment factor through its use of song and dance. The Fosse style with long legs, deadpan faces, provocative costumes, hats and gloves is probably more popular today than ever before.

Extract 3: Cabaret

An obvious link can be seen between the style of dance in the Kit Kat Club in *Cabaret* and the Fan-Dango Ballroom in *Sweet Charity*, but the girls in the Berlin cabaret are more decadent and not necessarily attractive. There are more sinister undertones running through *Cabaret*, as it is set in the time of the Nazi rise to power. The men of Berlin flock to the cabaret at night to escape the political turmoil. There are serious themes of anti-semitism, racism, bisexuality, homosexuality, prostitution and transvestism. The often tired-looking dancers enhance the bitter political flavour of the songs sung by the MC of the club. Chairs are a significant prop for Fosse and are used to dramatic effect by both Liza Minelli and the other dancers.

Costume defines Sally Bowles – in her bowler hat, stockings and green nail varnish – as being intentionally and self-consciously decadent, and enjoying life to the full at any given moment, a philosophy echoed in the words of 'Come to the Cabaret'.

Realism was a rule in the making of the film. There were no dances where there would not have been dances in real life – that is, they took place in club where dancing was expected. Musical staging is

Further study

In the film version (2002), Rob Marshall's choreography emulates the Fosse style – black, lacy erotic costumes, flying legs, pelvic thrusting, sharp hand movements and hat tilts, for example – but avoids using specific moves from the original.

Fosse did not choreograph the original 1966 stage show, but he did direct the film version (Allied Artist Films 1972), which we discuss here. The story was altered and songs were added ('Mein Herr' and 'Maybe This Time'). **You need therefore to focus on the film version to consider Fosse's choreography.**

The lyrics are by Fred Ebb, the music by John Kander and the book by Joe Masteroff, based on John van Druten's play *I am a Camera*, which itself drew on Christopher Isherwood's *Goodbye to Berlin*.

used on a set measuring ten by 14 feet, which is small but authentic to the type of club depicted. No more than six girls were used at a time and Fosse admitted that his task was to make the dances look like a 'down and out' guy had put them together; he moved away from his characteristic Fosse style and made the dancers look cheap. For example in 'Mein Herr', Liza Minelli is perched on a chair with one leg in a squat and the other extended out. The positions are not meant to look graceful or elegant; they are supposed to reflect the mood of the performers in the club. The other dancers are often draped over chairs and to be found in very difficult, sometimes painful and provocative positions with legs dangling and fingertips tapping on the floor. This is not the slick choreography of *Chicago*, but a development of 'Big Spender' from *Sweet Charity*.

Oscar Hammerstein II

Oscar Hammerstein II is one of the most influential figures in the history of the 20th-century American musical, and his working career spanned a significant part of the period you are studying. We have chosen to focus on him as a drama practitioner – however, as we have already noted, the nature of musical theatre means that the art forms work together and support each other in such a way that it is impossible to study the writer of the book or the lyrics in isolation from the music. Studying Oscar Hammerstein II is particularly interesting because he collaborated (at separate times) with two of the most gifted composers/songwriters for the genre – Jerome Kern and Richard Rodgers.

Oscar Hammerstein II was born in 1895 and came from a theatrical family; his grandfather (also called Oscar Hammerstein) had been a well known 19th-century impresario and his uncle, Arthur Hammerstein, was a successful producer of Broadway shows. The young Oscar Hammerstein II worked for his uncle as a stage manager on Broadway. The family was of Jewish extraction and, although not a practising Jew, Hammerstein must have come across some of the ingrained anti-semitism of the period, something that prepared him to tackle issues of race in his work.

Although he had studied law at Columbia University, graduating in 1917, Hammerstein was soon lured by the theatre, and by 1920 had begun work on writing the librettos for a number of minor shows. He was attracted by the conventions of operetta, and collaborated separately with three European-born composers who had all emigrated to the USA: Rudolf Friml (1879–1972), Sigmund Romberg (1887–1951) and Karl Hoschna (1877–1911). None of these collaborations came to very much and, even though he continued to work intermittently with Romberg, it was not until Hammerstein began his collaboration with the American-born composer Jerome Kern (1885–1945) that his career flourished.

Hammerstein's first collaboration with Kern was in the style of an operetta. *Sunny* was written in 1925 and took a completely different approach. While the plot was stylised, it could never have been described as operetta, as it contained so many bizarre

You will see that we have chosen one of the extracts from *Show Boat* to represent Hammerstein's early collaboration with Kern, and the other two from collaborations with Rodgers – *Oklahoma!* and *The King and I*. All of the examples from Hammerstein's work are available on video or DVD. Remember, though, that they are Hollywood film versions of the shows and not the original Broadway versions. Check with your teacher that the extract you are studying is **not** additional material inserted for the film.

Jerome Kern's music was quite different from the operettas of composers such as Sigmund Romberg. Kern had a gift for melody and an ability to write music that would capture the ears of American theatregoers.

elements including a ship, a fox hunt, a female gymnasium and a circus. But these were all elevated by the quality of Kern's score for the show and it was this more than anything else that ensured the show's success.

Kern and Hammerstein's next show was to prove the most important in establishing the musical as a serious art form that could both entertain and engage with the nature of society. *Show Boat* was composed in 1927 and is widely considered to be one of the masterpieces of the genre. We shall be looking at it in more detail shortly. Despite the success of *Show Boat*, however, Hammerstein's career effectively stalled afterwards and – despite the popularity of certain individual songs – no other shows from his collaborations with Kern reproduced its triumph.

Hammerstein began his collaboration with Richard Rodgers in 1942. Their first show – *Oklahoma!* – was based on Lynn Rigg's play *Green Grow the Lilacs*, and we have chosen this as the second example of Hammerstein's work. Hammerstein was significant as a lyricist and also as the writer of the books of almost all the musicals he wrote with Rodgers. While other lyricists were content to focus on songs, Hammerstein saw his songs as the means to move the plot and action of the play along. In each of the musicals that followed, the songs are used as a vehicle to move the drama along and reinforce its effect.

The scenarios themselves capture the essence of the American Dream in all its post-war fullness. *Oklahoma!* was completed during the Second World War but attempted to capture a sentimental view of American life. Plots of other musicals focused on the exotic locations around the world but effectively imposed an American cultural framework on the treatment of the subject matter. *South Pacific* (1949) was set in a tropical paradise; *The King and I* (1951) offers a stylised view of Siam (Thailand) and *The Sound of Music* (1959) takes a romantic view of Austria. In all cases, the element of fantasy is rooted in a style of music that is immediately recognisable as American.

Prior to his collaborations with Hammerstein, Richard Rodgers had been a songwriter in the tradition of George Gershwin, and his partnership with Lorenz Hart (1895–1943) had produced a number of enduring songs and a larger number of shows. Yet none of them had the impact of the shows he produced in collaboration with Oscar Hammerstein. Hammerstein was much more than a witty lyricist able to fit words to a pre-existent melody. He was able to set individual songs within the drama as a whole, and in so doing transformed the American musical from a variety show in which songs were conceived of as showstoppers, into a art form of style and craftsmanship that integrated music and drama in as powerful a way as operetta had done previously.

Extract 1: Show Boat

The first performance of *Show Boat* was appropriately in the Ziegfeld Theatre on Broadway yet, unlike the shows championed by Ziegfeld, *Show Boat* provides a continuous piece of musical

Show Boat

Richard Rodgers

Tip

You could decide to study both Rodgers **and** Hammerstein as practitioners for this topic. That way, you would have to study extracts from six musicals that they wrote in order to have three extracts for each. We have chosen not to do this, in order to give you a wider perspective on the historical development of the musical.

Tip

When you study the extracts from Hammerstein, you need to consider any potential differences between the works written with Kern and those written with Rodgers.

Show Boat was written in 1927, based on the novel by Edna Ferber. The music is by Jerome Kern, the book and lyrics by Oscar Hammerstein II. The original producer was Florenz Ziegfeld (of *Ziegfeld Follies*), someone perfectly equipped to handle spectacle, entertain and amaze audiences. The film version, made in 1936, is faithful to the stage musical ,although the song 'Ah Still Suits Me' was not in the original.

Hammerstein's concern with racial issues is also seen in his adaptation of Georges Bizet's famous opera *Carmen* for an all-black cast. Hammerstein's version was titled *Carmen Jones*.

theatre in which the songs reinforce the drama rather than indicating a break in it. It was *Show Boat* that finally released the American musical from the influence of European operetta. It was the first musical to deal with specifically American issues.

The plot is set over a broad time period from 1880 to 1927 and centres on three main characters. Cap'n Andy Hawks is the proprietor of a show boat called *Cotton Blossom*. His daughter Magnolia Hawks falls in love with a gambler called Gaylord Ravenal. They move to Chicago but split when Gaylord loses everything. Magnolia goes on to develop a career as a famous singer, however, and the couple are ultimately reunited on *Cotton Blossom*. The subplot deals with racial issues, which were keenly felt in the South, and the show was the first to engage sensitively with a multiracial cast. The show captures both the predicament of African Americans working on the docks along the Mississippi River and also the issue of mixed-race marriage, which was a punishable offence in 1927.

We have chosen the opening section of Act 1, as far as the end of Scene 2 (including the song 'Can't help lovin' dat man') as our extract. The whole of this opening scene deals with the relationship between Magnolia Hawkes and Gaylord Ravenal. Hammerstein resisted the temptation to produce a formulaic love song – the history of the musical was littered with these. Instead he approached the whole scene from a point of view of emotional reticence, so that the whole point of the song is to say 'I love you' through hints and gestures rather than explicitly. The notion of make-believe is carried through, so that the unthinkable – the daughter of the boat owner and the gambler falling in love – is suggested as make-believe. The melody has a sad yearning quality that captures perfectly the mood of the drama:

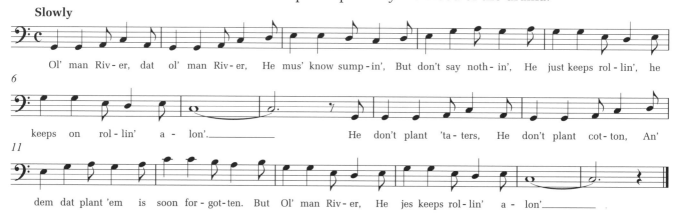

The opening chorus establishes the lot of black employees on the river and is set very simply using mainly tonic and subdominant harmony. However, when this re-appears, Kern reharmonises it using a chromatic bass, heightening the ethnic flavour and highlighting the community's feelings of isolation and rejection.

The extract also includes the solo and chorus 'Ol' Man River'. This gives a clear indication of the sensitive manner in which Hammerstein approaches racial issues in the play, as the score specifically asks for a 'coloured chorus'. This is established at the opening and is reinforced by the sophistication of Kern's music.

With *Show Boat*, musical theatre finally replaced musical comedy, the term used in the early part of the 20th century. The show's success was a result of the quality of the music, the realism of the plot and the integration of the two. There is a serious plot from which the music, songs, dancing and crowd scenes arise.

Extract 2: Oklahoma!

You will find that some books point to links between *Show Boat* and *Oklahoma!* They are both set in the same historical period – the turn of the 20th century – and in rural locations. The most important link between the works, though, is the way in which they integrate dance, drama and music in an absorbing and effective way. In *Oklahoma!* the element of dance was elevated to a new status through the involvement of the choreographer Agnes de Mille. The result of bringing her work together with that of Rodgers and Hammerstein was innovative and effective.

The plot of *Oklahoma!* is sentimental and focuses on the lives of ordinary people involved in a romantic triangle, albeit one that contains elements of danger. Curly and Jud are rivals for the affections of Laurey, a young girl living on a farm in Oklahoma with her Aunt Eller. The action of the play grows from her falling in love with Curly. As Curly is too embarrassed to return her affections, Laurey decides to spur him into action by agreeing to go to a box social with Jud Fry, a hired hand of whom she is afraid. At the social, Laurey and Jud argue and Jud goes off leaving Laurey and Curly eventually to realise their love and marry. On their wedding day, Jud starts a fight, falls on his own knife, and is killed. Laurey and Curly get married and there is a happy ending. There is a comic subplot in which the man-eating Ado Annie chases after both Will Parker and the peddler Ali Hakim.

We have again chosen the opening of the show as an extract for study. In the first act, Hammerstein takes considerable time to establish the emotional links between the characters rather than relying on the chorus to set the scene. It was customary to open a musical show with a large chorus number that had a number of attractive female artists singing and dancing. The exact opposite happens at the start of *Oklahoma!* where the focus is on establishing the narrative.

Only Aunt Eller is on stage – the opening song from the leading man, Curly, commences offstage and then grows louder as he rides on to the stage. This is an understated approach that shows Hammerstein's confidence in his ability to establish the form of the musical using his own techniques. It is almost three-quarters of an hour into the show before the first chorus number. The melody of the opening song 'Oh what a beautiful morning' is simple and effective. It uses a triple metre and has a lilting quality that sums up the mood of rural America.

As the opening extract is fairly short, it would be helpful to balance this distinctive use of music with the use of dance in the show. At the mid-point of *Oklahoma!*, Rodgers and Hammerstein introduce a ballet, choreographed by Agnes de Mille. The ballet represents Laurey falling into a deep sleep and dreaming of her impending marriage to Curly but this changes as Jud enters in a bullying manner. The nature of the dance used to represent this dream sequence is inspired by classical ballet and allows the heightening of the drama through the dance sequence.

Oklahoma! – written in 1942 – is based on a play by Lynn Riggs (1899–1954) entitled *Green Grow the Lilacs*. The music is by Richard Rodgers, the book and lyrics by Oscar Hammerstein II.

Further study

The film version of *Oklahoma!* was made in 1955 and stays close to the stage version, containing Agnes de Mille's ballet and other choreography adapted from the stage version.

The fact that *Oklahoma!* was the most significant musical since *Show Boat*, highlights the lack of significant musicals produced between 1927 and 1943. The one notable exception to this was *Porgy and Bess*, although Gershwin's masterpiece was more akin to opera than musical.

> " We agreed to start our story in the real and natural way in which it seemed to want to be told. "
>
> Oscar Hammerstein.

There are a number of features of *Oklahoma!* that set it apart from earlier musical comedies:

➤ The structure of the play allows character to be developed to a much greater depth than had previously been possible

➤ There is less reliance on the use of the chorus for big numbers

➤ The use of ballet and popular dance to reinforce the action is innovative

➤ The death of the Jud Fry could have alienated the audience, but is well handled

➤ Reprises of songs are used to reinforce and move along the dramatic content.

Extract 3: The King and I

In contrast to the gentle romanticism of many musicals, *The King and I* centres on a conflict between the two main characters, the aging King of Siam and the younger Anna, who arrives in Siam with her son and enters the king's palace as a governess for his children. The drama arises from a clash of cultures: the king is portrayed as something of a barbarian who needs the civilising influence of the western teacher. This inevitably sets in place a situation in which romance can develop from conflicts of culture and age. Yet the death of the King at the end is almost a catharsis – he is aware of his human failings and frailties, and dies knowing he cannot come to terms with his own character.

The extract we have chosen focuses on the clash of cultures that lies at the heart of the musical; it runs from the opening of Act 2 to the end of musical number 39 'Shall We Dance?'. This clash of cultures was nothing new for Rodgers and Hammerstein; they had explored related issues in *South Pacific*.

At the start of Act 2, Anna finally comes face to face with the reality of the king's polygamy, as she sees his many wives and children. Hammerstein's concern for racial equality shines through his lyrics. The first song in Act 2, 'Western People Funny' is not one of the show's best known, but it challenges the notions of civilisation prevalent at the time. Notice, however, that in the film version the song is used only as an underscore.

This is contrasted with Anna's dance with Sir Edward and the subsequent ballet – 'The Small House of Uncle Thomas', based on *Uncle Tom's Cabin*. Ultimately, this leads to the point where barriers between Anna and the King are broken down, as intimacy emerges in the singing of 'Shall We Dance?'. Here, virtually at the end of the play, there is physical contact between them.

The use of dance throughout the act builds on the use of ballet in *Oklahoma!* In *The King and I*, dance is used as a cultural phenomenon to develop the plot and also to move the action away

The King and I was written in 1951 and was based on Margaret Landon's *Anna and the King of Siam* (1943). The music is by Richard Rodgers, the book and lyrics by Oscar Hammerstein II; choreography was by Jerome Robbins. The film of the Hollywood musical was made in 1956 and is largely faithful to the content and style of the stage musical. The show was revived on Broadway in 1996.

> ❝ Nothing brought the Rodgers and Hammerstein musicals to life like a clash of cultures. Anna confronts the multiple wives and children of the King of Siam; they will be charmed by her, and she, in turn, will slowly change the social structure of Siam. ❞
>
> Kantor and Maslon

from reliance on drama and songs. As an example of the use of all of the art forms, this extended extract demonstrates how a wide variety of styles and approaches can be used effectively to reflect the cultural diversity of the show as a whole.

Leonard Bernstein

Leonard Bernstein (1918–1990) is perhaps best known for his composition of the music for the 1957 Broadway show *West Side Story* but that reputation alone does not come anywhere near doing justice to Bernstein's genius. Unlike the other practitioners we have discussed in this chapter, Bernstein did not only – or even primarily – work in musicals. The various works that we will consider as examples of musical theatre were referred to by Bernstein using a variety of titles: operetta, musical play, musical comedy, musical theatre. This reflects his breadth of interests: he was a composer, conductor, and musical writer and commentator whose eclectic musical interests echoed the diversity of American music in the 20th century.

Bernstein's initial connection with the Broadway musical was through his collaborations with the dancer and choreographer Jerome Robbins. Bernstein wrote the music for two ballets by Robbins: *Fancy Free* (1944) and *Facsimile* (1946).

Bernstein's reputation as a composer of musical theatre depends mainly on four works and these need to be seen within in the context of his entire musical output. His main impact on the musical life of the USA is generally considered to be as a conductor, and it was this that reinforced his exceptional ability to understand how to write for orchestra. After graduating from Harvard in 1939 he went on to study conducting with Fritz Reiner at the Curtis Institute and he quickly made a career for himself as a conductor. In 1943 he was invited at short notice to conduct the New York Philharmonic for a concert and later, in 1958, he became the principal conductor for that orchestra.

Bernstein wrote symphonic music, chamber music, vocal and choral music as well as works for the stage, although it could be argued that the stage works sum up Bernstein's energetic, theatrical personality. His first published work was the Clarinet Sonata (1941) and his Symphony No.1 followed in 1944, the year of his first foray into the world of musical theatre. *On the Town* was his first musical and provides one of the extracts we have chosen for study.

Despite the success of *On the Town* in New York, Bernstein's next attempt at musical theatre was not for another nine years. As an established conductor, Bernstein was called upon in 1952 to conduct a concert performance of Bertolt Brecht and Kurt Weill's *Threepenny Opera*. In the same year, Bernstein's short opera *Trouble in Tahiti* also premiered and 1952 was something of a reintroduction for Bernstein into the world of the stage. His engagements as a conductor had prevented him from being consistently involved on Broadway.

Web link

You can find a detailed discussion of Leonard Bernstein's music at the official website: www.leonardbernstein.com.

Bernstein's reputation as a composer of music theatre is not as a collaborator with a lyricist. While *West Side Story* brought him into an effective partnership with Stephen Sondheim, this was very much a one-off.

Bernstein as conductor

In some ways Bernstein's career is the opposite of that of George Gershwin. While Gershwin longed to move from being a songwriter to being an orchestral composer, Bernstein used his mastery of the orchestra as the basis of his musical theatre works.

Wonderful Town

In 1953, he produced *Wonderful Town* (which is totally unrelated to *On the Town* despite its similar-sounding title). Bernstein took on the project at short notice, weeks from the first performance, following the failure of the team who had been hired to complete the show. Despite its commercial success, none of the songs in *Wonderful Town* became well known and the show's success was probably due to the way in which it managed to evoke the arty atmosphere of 1930s Greenwich Village. Its main significance seems to have been to refocus Bernstein's mind on the challenges of writing for the musical stage.

Candide

In 1956, Bernstein returned to the world of musical theatre with *Candide*, although he saw this more as an operetta. In Bernstein's hands, the dramatic qualities of the European operetta were embraced and incorporated into the world of the musical. His musical language in *Candide* was as complex as his symphonic music of the period. The piece itself was something of a flop commercially, although this is due to the awkward nature of the drama of the book by Lillian Hellman (based on Voltaire's short novel) rather than Bernstein's music.

West Side Story

West Side Story is easily Bernstein's greatest success and proved the point that great musicals are often (although not always) the product of successful collaborations. The conception of Stephen Sondheim, Arthur Laurents and Jerome Robbins for the work presented an unrivalled opportunity to depict the reality of late 1950s New York in a way that the escapist fantasies of Lerner and Loewe and Rodgers and Hammerstein had never attempted.

Racial tensions and the possible clash of cultures form a recurring theme in musicals, from *Show Boat* to *West Side Story*.

Leonard Bernstein's success as a composer for the musical stage in *West Side Story* was never repeated. It was almost 20 years later, in 1976, that he produced his next – and final – musical, *1600 Pennsylvania Avenue*, a piece concerned with spreading racial tolerance. Bernstein worked with Alan Jay Lerner who wrote the book and the lyrics, but Lerner's former magic seemed to have deserted him and the book was roundly condemned as ponderous, although Bernstein's score was better received. The show ran for only seven performances but has since been recorded.

While Bernstein's output for Broadway was undeniably small, he brought to the musical a level of sophistication that went far beyond the musical contribution of any of his predecessors, and prepared the way for Stephen Sondheim's contribution in the final quarter of the century.

Extract 1: On the Town

On the Town brought together an effective team of collaborators although it was not the product of a musical partnership in the way that Rodgers and Hammerstein's hits had been. The team – all in their twenties – were united in the belief that the show should continue the trend in Broadway shows – established in *Oklahoma!* – that the plot, the music and the dances should be as integrated as possible. In particular, the power of the show was built on the energy that existed between the dance and the music. The result was an outstanding success that ran for 463 performances. You should notice, though, that despite Bernstein's understanding of

On the Town was written in 1944 (film version released in 1949). The origin of the work was the ballet *Fancy Free* (1944) on which Bernstein had worked with choreographer Jerome Robbins. Robbins had the idea for *On the Town* but the book and lyrics were by two friends of Bernstein, Betty Comden and Adolph Green, who went on to write the lyrics for *Wonderful Town*.

the possibilities of using the orchestra creatively, he was happy to allow five other people to work on the orchestrations – Hershy Kay, Don Walker, Elliott Jacoby, Bruce Coughlin and Ted Royal.

The plot of the show is very simple. It is set in New York where three sailors are on shore leave for 24 hours and have the time of their lives. They go on a breathtaking trip around the city, each with a different girl. The action of the musical takes place as the sailors pursue the girls and move around various parts of New York in search of fun and romance.

We have chosen to focus on Act 1, which contains many good examples of jaunty musical numbers aimed at moving the action along as the sailors move around New York. The opening follows the pattern introduced by *Oklahoma!* in that there is no big chorus number to open the show, although there is an orchestral overture that introduces the jazzy, urban rhythms of the music and dance. The use of the chorus in the opening number relies on the solo lines of the three workmen interspersed with the close harmony of the men's quartet, capturing the early morning feel of the opening. By contrast, the angular, jazzy rhythms of the show's most famous number 'New York, New York' (not to be confused with the song of the same name made popular by Frank Sinatra) establish the mood for most of the show. The show's other famous number occurs towards the end of Act 2 ('Some Other Time').

In 'New York, New York', the atmosphere of the city is captured through the strong bass lines, the sense of moving purposefully around the city and the syncopations of the melody. Songs such as this are almost more important than the plot in taking the action along, and Bernstein's music and Robbins' choreography partner each other perfectly. The end of Act 1 culminates in the Times Square Ballet, in which Robbins' choreography excels. The use of blue notes in the songs, the syncopated jazz rhythms and sharp orchestrations perfectly reflect the imaginative and lively dance sequences. The music embraces a huge range of styles – jitterbugs, rumbas, showtunes and ballads, all given a symphonic treatment. The show was also significant, not just for its artistic integration but also for its racially integrated cast.

Extract 2: Candide

Candide was produced in 1956, three years after *Wonderful Town* and the year before *West Side Story*, although there was some overlap in the composition of the two musicals. *Candide* is described as a 'comic operetta' in the score and the link with Europe is clear in the fact that the book by Lillian Hellman is based

> " Many thought that a Broadway show was an undignified sidetrack for Leonard Bernstein, pulling him away from serious music. But to Leonard all music was serious. His music for *On the Town* is unique in musical comedy history since it dramatises a mainly comedic, mid-20th century story in truly symphonic terms. "
>
> Adolph Green

Further study

On the Town was recorded in 1994 under the directorship of Michael Tilson Thomas. The CD number of the Deutsche Grammophon recording is 437 516-2 and the video is 440 072 297-3.

The extract for study is the whole of Act 2.

on the satirical short story of the same name, published in 1759 by the French writer Voltaire. While firmly within the conventions of American musical theatre, *Candide* was seen as being more akin to the spirit of opera and never quite captured the audience's imagination in the way that *On the Town* had done.

Lillian Hellman (1907–1984) was an American dramatist whose plays reflected her socialist and feminist concerns. As a traditional playwright, she struggled to translate her skills as a dramatist into writing comedy for the musical stage. Despite her achievements as a playwright, her book for *Candide* was widely viewed as a flop. As a result, the show ran for only three months on Broadway, although it was revived more successfully in 1974 with a new book by Hugh Wheeler.

In direct contrast to *On the Town*, there was hardly any dancing in *Candide* and this took away much of the element of spectacle associated with the musical as an art form. Moreover, there were relatively few memorable melodies and the potential for audiences to leave humming the tune of their favourite song was limited.

The plot centres on the young Candide, who is both immature and serious. She lives in a Duke's estate and is taught an optimistic philosophy by Doctor Pangloss that 'this is the best of all possible worlds' – this becomes the title of one of the songs in the show. That view is systematically undermined, and Candide comes to the realisation that there are flaws in such an outlook. Happiness has to be worked for and we should not just accept a type of fatalism whereby we think everything is happening for the best. The story is rich with action.

Act 2 is shorter than Act 1 and, having studied the opening of *On the Town*, note here how Bernstein moves the action along from the mid-point to the end of a show. The opening trio is in the style of a patter song – so beloved of Gilbert and Sullivan's operettas – with its witty rhymes although here the metre is expanded to take away the regularity of the lines.

> No doubt you'll think I'm giving in to petulance and malice
> But in candor I am forced to say
> That I'm sick of gracious living in this stuffy little palace
> And I wish that I could leave today
> I have suffered a lot and I'm certainly not
> Unaware that this life has its black side
> I have starved in a ditch,
> I've been burnt for a witch
> And I'm missing the half of my back side.

The act is punctuated by five instrumental numbers that function as entr'actes in the operatic sense, linking the style of the drama more with operetta than with musical. The constant changes of scene add to the light-hearted nature of the drama as the 'Schottische' is transformed into the 'Venetian Gambling Scene' with its single word lyric: 'money'. The final chorus – 'Make Our Garden Grow' – is truly operatic and uses a declamatory style of singing that moves through a number of different keys in proclaiming the final pragmatic message:

While *Candide* was not an initial success, it has been compared to the musicals of Stephen Sondheim as simply being ahead of its time and requiring public taste to catch up. Ironically, Sondheim was invited to work with Bernstein on the project but declined.

We're neither pure nor wise nor good
We'll do the best we know.
We'll build our house, and chop our wood,
And make our garden grow.

It is fitting that this message is delivered using a complex musical style since the whole dramatic journey of Candide during the piece is towards achieving the knowledge that we should not simply accept what happens.

Extract 3: West Side Story

West Side Story is not only the most well known of Leonard Bernstein's works but also one of the most famous Broadway musicals ever. It is one of the best examples of the integration of dance, drama and music, and represents the high point of the book musical. Bernstein's jazzy rhythms perfectly mirror Sondheim's lyrics and Robbins' dances. Because it is performed often, it is easy to lose sight of how distinctive a contribution it makes to the history of the American musical. The writing of *West Side Story* overlapped with that of *Candide*, and while the two works have relatively little in common, it is possible to trace the fingerprints of Bernstein's musical style in both. In contrast to the operetta-style of *Candide*, *West Side Story* is a musical play.

The plot derives from Shakespeare's warring Montagues and Capulets in *Romeo and Juliet*, transplanted into New York's West Side. Here the racial tensions between the whites and the Puerto Ricans are played out in the tragedy of the two lovers Tony and Maria. The tension of the rival gangs – the Sharks and the Jets – leads ultimately to the death of Tony as he tries to make peace between the groups.

The extract we have chosen is from the opening of Act 1, as far as the end of the song 'America'. The end of Act 1 has two dead bodies on stage and a further death at the end of Act 2, yet Bernstein's music lifts the sordid into the symphonic and elevates our fears into a spectacle of the highest order.

The instrumental prologue is quite different from any of the chorus numbers in previous musicals. The regular, almost menacing clicking and the syncopated chords lead into a jazz-inspired spectacular as the rival gangs prepare for war. This gives way to the Jet song which uses a waltz-type melody accompanied by more syncopated chords. The sense of uneasiness is captured perfectly by the music. Additionally, there is a significant amount of confrontational dialogue between the two groups spoken over the orchestral accompaniment. The mood is continued throughout 'Something's Coming' and this helps move the action ahead as it prepares us for the rumble. In this song, the regular rhythm of the melody in the previous number is shifted into the bass line while Tony's unsettlement is reflected in his tense, nervy rhythms. The dance at the gym and the mambo continue the dance-inspired action of the piece and there is no let-up from the quick tempi and complex rhythms. This gives way into a cha cha.

It is not until the meeting between Tony and Maria that the music calms down and the show's first big romantic number takes place.

First performed in 1957, the music is by Leonard Bernstein and the lyrics by Stephen Sondheim. As we have already noted, Bernstein's enduring collaboration was with the choreographer Jerome Robbins rather than with any of his lyricists. It was his work on *West Side Story* that did most to launch Sondheim's career in musical theatre.

Further study

There are a good many amateur productions of *West Side Story* put on by local societies each year. You could probably find one in your area but if not, the film of the Hollywood musical was made in 1961 and is largely faithful to the content and style of the stage musical. Remember that this show is extremely challenging and amateur productions seldom produce the technical accomplishment of the original intention.

Throughout *West Side Story*, the energy of each art form always moves the other art forms along. Each song is carefully constructed to be a piece of drama in its own right, although interestingly each song also works in its own right outside of the show.

This is a showstopper of the finest quality, but in this context, Bernstein is able to handle the elements of performance to ensure that such a broadly drawn number can still move the show along rather than stop it. It is in the song 'America' that the whole message of the musical is brought to life – they are all Americans yet the musical focuses on the reconciliation of warring factions. The music reflects this perfectly. Bernstein brings together the time signatures of $\frac{3}{4}$ and $\frac{6}{8}$ to ensure that the instability of these opposing Americans is captured in the constantly changing rhythmic patterns.

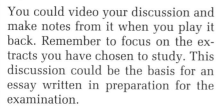

This song leads into another lively dance number and the ending of this is assumed in the score to be an audience-rouser in the marking 'applause segue' (go straight on during the applause).

And finally...

Once you have studied the three extracts from each of the three practitioners, you need to consider the similarities and differences between them.

Have open discussions in class about your experiences of the extracts and your reactions to them. Read reviews of the different works from which they have been taken. This is probably the most exciting part of this unit. Carry out your own research and converse with others in your class as well as the teacher. There are no right and definitive answers.

Think about the following elements:

➤ Development of the book musical as a coherent art form in which dance, drama and music all serve to move the action forward

➤ Antecedent of the form – knowledge of what came before and what influences can be seen in later works

➤ Relationship between the 'American dream' and the subject matter of the musical

➤ Cultural dimensions in the genre.

You should always have the nine extracts and your class notes to hand otherwise you will not be able to cite references – this is very important in the written examination.

Preparing for the examination

Preparing for examinations can be a frightening business. There are so many different sorts of fears that might crowd your mind, and it's easy to get muddled about what you should be doing. The purpose of this section is to help you improve your examination technique. No matter how much you know about the topic you've

> **Tip**
>
> You could video your discussion and make notes from it when you play it back. Remember to focus on the extracts you have chosen to study. This discussion could be the basis for an essay written in preparation for the examination.

studied, you can always get better at using the information to its best effect.

We're going to look later at a specimen answer, but first let's spend some time working through the principles of what you will be trying to do in this exam. This might seem rather unexciting but please bear with us and read this carefully. It would be a real shame if you were to spend a long time learning the factual content of this chapter but ended up not using what you know in the manner most effective for the examination.

The examination paper

What is likely to be different here from any other examinations you have taken is that you **answer only one question**. In Contextual Studies 1, you had to answer two questions so there probably seemed to be more choice. It also meant that you only spent a maximum of one hour on each question. The test here is about whether you can sustain your answer on a single question for two hours. In this sense, the paper is more like a timed essay than a traditional written examination.

Choosing a question

You have to prepare yourself for the fact that there is not going to be very much choice about which question you answer. You'll have studied only one topic, and within this topic there will be a choice of two questions. You need to pick one of these. This could be difficult, as both questions will be fairly broad and they may both seem to cover similar ground at first sight.

You need to spend five to ten minutes considering carefully which question to answer. The more you look at them, the more you will see the differences between them. You need to choose the one that best suits the study you have done.

The questions will not be trying to catch you out. The examiners have written them in a broad manner to ensure that everyone will be able to answer about something they know. However, the amount of detailed discussion will be up to you.

Writing for two hours

Let's face it, writing constantly for two hours is likely to be hard work. In fact, it's probably getting harder because most of us are getting more used to typing on a computer keyboard than holding a pen. You may find the act of writing for an extended period is itself challenging. If so, best to get some practice in at writing timed essays. No matter how fast you are on the computer, that won't help you in a written examination. You need to develop a strategy for writing effectively and easily.

You've probably been in an examination where someone has put their hand up to ask for more paper while you've still got five sheets of your answer book left. Don't worry – this has happened to most of us. You will be given an eight-side answer book and this is based on the amount that an average person can write in two hours. Average writing fits about nine words to a line, and there are about 25 lines to each side of the answer book. In total, therefore, you can

Tip

When you see the questions, spend some time going through the extracts you have studied and decide which of the two questions your extracts fit better. You will get more credit for answering the question with relevant examples rather than trying to make them fit a question for which they are less suited.

How much should I write?

Tip

Be concise – you need to make a point only once before moving on. Adapt your style to the number of words available.

probably get between 200 and 225 words per side. If you were to fill all eight pages of the answer book, the total number of words you would write is between 1,600 and 1,800. Compare this to the written commentary for the Community Performance Project, where you wrote 3,000 words – almost twice as much.

Types of questions

As we have already said, the questions will be general and will not assume that you have studied any particular works. Here are some specimen questions, some of them taken from the OCR website, some of them invented specially for this book. In the actual examination, you would only choose **one** of these questions to answer.

Postmodern approaches to the performing arts since 1960

1.   What contrasting uses of form and structure emerge within dance, drama and music since 1960?

   or

2.   'The art forms of yesterday no longer have any context. They simply exist to be used to speak to our society.' Is this view of postmodernism sustainable?

Politics and Performance since 1914

3.   'Performing arts practitioners have used everything from subversion to comedy to challenge socially-accepted norms.' Is there any common thread to creating political performance among practitioners across the art forms?

   or

4.   Discuss the view that during the 20th century, wars both great and small have been the greatest influence on political performance.

The 20th-century American musical

5.   'Drama with incidental music and stylised dance.' Discuss the extent to which individual songs and dance routines play a genuine part in moving forward the action of the musical.

   or

6.   Burlesque, operetta and variety show were all important influences on the development of the American musical, but what elements of each could be said to be discernable as the century progressed?

Planning an answer

Let's take a question from the specimen list above and plan out an answer. Planning is an important aspect of success and there is time in this examination to plan. You should allow around ten minutes to think through the question and plan out what to say.

 Discuss the view that during the 20th century, wars both great and small have been the greatest influence on political performance.

Consider the following points:

➢ How do we define war? It would be easy to think of the First and Second World Wars, but there have been many wars around the

Tip

The style of answer needs to be similar for all of these questions although obviously the content will be quite different.

Tip

The question is making an assertion that the most important influence on 20th-century political performance has been war. This is contentious and you are being asked to discuss the view. The answer that is mapped out here asks the question: What sort of war are we talking about?

world during the 20th century, and each of these could be said to have had some influence on practitioners. Some of the conflict situations never made it as far as war but nevertheless inspired works of art. If you think of the Bob Dylan songs inspired by the Cuban missile crisis, you'll see that there was no war as such but the fear of war (and rejection of it as a method of solving conflict) inspired Dylan to write the songs.

See pages 90–95 for more on Dylan.

> War does not have to be national. There are many other types of war: class war, gender-based conflict; the struggle for human rights; wars against terrorism and so on. Try to think broadly around the question. If you have studied Caryl Churchill, you may be very aware of how gender conflict inspires her work but less clear how other forms of war have done so. You could produce some quite impressive points about different types of war and the effects they have had. The little wars that everyone fights in terms of personal relationships would be helpful to think about. If you have studied Dario Fo, you'll know that the way in which he uses humour to satirise class war is based on styles that date back to Commedia dell' Arte.

See pages 67–72 for more on Churchill and 85–90 for more on Fo. Notice that here Churchill is used as an example of political performance, although earlier we used her as an example of postmodern practitioner.

> Are there other factors that could be said to be equally important or more important than war in influencing political performance? Your answer to this may depend on which practitioners you have studied, as there are various factors that could be said to inspire political writing.

> There could be a good argument that economic factors have been equally important. At a domestic level, the struggles endured by families and local communities are often engendered by economic need and the wish of each to survive at the expense of the other. Alternatively, you could take a view that the corruption of power is perhaps the most important factor in motivating practitioners to produce works that seek to change the minds and actions of their audiences.

Having considered all of these points, you need to make a plan for the answer. This could take the following format:

> Introduction – consideration of what is meant by war and the nature of war in the 20th century.

> The influence of national and international wars – examples of extracts that can be said to have been the result of wars organised by nations and races.

> The influence of the fear of war – pieces that play on the worries and concerns of an audience and that seek to persuade them of a particular course of action.

> The influence of conflict that does not lead to recognisable war – such as class, gender or race. Examples of practitioners or extracts that demonstrate this.

> Examples of practitioners or extracts that seem to indicate that other factors are more important than war in motivating their creators to produce the works they did.

> Conclusion – this is very important, as you need to make a concluding statement about what you believe, in the light of the discussion you have set out, to be the case. Don't sit on the fence. This doesn't have to be a personal statement along the lines of 'I think that…'. It is much better to take a line something like: 'The evidence seems to indicate that …'.

Covering the topic

Tip

Once you've made your plan, don't scribble it all out to make it illegible. It can be very helpful for the examiner to see what you had in mind as you were planning your work. It might even be that, if you ran out of time, you could still receive some credit if the examiner was able to see what you intended to do. If you put a neat line through it, the examiner will see that it's rough work, but will still be able to read it.

Using examples

> **Tip**
>
> Compare and contrast the examples. Simply talking about one after the other can be quite dull and is not likely to produce the highest marks. You may be familiar with more than nine extracts within the topic you have studied. You can mention as many relevant examples as you know – there may be extra credit for being able to show you have a very broad knowledge of the topic.

In the actual examination, you will have time to make a plan like the one above but you will also expect to fill it out with examples. You will have nine extracts with which you are very familiar. In most cases these extracts will be fairly long since together they are between four and six hours' worth of performance time. You could use these examples to prove a lot of different points and the test is whether you can organise your examples to argue for or against the question that has been set. As you work through the plan for the essay, try to group your examples under each point. You need to make sure that you use all nine examples if at all possible, but make sure that they are relevant to the point you're making – don't just throw an example in to make sure you've included it somewhere. You have to be discerning in the way you use the examples. Remember that they are meant to **exemplify** what is going on in the topic, and that the topic is bigger than the examples.

Sample essay

The following essay is a sample answer to question 5 from the specimen questions above. We have included some comments to give you an indication of the point of each section.

'Drama with incidental music and stylised dance.' Discuss the extent to which individual songs and dance routines play a genuine part in moving forward the action of the musical.

This is a helpful start. The candidate begins by taking a stand on the question which then sets the tone for their answer.

> The twentieth-century American musical has been seen by many as the only art form that really brings together the three arts of dance, drama and music. There is, however, a difference between bringing the art forms together in the same piece and actually making them work together so that the piece is stronger as a result. The quotation above suggests that the American musical is basically about drama and that dance and music are only present in a supporting role. This view is not supported by the history of the American musical in the twentieth century and I will be referring to examples from a range of musicals to show that the evidence does not prove that drama is the most important aspect of the musical. The book musical was an attempt to balance the art forms equally.

Very useful context that shows the historical basis for the candidate's points.

> At the beginning of the twentieth century, the most important aspect of the art form as it began to develop was spectacle. There are many types of performance that, it is suggested, preceded the musical as an art form. These include revues, variety shows, burlesque, minstrel shows and operetta. All of them were intended to provide their audiences with a spectacle which would take them into a fantasy world.

> Drama was by no means the most important art form in any of these styles. It would be more accurate to say that song and dance were the predominant features of all of them. The exception to this would be operetta where the plot and the content were as important as the singing, and dance was less important. In the other styles I have mentioned drama was not the most important aspect. One of the features of the variety shows was that there was little to hold the numbers together. Such spectacular shows as the Ziegfeld Follies depended on the sheer number of scantily-clad

troupes of dancing girls rather than any dramatic aspects. Although the bringing together of drama and music had appeared to some extent in Franz Lehár's 'The Merry Widow' of 1905, the biggest step forward was in 1927 with the composition of 'Show Boat' by Hammerstein and Kern. For the first time, the drama in the show was reflected in the way the music (in particular) developed. The musicals of the first part of the century had almost no interest in social realism. In fact, their relationship with the minstrel shows of the late eighteenth century would make them seem racist from our point in history. 'Show Boat' had a racially mixed cast and dealt with some major issues. The songs are used to move the plot along and the style of the singing perfectly captures the mood of the drama. For example in the song 'Ol' Man River', the sleepy river and the weary burden of the African Americans is captured perfectly in the style of the vocal melody.

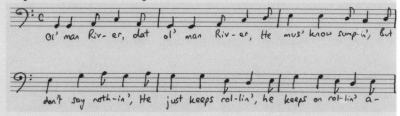

This link between drama and music was reinforced in Rodgers and Hammerstein's 'Oklahoma!' in 1943. Here the element of spectacle had given way to the sense of integration as the art forms were brought together. It may have seemed to the first audience that dance had been marginalised since the big opening chorus seemed

to have vanished in favour of a solo singer. Curly's song at the opening of the show is similar in purpose to 'Ol' Man River' from 'Show Boat'. The song has a memorable melody that matches the words and also takes the drama forward.

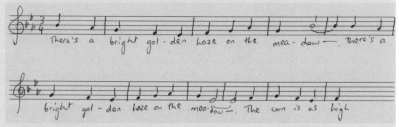

These two shows saw a re-balancing of the art forms and, significantly for the question asked here, an increase in the importance of drama within the art form.

Excellent bringing together of examples to make the point about the emergence of drama.

The role of dance in these musicals did, however, have some stylised aspects to it. The dream ballet in 'Carousel' and the ballet based on 'Uncle Tom's Cabin' in 'The King and I' are good examples of this. Yet they are based on set forms and are related to the action of the plot in a way that the dance routines of the early 1920s were not. George White's 'Scandals' for which George Gershwin had produced some music, had followed the model of the Ziegfeld Follies where dance routines were associated only with glamour and spectacle rather than artistic meaning.

In the musicals of the middle part of the twentieth century, the subject matter itself was derived from dance. For example, in Cy Coleman's 'Sweet Charity' of 1966, the show draws its life from a

This shows a good awareness of the styles of dance used. It would have been useful to have more specific discussion of style in the Rodgers and Hammerstein works but the answer makes the point fairly well.

This makes some good points about the relationships with earlier plays. It would have been helpful here to have had more detail on the song 'I could have danced all night'.

story of a dance hall hostess who wants a better life, and Bob Fosse's choreography reflects the rhythms of the various songs in the show. The explicit lyrics and gestures of 'Big Spender', for example, complement each other very well. The military strut that accompanies 'I'm a brass band' is also evidence that, while he was capable of producing stylised dance, Fosse was not limited by the style of any one dance. Fosse was able to develop his breadth of dance style in Kander and Ebb's 1975 show 'Chicago' where he is able to integrate the vaudeville double act that occurs within the story line.

In a number of musicals written in the 1950s there was a strong relationship between the three art forms as by this time the drama of the shows had become established and was well advanced from the flimsy plots and one-dimensional characters of the early part of the century. This was due to some extent to the way in which a number of the most important musicals of that decade were based on existing books or plays. In Lerner and Loewe's 'My Fair Lady', for example, the use of George Bernard Shaw's play 'Pygmalion' provides a strong dramatic structure on which the collaborators based their work. Yet the skill of the team is seen in the way that the songs help to move the action along. Songs such as 'All I want is a room somewhere' and 'I could have danced all night' form an integral commentary on the story of Eliza Doolittle's transformation from flower girl to society madam. In the same way, the dance work (such as in 'I could have danced all night') ensures that the drama is interpreted and broadened by rather than simply interspersed with songs and dances.

This is seen at its best in the work of Bernstein and Sondheim in 'West Side Story'. This is based on Shakespeare's 'Romeo and Juliet' although, unlike 'My Fair Lady', the book does not rely on the dialogue of the original work. Arthur Laurents' book takes the drama into a new context and transposes Shakespeare's Italian story of the warring Montagues and Capulets into New York's West Side in the 1950s. Yet the drama is almost incidental to Bernstein and Sondheim's music and lyrics. For example, the extended opening scene of the musical uses a complex range of jazz dances choreographed by Jerome Robbins to establish the story through dance. The jerky, angular rhythms of these dances are perfectly related to the music of these dances. In fact, unlike other partnerships of the previous part of the century, Bernstein's most frequent collaborator was not a lyricist or writer of the book but the choreographer Jerome Robbins.

This meant that Bernstein's musicals tend to approach the style through music and dance and they are the best example of why the quotation in the question of this essay is wrong. In fully integrated musicals such as 'West Side Story', the drama is simply one component of the whole thing. For example, the song 'America' is a central number in the show which deals with the question of what it means to be an American. It focuses, sometimes comically, on differences between native-born Americans and Puerto-Ricans. The song makes extensive use of constantly changing rhythms and moves between $\frac{3}{4}$ and $\frac{6}{8}$ time. This makes the music spiky and energetic and the dance number accompanying this reflects this perfectly. The setting is urban and littered with signs of deprivation and the use of space and levels within Robbins' extended dance sequences interprets this very well. The conflict between the two rival gangs, the Jets and the Sharks, is a major factor in many of the numbers in the show and the drama is created through the music and the dance rather than being added to it afterwards. In the Jet song at the start of the show the syncopated rhythms and the finger clicking create a mood in which the highly organised jazz dance movements move the action of the show forward. Throughout the show, Stephen Sondheim's lyrics create rhythms that also ◄—— enable Bernstein to produce interesting and complex melodic lines. These are the basis for Sondheim's own musicals in the last quarter of the twentieth century.

> Very useful pointer to Sondheim's musicals even though the candidate has not studied these specifically.

These examples all disprove the view taken in the question that the heart of the American musical is drama and that incidental music and stylised dance were additions to create a better sense of entertainment. While it is possible in the early part of the century to find examples of musicals where songs and dance routines are the dominant feature of the show, it is difficult to find many examples of musical plays where the drama dominates the other art forms. In fact, in the range of examples I have used in this essay, the opposite seems to be true. The history of the musical in the twentieth century is one in which drama has sought to emerge in an art form that is more associated with music and dance.

Comments

This is a strong piece of work that could be written in the space of two hours. It has both strengths and weaknesses:

Strengths

➢ The answer is well-related to the question and keeps coming back to why the candidate disagrees with the statement in the opening. This is based on a good range of evidence and the candidate has clearly studied enough extracts to be able to give good coverage of the topic.

➢ The answer covers the scope of the whole period and uses appropriate examples.

➢ The answer has a good theme running through it and the points between paragraphs are well related.

➢ The musical quotations help to enhance the answer.

Weaknesses

➢ There could be more sustained reference to the book musical.

➢ The examples themselves are not always discussed in the same depth; the dance examples from Bob Fosse could have benefited from being discussed in the same level of detail as the song 'America'. However, there are plenty of references to dance and all three art forms are covered.

➢ The examples need to be as specific as possible; some are very good, but others are not so specific.

Student Devised Performance

What do I have to do?

This unit is about devising a piece in response to a commission, and performing it to a visiting examiner and an invited audience. You'll be assessed on your ability to work to the commission, your ability to devise a role for yourself and the level of your performance skills.

You've been doing a great deal of performance work during the course so far. Quite a lot of it has been about acquiring skills and being assessed on your understanding rather than on the performance itself. This unit is where all that changes.

By now, your performance skills should be at their most developed. In the previous units, you'll have learned how to devise your own material, how to develop your performance skills in the three art forms, and how to imitate the style of practitioners in your own work. The Student Devised Performance unit is **synoptic**, which means that it sums up everything you have learned during the course and helps you to bring together the whole experience in one performance. That's a tall order, but in practice it means demonstrating to the examiner who comes to watch your performance what you have learned during the whole A-level course: skills, approaches, theory, practitioners. You'll need to show that you have mastered all the skills you have learned, and that you're able to talk about how your previous experience has helped you create this new piece.

Over the following pages, we're going to have a brief look back through the whole A-level course. If you're going to show as much as possible of what you've learned, you need to reflect on what that learning consists of. You'll need to spend some time reflecting and revising, but first let's have a good look at what the examiners want you to produce at the end of the unit.

Getting organised

In January of your A2 year, your school or college will be sent a list of 20 commissions by the exam board. Your group needs to choose **one** commission from that list, and this will become the basis of the work you do for the unit. You'll therefore need to be sure you choose one that you all like, as you'll be spending several weeks working on it.

The assessment is based on group work, and you'll work in groups of between three and seven to devise an original piece based on the commission that your group chooses. Your piece will last between 15 and 30 minutes, depending on how many people are in the group.

> **Tip**
>
> Don't feel that you're starting from scratch. Before you start doing any work at all on this unit, you need to review which skills you've learned during the course (see pages 123–137). The visiting examiner may ask about your previous work in the discussion before the performance.

> **Tip**
>
> Remember what we said for earlier units – that it takes about one hour to produce one minute of performance material. Expect it to take up to 30 hours to devise, rehearse and perform your piece for this unit.

You're probably wondering what the commissions look like. We'll give some examples later on, but they are all very simple and allow plenty of scope for you to devise a performance. There are **five categories** of commission that will be set on the list, and there are **four choices** in each one – and you only have to find one, which means that there's quite a good chance of finding one your group likes the look of.

The categories of the commissions are:

Categories of commission

➢ **Pictures**: you'll be given the titles and you'll have to look them up in named books.

➢ **Historical events**: you'll be given the name of a historical event.

➢ **Poems**: you'll be given the titles of poems to look up in named books.

➢ **Stories**: these will be titles only and you'll have to find them.

➢ **People**: you'll be given names only and you'll have to look up who they are.

All of these are very broad and will require you to do a lot of research to make sure you know about the one you choose in great depth. We'll say a lot more below about the sort of research you need to do. It isn't just knowing about the commission that's important: it's knowing what performance potential the commission has.

Revising your skills

Before you spend any more time looking at how to work with the commission, you need to make some plans as to how you will revise what you've done so far in the course. It's crucial at this stage to take a thorough look back at what you've already achieved in order to ensure that this piece really is of the highest standard possible.

This recap of what you've learned so far is not just about practical skills. We'll be thinking about those as well, but first let's have a look at what the exam board says about subject content to remind you what you've been learning during the course. That way, you can be sure that your piece will be truly synoptic as you go through a checklist of what you have covered.

 The exam board states that the course covers four areas:

➢ Performance repertoire

➢ Performance styles and genres

➢ Performance skills

➢ Performance processes.

Let's look through each of these areas, with questions for you to consider as you review your work.

Performance repertoire

Studying performance repertoire is important because it helps you to engage with techniques for devising performance material. It's common to struggle when you come to devising your own material – perhaps because you can't decide what your piece is going to be about, or because you have plenty of ideas but you don't know how to structure them. You'll find that these two issues – **content and form** – are essential to what you're trying to do in your devised performance. How do the practitioners you've studied deal with them? Think back to the pieces that you've studied during the course. What were they about? Powerful pieces of drama are often about fairly commonplace themes: it's how the playwright deals with them that makes a play original. Songs are often about fairly predictable themes: the originality usually lies in the way that the songwriter organises their material. Dance pieces may have a storyline, but are sometimes simply about the organisation of movement to create interesting patterns and use of space.

By studying repertoire, you'll have learned about structure. You will almost certainly have looked at the form of a dance, a song or a play. Think back to techniques you have come across that would help you to structure your own piece. During the course, you've been studying:

➢ The work of significant choreographers, composers and playwrights, and a range of performance repertoire

➢ The definitions, uses and characteristics of different styles and genres.

 Think about...

☑ You will have studied a number of pieces during the course. List them, and make **short** notes about what you think could be useful from them when working on this new piece.

☑ Do the pieces that you have studied have anything in common or do they all represent completely different approaches?

Performance styles and genres

As well as specific pieces of repertoire, you'll now be familiar with the bigger picture – the styles within which practitioners were working. Think back to the conventions of different styles. Perhaps you looked at epic theatre in your study of Brecht, or physical theatre, or Tin Pan Alley songs. Think about how practitioners work within a style. Quite possibly the styles that you've studied are very different from one another, and the challenge for you is to make sure that you don't rely on approaches that will clash. For example, it's probably best to avoid having a section of your piece in the style of physical theatre only to follow it with a 1930s American-style song. Although you will be familiar with a range of styles, you don't have to use them all: select what works best. You've been studying:

➢ Theoretical and practical issues in performance styles

➢ Ways in which intentions are realised in performance work

➤ Methods of creating performance work in a given style or genre

➤ Use of conventions and methods of creating performance work for a variety of situations, contexts and audiences

➤ Relationships between the three art forms of dance, drama and music.

 Think about...

☑ Which styles and genres have you studied?

☑ Which of these would you feel comfortable using?

☑ How successful has your practical work been in these various styles? List what went well and what could be improved for each one.

☑ What strengths and weaknesses are there in the relationship between performer and audience in the pieces you have produced so far?

☑ What relationship is there between the art forms in the styles you have studied? Can you identify this easily or has it always been a bit of a struggle to see much in common between them?

Performance skills

In some ways, this is the aspect of the course about which you will be most concerned. You need to ask yourself how good your performance skills are. We're going to devote a whole section to this later on in the chapter, but at this stage, find any videos of the practical work you've done on the course. This can be quite a sobering experience, but do watch everything you have, in the order in which you did it. Try to see whether there are any generic elements that either work really well or hinder an effective performance. You've been studying:

➤ Performance skills in dance, drama and music

➤ Performance techniques and the appropriate technical vocabulary to discuss them in each of the art forms.

 Think about...

☑ Make a list of your strongest skills in each of the three art forms. Have you worked across all art forms or are you trying to avoid performing in one of them?

☑ Which skills have you worked on that still need further development?

☑ How confident are you in using technical vocabulary when you discuss your practical work?

Performance processes

Think back to the very first unit in the course, the Language of Performing Arts. There, you learned about the performance process of improvising–rehearsing–performing. Although this process is not mentioned much in the other units, it is the foundation for working effectively to create pieces of original work. Think about how effective this process has been for you. Do you know how much time to devote to each phase or do you always

Tip

While it is not a requirement for this synoptic performance that you work in all three art forms, doing so would be an ideal approach.

Go back to the list of words in the Language of Performing Arts unit. Are you now completely at ease with them or are there some that you would never use because you're not confident what they refer to? See pages 12–39 of the *OCR AS Guide* for a detailed exploration of these terms.

find (for example) that there is never enough time for rehearsal? Think back to the six pieces that you've devised so far: four short pieces in the Language of Performing Arts unit, one devised piece in Performance Realisation and an extended group piece in the Community Performance Project. How effective was the process in those pieces? What can you learn from your achievements and mistakes?

You have been studying various approaches to devising a performance. This should include understanding of:

➢ The development of performance ideas

➢ Stages in the devising of performance work

➢ Methods of refining work into a coherent structure

➢ Interaction of the art forms of dance, drama and music

➢ Rehearsal methods and discipline

➢ Working to performance deadlines.

 Think about...

☑ How well have you grasped the performance process of improvising–rehearsing–performance?

☑ How good are you at developing ideas rather than just going with the first thing you thought of?

☑ How much refinement and rehearsal do you usually put into your pieces? Do you spend huge amounts of time devising them and leave no time for rehearsal?

☑ Do you always start your work with the same art form and then try to slot the other two in?

☑ How well do the art forms fit together in the pieces you have devised so far?

☑ How disciplined would you say your rehearsal process has been for the pieces you have devised so far?

Performance studies contains a strong element of evaluation, and you need to be able to answer these questions honestly if you are going to be successful in the piece you are about to devise.

Reviewing and developing performance skills: dance

By this stage in the course, you have probably choreographed several short pieces of dance, either in a group or on your own. Look at this work on video and discuss what skills are needed for each performance. The following points could form a basis for your discussion.

Describe the opening

Does your piece begin in darkness or light? Are the dancers already positioned on stage or do they enter while the lights come up? Does one dancer follow another? Does the entire ensemble appear in the opening section? How do the dancers take up their initial positions? How do they hold themselves? Where is their eye focus? How do they connect with the audience, if at all? Do the dancers enter the stage one by one or in pairs?

The opening to any piece is extremely important. It goes without saying that this is where the performers create their first impression on the audience. Each performer must be completely ready for the first moments of the piece. They must know exactly where they are to be on the stage, how to get there and how to hold that all-important opening pose. It may be that each dancer is moving right from the start. Each dancer should communicate a sense of purpose in those opening moments and be able to create an atmosphere on the stage.

Perhaps you are using silence to create tension when the dance piece begins. The dancer must be able to use a pulse or counts in order to perform the required movements at the correct time. How have you achieved this in the past? Did you use a metronome or simply have someone counting aloud? Once the opening had been choreographed, how did you rehearse in order to polish the performance?

Energy

Are energy levels sustained throughout the piece? Sometimes a piece is dynamic in the first few minutes with lots of action to attract the audience's attention, but this level of intensity then diminishes and the audience loses interest. How do you build up to a climax in the piece? Do you introduce a motif in section one and then build on this throughout the other sections? Perhaps one dancer performs the motif in section one and then two dancers pick it up in section two and so on until the finale, where all the dancers are performing the motif in unison and then canon. Look back over **compositional devices** that you may have used in past pieces in order to structure the work and keep the audience curious as to what is going to happen next.

Stamina, strength and flexibility

In order to have sufficient stamina to perform a piece, you need to rehearse the entire piece on a regular basis leading up to the practical exam. You should also carry out extended warm-ups and attend extra classes if possible in order to develop the necessary strength and flexibility for the dance styles in your piece. You may well have had a period of revision for exams in January when you were not taking part in practical sessions at school/college. You will need to start each lesson with a warm-up to get your self back into shape. This should be followed by improvisation in order to bond with other members of the group and get your imagination working.

> **Tip**
> There is a risk that you will sit around and discuss ideas for the commission for too long. Once you've chosen a commission, move the chairs and tables to the side of the room. Come to class dressed for practical work and use your time in lessons to devise from the commission.

Remind yourself of the five elements of dance:

➤ Motif

➤ Action

➤ Dynamic

➤ Relationships

➤ Space.

The language of dance

How did you apply each of these when creating your first dance piece in the Language of Performing Arts unit? How might you apply them to an aspect of your commission?

Imagining that your commission topic was the nuclear explosion at Chernobyl, work through the following exercises.

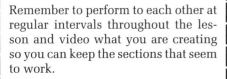 Experiment with creating the idea of an explosion by using different levels and showing the shapes of a nuclear cloud. Using some of your research, such as photographs, devise five appropriate **motifs** from which to work.

Experiment with using different **relationships** of dancers. For example, as an ensemble form a still tableau to represent the explosion then allow the tableau to move to mirror the formation of the cloud.

Break the group into smaller units, and work in pairs and trios to show the workers' reactions to the first signs of the explosion. Give each pair or trio 32 counts for their devised section.

In order to work on **actions**, you will need to revise the basic actions that you learned in unit one:

> Stasis (stillness)
> Travelling
> Turning
> Falling
> Jumping
> Gesture.

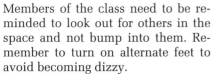 You could use the warm-up session at the beginning of the class to develop **travelling** ideas. Begin by walking briskly around the space with your teacher issuing instructions on when to change direction. Then use a figure of eight. Try a serpentine pathway. Let one member of the class lead and keep finding new pathways. Then let other members of the class take the lead. Go through a range of travelling steps – hopping, skipping, jogging, running, dodging, walking backwards, rolling across the floor, gliding, galloping. Ask members of the class to come up with their own ideas.

Move on to **turning**. Try half turns and then full turns. Try to turn on one foot then two. Sit on the floor and spin on your bottom. See how many spins you can do and experiment with different ways of coming out of the spin.

Break dancers will be able to spin on their backs. Try standing up and turning while holding a partner.

Before experimenting with **jumping**, you must warm up your feet and knees as well as your muscles in order to avoid injury. Carry out pliés in second position and then lift one foot off the ground while paying very careful attention to the way the foot is lifted, by bending the knee and lifting the heel then the toe. When replacing the foot, the reverse action must be carried out, placing the toe then the heel, and the knee must be bent. Practise this several times on each foot until correct.

Tip

Remember to perform to each other at regular intervals throughout the lesson and video what you are creating so you can keep the sections that seem to work.

Tip

Members of the class need to be reminded to look out for others in the space and not bump into them. Remember to turn on alternate feet to avoid becoming dizzy.

Tip

Ballroom dancers will be able to offer ideas on turning. You could also watch a video of *Strictly Ballroom* by Baz Luhrmann (1992). If you can get hold of Fred Astaire and Ginger Rogers films, these might be useful for demonstrating turning as a couple. Ballet dancers could demonstrate pas de deux, or again you could watch examples on video. Look at traditional ballets as well as considering perhaps the male duet in Bourne's *Swan Lake*.

Once you have warmed up, try some simple jumps with feet in first position and then second. Alternate first and second, and do eight jumps in each position, then four, then two, and finish with singles.

You can now try bigger jumps. Perform these at your own pace and use a deeper knee bend. Try to perform jumps that you have learned throughout the course. Those with ballet training can perform jumps that turn in the air. If you are unused to these, then practise by jumping from two feet to two feet, simply up and down, remembering to land with knees bent. Then progress to jumping up and turning 45 degrees in the air. If you feel confident, try 90 degrees, then 180 degrees, then 360 degrees so that you can now jump and turn a complete circle in the air, landing back where you started.

Further study

Look back at some of the videos of dance companies you have watched. For example, watch both the traditional version and Matthew Bourne's version of *Swan Lake*. Also watch Bourne's *The Car Man* and *Nutcracker*. Consider how jumps and turns are used in these pieces, and experiment with some of them (although always experiment under the supervision of your teacher). Look at what you studied for Contextual Studies for some more ideas. Discuss all the performances you have seen and the different styles of dance. Consider how different companies such as Stomp and Tap Dogs compare to a traditional ballet company.

 Try some **lifts**. Remember that men can lift men and women can lift women. Look at American musicals and ballets for ideas. *Seven Brides for Seven Brothers* has some high energy numbers involving acrobatic movement as does *Singin' in the Rain*.

In order to practise falling, you should put mats on the floor and carry out a few trust exercises in pairs, with a third dancer standing by to assist.

Practise **falling** backwards into another dancer's arms. This can be executed with the faller going straight back and being brought gently to the ground or with the faller being turned after being caught and then being placed on the ground. Three or four people can stand in a line and catch one person falling into their arms.

Gesture can be worked on when considering character. A low status person might bow low to a high status character who only nods their head. Consider daily routines such as washing, brushing teeth, making meals, or waiting for a train or bus in order to create gestures that your character might perform.

Further study

Lea Anderson and Matthew Bourne both use gesture very effectively in their work. Look at *Flesh and Blood* and any of Bourne's pieces. Consider how Bourne uses the royal wave in *Swan Lake* to great effect.

Once you have revised and discussed past work and have started improvisation, you need to remember to focus on the commission during the devising stage. During rehearsal, keep the following points in mind for your performance work:

➢ Concentrate on transitions and make sure that they are quick, smooth and seamless.

➢ Make sure you show clear alignment of the body, strength and focus.

➢ Use appropriate eye focus and do not let the eyes wander. Decide where you are looking and why, and keep that intention. Facial expression can be blank if appropriate, but this must be discussed and decided on by the group.

➢ Use contrast to vary the dynamic and choose music very carefully. If the music is devised, then work closely with the musicians during the composing stage.

➢ Consider costume and make-up early on in the process. Try out costumes and make sure that you can move in them.

Tip

Remember to sit out and watch each other and use the video during rehearsal so that you can watch your performance and adapt facial expressions if necessary.

See page 11 of the *OCR AS Guide*.

> Use the performance space sensibly. Do not perform in only one area of the stage unless you have a specific reason for doing so that is related to the commission. Look again at the nine areas of the stage and see if you have used them effectively.

Reviewing and developing performance skills: drama

As with dance, it is worthwhile revising the elements of drama from the Language of Performing Arts unit:

> Characterisation

> Dialogue

> Physicality

> Proxemics

> Tension.

Look at videos of your past work in drama and consider the performances' weaknesses and strengths. You might look at the drama piece and the integrated piece from the Language of Performing Arts unit, and at the Community Performance Project, as well as any devised work from the Performance Realisation unit. You will need to discuss the styles you used and your intentions at the time. Consider now whether you achieved your intentions and how the drama performances could have been improved. You are now older, wiser and more confident. List the weaknesses of the earlier performances and offer suggestions for improvement, but always remember that this is constructive criticism aimed to help you avoid making some of the same mistakes again.

Once you have decided on your commission and have an idea of the characters you are going to include in your piece, you will need to start working on **characterisation**.

A character profile can cover the following and more: gender, age, name, address, type of residence, social status, marital status, family ties, educational background, religious beliefs, political persuasion, favourite food and drink, favourite clothes shops, hobbies, sports played or followed, music taste, and state of health.

You could start with **hot-seating** as you may have done in previous units in order to create a character, then try writing a **character profile**.

You could write this out in a list or you could **illustrate** the character and create a short **storyboard** to show a day in their life. However you approach the development of your character, try to consider and discuss as many angles as possible.

Tip

Remember to video all the improvisations so that you can watch them through and discuss what worked and what didn't.

Once each member of the group has established at least one character each, set up a **scenario** that is appropriate for your commission. Taking again the example of the Chernobyl nuclear explosion, imagine that these characters work in the nuclear plant, whether on the floor or in the offices. Improvise around the idea that one worker is suspicious that something in the plant is not working as it should. The scene could be set in the works canteen over lunch. You might have one character in a position of authority, who knows that something is indeed wrong but is not allowed to tell the workers. He could let the audience in on the secret through a soliloquy in which he worries about not being able to tell someone. This would create dramatic irony and tension. You could follow this improvisation with another set after the explosion at the hospital, where the families are waiting for news of their loved ones.

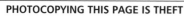

Consider the character's **physicality** at all times: the way they stand, sit and move. Each time you work through the improvisation, you need to stay in your character and talk and move as they would. This is where your character comes alive as a fully rounded person. For instance, in the canteen you must know what to order for lunch because you have thought about what your character eats and drinks in the hot-seating session. Experiment with how your character pulls the chair from under the table, how they sit and hold the knife and fork, and so on.

 Now try creating the comical character of a woman who is obsessed with wanting a flat stomach, and so is constantly holding it in, patting and stroking it, or pulling a jumper down over it. It might be a big, baggy jumper or a jumper that is too small and keeps riding up. The character is obsessed with diets but never loses any weight. She talks constantly about what she has or hasn't eaten, what she might eat later and how many calories it contains. She eats chocolate secretly, so the audience might catch her eating but the other characters on stage only have their suspicions. She switches from a reflective mood in which she is totally self-obsessed and shut off from life to being over-alert and fully attentive, much like a daydreaming schoolgirl.

> **Tip**
>
> It is sometimes easier to think of someone you have observed and mimic their behaviour if you cannot create the behaviour yourself. Remember that everyone has their funny little habits or idiosyncrasies. Watch the way people use their hands to gesticulate when talking. Observe how people play with their hair, their mobile phones or the handles on their bag. It is often the trivial aspects of a character that help make them real for an audience.

 Begin working on dialogue. Staying with this same character who lacks self-confidence and is forever trying to improve herself without success, consider how she might speak.

Look back at her character profile. Choose a topic for her to speak on for one minute, for example speed-dating or even diets. Put her with another character, perhaps someone who does not really like her, because they have known her for several years as a colleague and heard it all before. They could stand in a queue for morning coffee. Try this exercise with each character in the group and keep changing the roles.

> **Tip**
>
> Video the monologues so that you can use them later for scriptwriting.

 Set up a duologue around a machine that has broken down. One person is trying to fix it and the other is giving advice. The one trying to do the repair becomes more and more agitated by the constant flow of suggestions. See where the improvisation leads. Remember that shouting and screaming is never very interesting – there is nowhere to go after such an outburst. Keep the tension without the high-pitch argument that might ensue. Remember to keep in character – you personally might get very angry in such a situation and shout, but you must consider what your character would do and say. What vocabulary would they use? Would they be polite? How close would the characters be in physical terms and how might this use of **proxemics** betray the relationship between them?

Once you have created some dialogue, start working on **vocal delivery**. There are several aspects of vocal delivery to revise at this stage:

> ➤ **Volume**. This is dependent on your performance space, as some stages require more projection than others. You must also be careful about where you stand on a stage so that your voice doesn't get swallowed up by the ceiling.

> **Tip**
>
> You will need to practise in the space and let someone stand in different positions in the auditorium to see if you are loud enough.

> **Direction**. You should always know exactly who you are addressing when speaking, whether it is directly to the audience or another character, or an aside. Make sure that your direction is executed cleanly so that the audience are clear.

> **Clarity and diction**. The audience needs to understand what you are saying but think also about keeping true to whichever accent or dialect you have chosen to use.

> **Use of pitch**. Pitch is often indicative of emotion. In simple terms, an angry person's voice will be higher than when they are calm. A child's voice has a higher pitch than an adult's.

> **Intonation** refers to the way the voice goes up and down across a sentence and can be likened to a melody. Listen carefully to the way your friends' voices rise and fall across a sentence. How does this differ when they ask a question?

> **Pace**. When delivering a poem, you need to take into consideration the metre of the lines and any rhyme scheme as well as the content. You need to look at the punctuation marks and where you should take a breath. Which words should be emphasised? Where do the stresses appear on the words?

Look at a speech from Shakespeare and practise different speeds at which to deliver the lines. Where should you slow down or speed up and why? Are there any cases of enjambment, where one line spills over into the next and you are forced to take a breath later on?

Remember to integrate the drama with dance or music or both, and try to create a performance piece that does not have tokenistic drama. Choose your style carefully and list its stylistic features before starting to devise. Look back over the Contextual Studies units from AS and A2 as well as your Community Performance Project to revise what you learned about other practitioners and their styles. Consider performances that you have seen and look at the reviews you wrote or read to remind yourself of stylistic features and useful devices.

Tip

Music should not be an afterthought. Starting with music can be an excellent way of being creative and original in your work.

Reviewing and developing performance skills: music

It would be fair to say that a lot of students struggle with how to use music effectively in a combined arts piece. That said, it needn't be too difficult as long as you treat music as an important part of the piece rather than as something you try to add later on. So, let's look back at what you've learned so far and the ways in which you might be able to use your musical skills in your piece.

Let's start – as we have done with the other art forms – by thinking about the elements of music that you explored in the first unit, the Language of Performing Arts. Find the recordings of the music you produced in that unit and in other parts of the course, and look at how you used the elements of music in those pieces.

Rhythm The most important aspect of rhythm in a piece is to provide a backbone to what is going on and to keep the music moving. Rhythms might be regular, irregular or syncopated. You might choose very simple rhythms or very complex ones but normally it is important that there is some variation in the rhythm. You may have one rhythm that repeats – an ostinato – but to create maximum effect you should normally try to create contrast.

How could you use rhythmic work on its own in your piece?

> You could use strong rhythms to create a sense of ritual if that is appropriate to your piece. Drumming can be a very effective way of creating a climax or of introducing episodes in a piece.

➢ You could use interlocking rhythms as a way of building tension, or moving the action of a piece forward.

➢ You could use clapping rhythms as a powerful way of emphasising a moment in the piece – especially if the rhythms are clapped in unison.

 Devise a fast-moving 60-second piece that uses only hand claps. You should include syncopated rhythms and everyone should have a different rhythm. This will create polyrhythms, and could accompany some dance work.

Melody

A lot of people assume that music is just melody – they think that being able to hum the tune is all that matters. There is certainly a place for melody in devising your work but remember that this does not have to be restricted to singing. Think about the following ideas:

➢ A motif – a short snippet of melody – can be very helpful in building up a mood. For example, you could have the motif recorded to use as a backdrop to something else; you could also decide that when it is repeated it could be made longer, or quicker, or slower. A motif could be associated with a particular person or character – this is known as a leitmotif.

➢ A slow melody, unaccompanied, played on a violin or an oboe (perhaps pre-recorded on a tape or computer) can be an excellent way of creating a reflective mood. The melody could be used as a theme to bring this mood back later in the piece.

➢ You could have a melody in a song – but have a look at what we say about songs later on. They can play an important part in a devised piece but they can also wreck it – so be careful.

 Compose a simple, short melody that would create an atmosphere of fear or brooding, to use as a motif for a sinister character.

Harmony

Harmony can be associated with singing – hymns are often sung in four-part harmony, for example. Or it might be that your piece uses chords for a particular effect.

➢ You could use a short phrase in two-, three- or four-part harmony. This could be hummed or sung to a syllable such as 'do' or 'la'. You could create a particular mood by singing a line from a hymn in parts. Or you could select a line of text to sing in harmony – perhaps from a poem if that is what you have chosen for a commission.

➢ You could use a repeated chord sequence, perhaps to create a particular musical style such as 12-bar blues. This would have to be appropriate to the style and intention of the piece, though.

➢ You could use non-functional harmony. This means that you choose chords because of the particular 'colour' they have. They are not a chord progression, as they do not lead anywhere, but they help to create a particular mood. You could decide to use a string sound on the synthesiser or computer to add to the effect of these chords. You'll also need to think carefully about how quickly the chords move from one to another – this is known as the rate of harmonic change.

 Make up a chord sequence using between six and eight chords. These chords should be chosen for their 'colour' rather than as a progression. Try making them different lengths.

Timbre

You may be used to using live instruments in your work or you may have relied heavily on recordings. Both are equally valid but you need to think about the advantages and disadvantages of each. In both cases, you will be able to choose the particular sound that you want for your piece, but if you choose a live instrumental sound, you will obviously need to have someone in your group who is able to play that instrument. It does not matter, though, if you decide to use a sound from an electronic source. The important thing is that you make effective creative decisions about the various timbres that you wish to use.

Think about some of the following suggestions:

➢ Decide on the mood you want to create at any given point in your piece. An oboe sound can help to create a plaintive or reflective mood whereas a trumpet sound might be used to suggest a sense of pageantry, patriotism or ceremony.

➢ Think about how you want to combine timbres. The human ear quickly tires of hearing the same sound for an extended period of time (remember this when crafting the dialogue too) and you need to provide variety and contrast. Be careful about putting timbres together; you can easily end up drowning one of the timbres out completely if you mismatch them. A flute sound is likely to be swamped by an amplified electric guitar, and singing accompanied by a trumpet becomes indistinct.

Tip

Live music can be really effective but you need to consider how you use instruments in the piece. Suddenly grabbing a euphonium to play a few notes in the middle of a staged argument might look ridiculous. If you write the music, make sure that you identify it as an original composition to the examiner so that you receive the credit you deserve.

 Use an electronic keyboard to create four motifs that represent different characters. Use a different timbre for each one, for example oboe, trumpet, violin.

Texture

The texture of music is where you have the greatest potential to be creative. You can create contrast and interest simply by changing the texture of the music, by moving from one or two sounds to a large number, following a solo with a tutti passage. One of the greatest challenges in using music in an extended devised piece is having enough variety.

'Tutti' refers to the entrance of full orchestra in a piece, as distinct from a solo passage.

Think about the following and ask yourself how effective you have been so far in creating interesting musical textures:

➢ How much contrast is there in the pieces you have composed previously? Do they rely on the same number and type of sounds throughout? If so, how have you created contrasting sections? If you haven't, how interesting are those pieces as you look at them again?

➢ Link changes in texture to changes in the structure of the piece. For example, if you were trying to produce a piece in rondo form (ABACADAEAF and so on) you might want the texture of

Tip

You don't need to produce radical changes between sections. If there is too much change, the effect can be quite unsettling – but perhaps that's what you want to create?

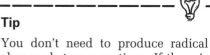

the 'A' section to be similar each time it returns, so as to create a sense of reassurance for those listening to it.

 Compose a 15-second piece that uses a texture comprising at least six parts. Use this as transitional music between episodes.

No matter how you use these elements to create music, you will find that it's the style of the music that makes the most impact, not the individual elements. Rhythm, for example, works within a given style. Whether it is slow or fast will be less noticeable to an audience than whether it is used in a piece of African drumming or a piece of swing.

So what styles of music have you been creating during your course so far, how do they use all the elements of music and – most importantly – how could you use these in your Student Devised Performance? Let's think about the types of music that you might have been working on. These are only examples, so look back at the music that you have worked on in each of the units so far and look at how effective each has been. More importantly, ask yourself whether there are ways of using music that you haven't used yet.

Songs. If you're able to write effective songs, there's every reason to include them. However, think carefully about the following:

➤ Songs are non-naturalistic and can turn the overall piece into a musical, especially if you adopt a style of singing that sounds like a West End show.

➤ Songs can be used to comment on something that is happening in the action. You might find that folk songs or protest music are a good way of commenting in a style that is less 'glitzy' than show-type songs.

➤ Songs should be carefully crafted and you should be able to sing the melody in the same way each time you perform it. Examiners can get very irritated with songs that sound as if they're being made up on the spur of the moment.

➤ You don't have to create a 'whole' song. You might find that one verse is as much as you need. If you've taken a poem as your commission, you could simply take a few lines from the poem and create a melodic structure for those words. This can be an effective method of linking your piece with the commission.

 Find a political poem and make a protest song out of it. Use solo acoustic guitar and voice, perhaps with tambourine and harmonica.

Rhythmic and melodic motifs. We have already seen that rhythmic work can be highly effective at creating a sense of power or tension. You could use some of the techniques of Stomp or you could use interlocking rhythms of wood blocks. The important thing to think about is why you want to use them. Melodic motifs can also be used to good effect.

Style

> **Tip**
>
> Remember that the music you use in the Student Devised Performance doesn't have to be actual 'pieces' as such; you might decide to use music in short bursts throughout the piece.

➢ If you've chosen a poem for your commission, think about the rhythm and metre of the words in each line. You could create a rhythmic motif from the rhythm of the words. This could be a very sophisticated device for moving the piece along.

➢ Rhythmic motifs can be combined with dance motifs to create powerful and effective sections. Try not to separate rhythm and movement – the two are much more powerful in combination.

➢ Rhythms can be used to suggest a particular period. For example, swing rhythms could be used to suggest the 1920s, techno rhythms could suggest the 1990s.

➢ Think about the difference between rhythm, pulse and tempo. You might want to use a complex rhythm but a slow pulse. Be clear about what you are doing and why.

➢ You might want to create a motif from a snippet of melody combined with an interesting rhythm. You could link this to a particular character in your piece.

Vocal pieces other than songs. There are many interesting and exciting ways of using the human voice in performance. Not everyone can sing in tune, so don't feel that you have to sing. You can use extended vocal technique to create interesting vocal textures and these might be highly effective in creating a more vivid, raucous sound appropriate to a particular moment. Consider the following:

➢ If you have chosen an abstract picture as your commission, you might want to create non-naturalistic vocal sounds. You could deliberately create discordant, clashing textures that suggest chaos or madness. These could be varied in volume and intensity or combined with movement and varied use of the space to threaten or challenge the audience.

➢ You can create a sense of stillness or reflection by having each person in the group hold long notes and perhaps increase and decrease the volume to produce a sense of ebb and flow.

➢ You could have some heightened dialogue spoken over this type of sustained textural work. This could create a powerful non-naturalistic epic style.

Choral speaking. Don't be afraid of using choral speaking but don't overdo it. It's hard to speak in unison with others so you'll have to practise, but it can be powerful if particular lines are spoken chorally to heighten what is said. If you decide to use choral speaking, make sure that it has attack, is well coordinated and that there is no sense of embarrassment or holding back from anyone in the ensemble.

Soundscapes. These are often put together by students who have no idea how to use music and end up simply making a tape with a few sound effects on it. However, soundscapes can be effective if used for a particular purpose and as long they are not the only music in the piece.

Finally, whatever music you decide to use in your piece, remember the following points:

➢ It should be integral to the piece and never a bolt-on extra that is stuck in at random.

Tip

Try to avoid having everyone sitting around the computer and keyboard simply pushing keys to create a kind of sonic improvisation. There isn't really very much skill involved in that.

- ➤ It should be stylistically relevant to the piece.

- ➤ Everyone must do something different in the music so that the examiner is clear on who has done what – it just isn't possible for five people all to have written the same tune.

- ➤ Think about the balance between live and recorded music in your piece.

Working to a commission

Watching a piece of performance work is a bit like looking at a well-crafted building: once it's finished, you can see an impressive product, but you can't see the most important bits – the foundations. Without solid foundations, the building would collapse, and no matter how impressive the architect's intention, a pile of rubble impresses very few people. Now that you are preparing your final performance, the foundations are vital. As well as spending time revising your performance skills, there are therefore some very important decisions to be made about the **content** of the performance. This content has to come entirely from the commission that you have chosen.

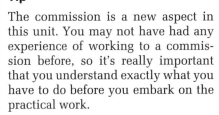

Tip

The commission is a new aspect in this unit. You may not have had any experience of working to a commission before, so it's really important that you understand exactly what you have to do before you embark on the practical work.

What exactly is a commission?

If you've studied visual art or music you may already be familiar with the word 'commission'. Artists and musicians are used to being commissioned to produce a piece of art or music. The process usually works something like this: someone (occasionally referred to as a **patron**) approaches an artist or composer and asks if they would be interested in receiving a commission to produce a specific piece; it may be that a portrait is desired or a piece of music needed for a particular occasion. The crucial thing is that the person giving the commission has specific expectations of what the person receiving the commission will produce. If it works well, everyone is happy.

A commission is a specific instruction to produce a piece of performance that someone else wants. The person working on the commission should have a good idea of exactly what is required before starting work.

However, often things do not progress that smoothly. There are plenty of examples of commissions being misinterpreted, misunderstood, or just plain ignored. Someone commissioning an artist to paint their portrait might expect the end result to be a pleasing, perhaps flattering representation. If the artist has chosen to emphasise the subject's large nose or receding hairline, the end result may be decidedly unflattering. There is no shortage of examples of patrons refusing to accept the final work because it was not what they intended. There must be no misunderstandings. Be absolutely sure what is expected before you start work on the commission.

A professional artist or musician will expect to be paid a sum of money for producing the commission and this will also be specified before work begins.

How does a commission differ from a stimulus?

A commission is **not** the same as a stimulus or a starting point. Let's have a look at the differences.

A stimulus might be a phrase, a line from a poem, a quotation and so on. It is fairly general and allows you plenty of scope for coming up with ideas for creative work. For example, you might have been given a stimulus such as 'Blue is the colour of...' which could have set you thinking about all sorts of things – blues music, changes in

A stimulus

A commission

Some candidates think that sticking to the commission is too straightforward and possibly boring. The opposite is true – keep coming back to the commission and you'll find huge possibilities while remaining focused.

mood, blue sky thinking, once in a blue moon. The possibilities are endless.

A **commission** is much more specific than this. You'll find that the exam board does not set general commissions. They are all very specific and you need to treat them accordingly. With a stimulus, you can be as creative as you wish and it doesn't matter too much if you wander away from it – after all, it's only intended as a starting point, a kind of hook on which you can hang your ideas. With a commission, you are expected to stick precisely to what you've been asked to do. We'll see exactly how this works with different types of commissions later but the basic rule is: your audience needs to be able to follow what is happening in the piece through a combination of watching the performance and reading your programme notes. They won't be present at the discussion with the examiner beforehand so don't rely on the discussion to get you any marks if the examiner can't understand what's going on from the performance and the programme notes.

One more thing: the title of the piece should be the same as the commission. That sounds obvious but some candidates have tried to be creative with the title of their piece and have ended up confusing both the examiner and their audience. Keeping the titles the same should make it easier to remember that the purpose of your piece is to work within that commission to interpret it.

What sort of commissions can we choose from?

Think back over the course so far. What type of commission is likely to produce your best work? It's possible, of course, that each member of the group has different strengths and that you cannot make a general decision like this, but you need to appreciate that there are different skills involved in each type of commission. Someone who responds well to a picture and can see all sorts of interesting images in it may respond very differently when it comes to interpreting a historical event. Similarly, working on the life of a specified character is very different from taking a poem as your commission.

As noted above, there are five different types of commission with four options in each category: 20 commissions in total.

✦ Pictures (titles only)
✦ Historical events (names only)
✦ Poems (titles only)
✦ Stories (titles only)
✦ People (names only).

There are two crucial questions that you need to ask as you look at each of the commissions:

➢ What performance possibilities are there for this commission?

➢ Is it possible for our group to work creatively while staying within this commission?

Obviously, all of the commissions have performance possibilities but your group may struggle to think of them. For each commission, you need to make a rough list of any possibilities you think there are and then assess how well those match the skills and abilities of your group.

Tip

Don't decide too quickly on which of the commissions to choose. The exam will take place at some point between early April and late June, so you've got time to experiment with one or two ideas before making a final decision.

Beware of going for what you believe to be an easy option, however. For example, you may be very drawn to a historical event because you feel your group is good at drama and you want to retell the story, but that might be a bad reason for choosing that commission if you end up producing a piece of narrative drama with no space for any dance or music.

What do we do with the commission we've chosen?

Once you've decided on your commission – and it's vital that everyone in the group is committed to the choice – you need to do some research into the specifics of it.

Research is a word that gets used in different contexts. It's often used to describe the sort of work that goes on in universities where people who know a lot about their subject undertake original work to discover things that no one else knows, but this sort of original research isn't what's required of you here. The sort of research you need to undertake is much more like a form of exploration: you need to explore what you can find out about the commission itself and you also need to explore what possibilities the commission has for performance. Let's look at these separately.

This is the easy bit. You simply need to find out as much as you can about the commission. The examination paper tells you almost nothing about any of the commissions. It's up to you to look them up and find out as much as you can about the one you've chosen. This can be from a variety of sources: books, journals, magazines, websites, CDROMs. As a group, keep a central file with all of this information in it.

Once you have all of the information you need, be disciplined and stop looking for any more. It's always tempting to spend too long gathering more and more information, but you don't need to know everything there is to know about your commission – just enough to devise a piece. What matters most is what you do with the information you have discovered.

So spend some time looking at what you know about the commission and what possibilities that has for performance. There is no point in knowing *about* the commission if that knowledge doesn't help you to create a better piece. Ask yourself which skills you could use to demonstrate your knowledge of the commission. What dance skills could bring it to life? How could drama be used in a way that doesn't simply tell the story? How can music be used? Is singing appropriate in this sort of piece?

How literalist do we have to be with the commission?

There are two extremes and you need to be careful that you don't fall into either of them. At one extreme, you go for a literalist interpretation. For example, imagine that your chosen commission is *The Battle of Agincourt*. You could simply decide to re-enact the battle and bring the story to life, including the characters of Henry V and others that you wanted to include. This is called **animating** or acting out the story. You could get some marks for doing that but you would probably find that the best you could hope for on your group mark for the commission was about 14 out of 25 – and that's if you did it really well. The reason for this is that examiners are not looking for a simple re-enactment of the story. At the other extreme, imagine a group of students who have taken the same commission and not taken it literally enough. Their piece is about a man called Henry who battles with his wife over the pub they run called *The Agincourt*. That would be all right in the case of a stimulus, but of no use at all for a commission. This approach

Exploring the commission

Tip

Research into your chosen commission is vital – but that doesn't just mean going on the Internet. Visit libraries and see what you can find. It's also important to keep in mind that information on the Internet can be unreliable. Be careful about which sites you visit and what you believe.

Find out more information

Tip

Don't duplicate information in your central file. If you print out information from a website, only include what is relevant. Don't be afraid to throw away the bits you don't need.

Look at performance possibilities

It isn't just knowing *about* the commission that's important: it's knowing what *potential* the commission has for you to create a performance on it.

would score a very low mark for the commission – possibly only four or five out of 25.

So the challenge of the activity is: keep within the 'facts' of the commission while still being creative. You're not simply trying to bring the commission to life in a literalist way, but even that would be better than using it so loosely that the audience is bewildered as to what's going on.

Sample commissions

We're now going to look in turn at each of the five categories of commission in order to give you a better idea of what might come up and how you might choose to approach each one. For each category, we've provided an example of a commission that has been set by the exam board in the past. Read through the suggestions we make for working to each commission and think about how you could develop the ideas.

Pictures

You don't have to be studying A-level art to decide to work on one of the pictures; you just need the ability to transform a still image into a piece of live performance. This is easier said than done because everybody 'sees' pictures in their own way. The philosopher Ludwig Wittgenstein had a theory of 'seeing-as'. What he meant by this is that we all tend to try to see things that may not be there intentionally. For example, if you watch the clouds changing shape in the sky, sooner or later, you will see a shape that reminds you of something – the shape of a face, a map of Australia, an elephant. Obviously, these shapes are not really there: our memories associate shapes that we're seeing with things that we've seen before. The same can be true of pictures. We have to be careful that we don't just 'see' things that are nothing to do with the picture, things that we've superimposed on to it.

The types of pictures set in the commissions vary considerably. Sometimes they are **representations of historical people or events**. Examples of recent commissions include Jean-François Millet's *The Gleaners* which depicts characters gleaning (gathering leftover grain) in a field or Pieter Bruegel's *The Tower of Babel* which depicts the story from the book of Genesis in the Bible. Other pictures have been more **surrealist or abstract** and have allowed interpretation to arise from the images in the picture. The crucial thing is that whatever is in your piece has to grow from what is in the picture. Don't waste time making things up that are nothing to do with the commission.

Pictures by Salvador Dali have been set several times by the exam board in the past, and they are often very popular with students. One recent example is *Swans Reflecting Elephants*. Find a copy of the picture and think about how you might use it as a commission. Your initial research would tell you that the artist was a surrealist who was interested in psychoanalysis and dreams, but what you would really need to explore is how to produce a performance from this picture.

Tip

Don't just make up a story using characters from the picture. If the picture includes people, use them in that context.

Swans Reflecting Elephants

Web link

There are many copies of it on the Internet. Try, for example: www.virtualdali.com/37SwansReflectingElephants.html.

Some students always go for the first idea they think of and this can be very dangerous. The central image of the painting is the reflection of the swans as elephants. When it was set, this led some students to produce pieces about eating disorders as they took the idea of what could be seen in the mirror. This was nearly always disastrous as it had little to do with the actual picture.

Let's make a list of some of the obvious features of the picture that you could use in performance:

➤ There is no obvious story so it would be best to leave any narrative dimension of the picture to one side – focus on what is in the image.

➤ There is a central image based on reflection: this might lend itself to some creative dance work, perhaps based on the shapes of the swans themselves.

➤ There is scope for creating an ensemble of six here – look at the relationship between the characters and the image. There are three figures occupying the central area – this could be a good indication of the proxemics of some scenes.

➤ There are natural levels in the picture – look at the relationship between the mountains, the swans and the lake.

➤ The colours of the picture are organised so that the earth is heavy and brown, and the sky is clear and blue. You could think about how this could be reflected in the texture of the piece.

From these observations, it would be unwise to start with a narrative drama approach. The points above lend themselves to a dance-based approach. From that, you could easily adapt the piece to embrace music as well. Remember: the piece doesn't have to be *about* anything: it could just be a piece that explores the imagery, texture, shape and colour of the picture. You don't have to create a story.

Historical events

You could be forgiven for taking a narrative approach when dealing with historical events – after all, in most cases there is an obvious story for you to latch on to with characters and plot. This may be appropriate in some instances, but remember that you have to show your ability in at least **two** art forms and therefore creating a dramatic plot may mean that dance and music look like added extras when it comes to performing the piece.

Some of the historical events that the exam board has been set have been within the 20th century; others have been much further back in time. Examples have included straightforward 'happenings' such as *Hong Kong reverts to Chinese rule*, *The Conquest of Mount Everest* or *The Signing of Magna Carta*. In other instances, the event has contained an element of controversy or historical enquiry, or the potential for some type of political dimension. Examples of this include *Poll Tax Riots*, *Bloody Sunday* and *Did they really Land on the Moon?* – each of which has the potential for a political slant on the event itself.

If you studied Political Performance for Contextual Studies, you will probably find that you know a great deal about the way in

Tip

It's tempting with a historical commission to re-enact the event itself. You could incorporate aspects of historical detail but you would probably do better if you were to expand this with some sort of commentary.

Tip

Although it's tempting to move away from the actual event completely, it's a temptation you should avoid. The examiner is likely to ask you about the link between the commission and your piece, and you don't want to look as if you've abandoned the original commission.

which the art forms can be combined in an attempt to persuade an audience about a political point.

Poll Tax Riots

You need to look very carefully at the exact title that has been set. It would be tempting to think that the commission refers exclusively to the riots that took place in the late 1980s when the Conservative government attempted to introduce a tax to cover the costs of living in a local authority. But a closer look reveals that there is no date on the commission and it would therefore be helpful to consider whether this has ever happened before. Research will reveal that similar riots took place in 1377, 1379 and 1380 in England, and led ultimately to the Peasants' Revolt of 1381. Clearly the context is British, although there would be scope for considering whether similar taxes had been introduced in other countries. Some of the possibilities that immediately present themselves are:

➢ The role of political song – can songs be devised to form the backbone of a political piece (in the way that Brecht used songs in his plays)?

➢ Given that poll tax riots have been both a medieval and a modern phenomenon in Britain, is it possible to interweave the stories?

➢ How much of the story could be told through movement-based scenes, perhaps relying on such conventional approaches as pageant or mummers plays?

➢ The use of space – riots can be a good way of involving large numbers of performers but the most you will have in your group is seven. What can you achieve with only seven people that will capture the nature of a riot?

➢ Political work can lend itself to an episodic structure – is it possible to intersperse songs and/or movement and take the focus away from story? You could create character in ways other than simply telling a story.

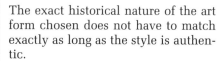

Tip

The exact historical nature of the art form chosen does not have to match exactly as long as the style is authentic.

Poems

Poems are always popular with students, but the main reason for this is that many of them present a scenario with ready-made characters. While this can be highly original (after all – poems tell us very little about actual people and there is plenty of scope for creating characters) it can also encourage you to work too loosely. You need to be completely honest about what is in the poem rather than using it as a peg on which to hang ideas that you already had before you started work on the commission. Some poems chosen by the exam board are by poets from before the 20th and 21st centuries, such as John Donne or Rudyard Kipling, and therefore the nature of the language – its style, rhythm and pacing – will be an important characteristic. In contemporary poems, the scenarios may be what stick most easily in your mind.

Wendy Cope: Lonely Hearts

'Lonely Hearts' from *Making Cocoa for Kingsley Amis* (Faber 1999).

Wendy Cope (born 1945) is a former teacher whose humorous verse has a way of capturing contemporary scenarios in a recognisable way without labouring points of detail. Read through the poem 'Lonely Hearts' below.

Can someone make my simple wish come true?
Male biker seeks female for touring fun.
Do you live in North London? Is it you?

Gay vegetarian whose friends are few,
I'm into music, Shakespeare and the sun.
Can someone make my simple wish come true?

Executive in search of something new –
Perhaps bisexual woman, arty, young,
Do you live in North London? Is it you?

Successful, straight and solvent? I am too –
Attractive Jewish lady with a son.
Can someone make my simple wish come true?

I'm Libran, inexperienced and blue -
Need slim non-smoker, under twenty-one.
Do you live in North London? Is it you?

Please write (with photo) to Box 152
Who knows where it may lead once we've begun?
Can someone make my simple wish come true?
Do you live in North London? Is it you?

Each stanza offers a caricature of people the writer might wish to meet. Look closely at the structure of the poem. There are two lines that are each stated four times, so that eight of the 19 lines rely on restatement. This could be an important feature of the piece that you create. The two lines are: 'Can someone make my simple wish come true' and 'Do you live in North London? Is it you?'

Some possibilities from this poem are:

➢ The recurring lines could become snippets of dialogue or they could be used as choral speech to heighten significant moments of the performance. The two lines have rhythm that gives an added dimension.

➢ It would be possible to create characters from the poem, but this may not be the most effective means of creating performance. This would almost certainly lead to your group inventing five or six characters that matched the descriptions in the poem. You could get a few marks for doing this but since they are not named, you do not need to create them as fully-blown characters.

➢ Staying with these two lines, you will see that they both contain ten syllables. When you're looking at poetry, always look at the metre of the lines as this can contain an obvious musical element. The style here has links with the iambic pentameter used by English poets over the centuries: can anything be done using this rhythm?

➢ The poem might lend itself to an episodic structure: perhaps each stanza could become an episode.

➢ The use of space could be interesting here – you could use chairs within the space to create 'centres' where performers sit to create a semblance of their character.

Stories

Stories often prove to be popular commissions, though this doesn't mean that they are easy. Most of the stories chosen by students are what might be termed fairy stories. It is sometimes thought that fairy stories are only suitable for performance to young children but this is by no means the case. The writer C. S. Lewis (perhaps most famous for *The Chronicles of Narnia*) was a highly respected academic who wrote many works on language and theology. Yet he firmly believed that fairy stories were a powerful way of conveying truth. He once spoke of his embarrassment in reading fairy stories when he was a teenager but commented on how as a mature adult he read them openly. So it is no surprise that they are popular vehicles for communicating to an audience. Because they are effectively make-believe – in the best sense of the term – and therefore essentially non-naturalistic, they have the power to embrace all the art forms.

This means that you don't have to use the story exactly as it stands. You can be as creative as you want, as long as it's obvious to your audience and the examiner what is going on. Fairy stories can be seen as allegories and you might decide to weave a modern story into the framework of the existing story. Or you might want to use the story as it stands but tell it through dance and music rather than simply creating narrative drama. Then again, you might decide that you want to take the framework and characters from the story but set it in a particular time or place or even adapt the style. For example, you could take a fairy story and turn it into a political piece along the lines of George Orwell's *Animal Farm*. There are endless possibilities with stories – don't be afraid to use them creatively. There's a huge variety of stories that are set as commissions. These range from European fairy tales such as *Hansel and Gretel* and *Goldilocks and the Three Bears* to stories from around the world, into which you may need to undertake considerable research.

Hansel and Gretel

See pages 153–155 for an example of how one group approached this commission.

This story operates at a number of levels but there are two elements that define it: the characters and the situation. The characters are: Hansel, Gretel, the Father, the evil Stepmother and the Witch. The situation is fairly far-fetched: the evil stepmother gets rid of the children in the woods, where they find a witch's cottage and get taken prisoner, but manage to kill the witch, escape and return home to live happily ever after. The question arises: how can the characters and the scenario be adapted within the confines of the commission? They could be brought up to date but retain the same names. The scenario could be adapted so that it is contemporary: exactly the same things happen, but in a situation of marital breakdown where the children are taken into residential care but are treated badly. The programme notes would need to make it clear exactly what was happening and there would be a need for the audience to be constantly brought back to the original tale.

People

The people who are used for commissions are drawn from performing arts and entertainment backgrounds. This is done deliberately in order to enable you to draw on your pool of skills where appropriate. For example, if the person specified is a famous singer, it would obviously be wise to consider including some singing in the piece; if the commission was a dancer, it would be wise to incorporate significant amounts of dance. Examples of people who have been set in recent years include the cellist Jacqueline du Pré, the comedy duo Laurel and Hardy, the dancer Isadora Duncan and the clown Joseph Grimaldi. In each case, there was ample opportunity for candidates to demonstrate practical skills through incidents in the lives of these people. Some students get side-tracked here so let's be clear: don't take peripheral aspects of their private life and construct a soap opera. Start by considering the most obvious thing about that person and develop it from there.

Once you've done some research about the life of Joseph Grimaldi (1779–1837) you'll know about his tremendous acrobatic skills, and you'll see that his life therefore easily lends itself to a very physical piece. Avoid the temptation to produce a piece about a sad clown, riddled with self-doubt. However, you might want to have this as a secondary theme running through the piece. Our advice with using a person as a commission is always to start with practical skills associated with the person or people, rather than constructing a narrative story that could focus on drama at the expense of the other art forms.

Joseph Grimaldi

Devising the structure of the piece

No one wants to be bored when they watch a piece of performance. One of the comments most frequently made by candidates when speaking to the examiner before their performance is that they are worried about boring the audience. The structure of the piece is crucial to ensuring that this doesn't happen. The danger is that some sections will be far too long, others far too short, that some unimportant ideas are done to death while other major aspects are almost ignored. A poor structure can affect the pace, timing and impact of the whole performance. You need to make sure the structure for your piece is well thought-out so that it helps you to achieve what you want to achieve.

> **Tip**
> Structure is one of the most important aspects of a piece of performance. Audiences need to feel that the piece is 'going somewhere' rather than simply moving along aimlessly.

Following the earlier analogy from architecture, think now about the structure of a building. When you gaze at a large building – a cathedral, for example – you can be overcome by the sheer size and grandeur of it. It's likely that you won't be analysing the way it is put together – you're more likely to be impressed by the totality of the experience. But we know that all buildings have a very definite structure, and that much careful consideration and planning is done long before any building takes place.

Building your piece

Devising a performance is rather like planning a building. You need to have some clear ideas about the structure and the way you want to put your ideas together. There are, however, two essential differences between designing a building and designing a piece of performance.

➢ It would be impossible to begin work on a building unless all the plans were in place at the outset – you can't expect the builders to make up bits as they go along. In a piece of performance, however, it is quite usual for adaptations to be made in the light of suggestions made by the performers.

➢ It is possible for the eye to take in the whole of a building in one go – you look at it and you can see how things are put together.

> **Tip**
> At all times, keep in mind the audience and the effects created for them by various devices and techniques. What are you saying to the audience? What are you trying to convey, be it abstract or naturalistic? Are you succeeding in creating an effective piece of performance? At pre-arranged points in the course, try out your ideas in front of an audience so that you can see how the ideas that evolved in rehearsal actually work in live performance.

Performances exist in time and you have to watch or listen to the whole piece before you can get an idea of how the structure works.

In spite of these differences, though, it is possible for your group to make some effective decisions about structure before you start work. At the very start of your work in performance studies, you learned about the performance process of improvising–rehearsing–performing.

Now, more than ever, it is vital that the structure is determined during the improvisation process. This process is like a cycle: you start with a basic idea and then you experiment. In the light of experimentation, you modify the structure, experiment again and so on. But how do you know where to start? The answer is: **take the commission as your lead**. Different types of commissions will call for different structures. Let's look at each of the types of commission and think about how the commission could lead you to a suitable structure. It's a good idea to try to think in terms of how you can create short sections, or episodes. Think about sections rather than scenes or you may find yourself being drawn too heavily towards a drama-based approach.

It can be difficult to decide on the length of an episode. If your piece is 24 minutes long in total, for example, you need to balance the sections to avoid ending up with 12 short sections of two minutes each. You need to make sure that transitional sections are shorter than the main sections, and take care to balance longer, more powerful episodes with shorter, more fast-moving sections.

Pictures

If you have chosen a picture for your commission, look at it carefully, to the extent that you see everything about it. Move your eyes steadily across the picture and spend several minutes in silence concentrating hard on taking in everything that is there. Then try to answer these questions:

➤ What is the structure of the picture – what is your eye most drawn to? Is that the centre of the picture? What is the context?

➤ Are there recurring themes in the picture? If so, could these be used as a structural device in your piece? What is the balance between things that appear only once and things that are duplicated in the picture?

➤ How are light and shadow, black and white, or colour used in the picture? Do these give you any clue as to how you could structure your piece?

➤ What levels are used in the picture – could these be translated into scenes or episodes?

➤ Is there any physical movement implied in the piece that could become a motivic device which you could use to structure your piece?

➤ Is there an implied story to the picture? Be careful not to invent one if there isn't but you should feel free to use the context of the picture if it has a naturalistic dimension to it.

➤ What possibilities are there to work within all three art forms? Although individual members of the group only need to

> You should be quite familiar with this process by now as you will have experimented with it in a number of pieces – four pieces in the Language of Performing Arts, one piece in Performance Realisation and an extended piece in your Community Performance Project.

Tip
You could, for example, equate darkness with intensity and light with relaxation.

demonstrate two art forms, it would be advisable for the piece as a whole to cover all three art forms.

Historical events

Historical events need an exact definition in terms of the period of time they occupy. You will find that some of the commissions are much more specific than others regarding the time that the event occupied. For example, the conquest of Mount Everest covered a relatively short period of time whereas the occupation of the Channel Islands in the 1940s went on for several years. This is an important distinction, as your piece will last a maximum of 30 minutes and you need to decide how – or if – you will portray time in your piece.

Look at the factual research that you have undertaken on your chosen commission and ask yourself the following questions:

➤ What period of time is covered by the event?

➤ Is it possible to cover this effectively in a naturalistic manner or would it be better to avoid simply telling the story in order to ensure that the art forms are fully integrated?

➤ Do you want to take episodes in the order that they occurred or could you play around with the historical time line – start at the end, jump to the beginning and work back?

➤ How many characters are involved in the event? Think about this in relation to your group size (minimum three, maximum seven). Does this mean that some characters need to be omitted – or introduced – or do you need to multi-role to cover the event effectively?

➤ Is there anything controversial about the event? If so, could this be the clue to your structure. Remember that a good structure takes the audience to where you want them to go. You could create some intrigue or mystery by the way you structure the piece. In the commission *Did they really Land on the Moon?* it would be possible for the piece to convince the audience that either the whole thing was a hoax or that there was no room for doubt, simply by the way in which you organise the episodes.

➤ What possibilities are there to work within all three art forms?

Poems

Poems have a structure of their own and this can be a valuable place to start when creating a performance piece. The lines in the poem are likely to be organised into couplets, stanzas or sections, and you need to decide whether this structure could be reflected in your piece. Ask yourself the following questions:

➤ How is the poem organised overall? Are there individual sections that could be turned into performance episodes?

➤ Are there repeated lines that could be used as a structural or thematic device in your piece?

➤ Is there a rhythmic structure to any of the lines that you could use to create some music?

➤ Could any of the words be set to music? You are not allowed to use large chunks of the poem but it might be effective to take a line and repeat it as a choral motif, or a short musical motif that could be passed around the ensemble. Or you could use a repeated single line to indicate a change of episode, such as 'Can someone make my simple wish come true' in the Wendy Cope poem.

➤ Is the poem telling a story? If so, you need to decide whether your piece will also have narrative elements. Don't just animate the poem, though. Be creative.

➤ What possibilities are there to work within all three art forms?

Stories

Like poems, stories have a natural structure, and this can be very helpful in deciding how to structure your piece. However, stories differ in length and the amount of detail they give. Also, in the case of folk tales, there are often different versions of the same story. Which one will you choose? Are there enough similarities between the stories to create a composite version that includes elements of all of them? Look carefully at the story you have chosen and answer the following questions:

➤ What is the structure of the story?

➤ Where are the significant moments in the story?

➤ Can these be turned into transition points in the performance?

➤ How many episodes would there need to be?

➤ How much potential is there for dance and music in this story?

➤ What characters are there? How could these be covered in your piece?

➤ Is it possible to use a 'parallel story' approach whereby a contemporary version is interspersed with the original?

➤ Is it possible to change the setting of the story to a different period of time? Could this be done through dance or music?

People

Choosing a commission about a person offers plenty of freedom because you can choose which aspect of the person's life or career to focus on. You'll need to have done some research about the person's life before you start, but you'll find that this will almost certainly produce a great deal of material from which you will need to select carefully. Ask yourself the following questions:

➤ What is this person's most well-known contribution to the world of performing arts?

➤ Does our group have the potential to include these skills in our piece?

➤ What aspects of the person's life will our piece focus on?

➤ What is the time span of our chosen aspects of that person's life?

➤ Are there significant moments that we can use as separate episodes?

➤ How can we avoid simply producing a documentary?

➤ Is it possible to take an original angle – perhaps by juxtaposing scenes from contemporary events or episodes?

➤ What possibilities are there to work within all three art forms?

Working structure

Regardless of the type of commission your group has chosen, you should now make a preliminary plan about the type of structure you intend. This can be modified as necessary but you must start with at least some broad idea of the overall plan. Try to balance the art forms as much as you can when you work through the structure.

You'll see that we keep guiding you away from drama as a starting point. This is to ensure that you make full use of dance and music.

For example, for Wendy Cope's poem *Lonely Hearts*, you might come up with the following plan. You could use this type of working sheet for your own piece.

Wendy Cope 'Lonely Hearts'
Preliminary structure: open to discussion and reworking in the light of practical improvisation
Number of candidates in group: five
Length of piece: 20 minutes

Choral speech	Based on line 'Can someone make my simple wish come true'. Builds into rhythmic motif using ten beats	Two minutes
Dance section	Presents five characters using physical theatre techniques	Three minutes
Transition	Based on 'Can someone make my simple wish come true'	Two minutes
Dramatic episode	Five characters seated, each presents line from poem, works into tableaux	Three minutes
Transition	Vocal harmony and movement based on 'Do you live in North London? Is it you?'	One minute
Dance episode	Five characters, 'where do you live' and 'is it North London'. Sound track created in music studio using speech samples – instrumental lines also recorded imitating speech melodies.	Three minutes
Dramatic episode	'Can someone make my simple wish come true' – based on no more than two lines of dialogue, each with ten syllables.	Two minutes
Climax	Vocal harmony and choral speech interspersed – increase pace and volume to a point of climax. Fortissimo, then cut and blackout.	Four minutes
End		

The style of the piece

So you've chosen the commission you want, you've done some factual and historical research, you've got some ideas and you've made a preliminary plan of the structure. There's one more thing to consider before the practical work begins: the style of the piece.

Remember that this unit is synoptic, which, as we've already seen, means that your piece has to sum up the wide range of work that you've done during the course. We asked you earlier to review the repertoire, styles and genres that you've covered during the course. Now's the time to go back to that list and have another careful look through it.

It might not seem very promising initially – after all, some of the practitioners you've studied may not have very much in common. Remember, though, that the purpose of this unit is not simply to create a big piece in which you use *all* of these things. The style of your piece is almost certain to be eclectic, bringing together different stylistic trends in different sections, and there is no problem with this in principle. You need to make sure, however, that the piece is coherent, and simply bringing together some of the styles you've studied before may not achieve this. For example, if you studied Lloyd Newson and George Gershwin for AS, it might be strange if you now wanted to juxtapose a section involving physical theatre with a song in the style of Gershwin, unless, of course, you wanted to create a particular effect by doing so.

Look at your proposed structure for the piece and try to match it against styles and techniques in which you have strengths as a group. Then try to imagine the effect that bringing these things together will have on an audience: you need to make sure that you don't confuse the people watching your piece – or, worse, make them laugh unintentionally.

Creating a role for yourself

As we have already seen, in the assessment of your work, 25 marks are awarded for the link with the commission. Everyone in the group will get the same mark for the piece. The remaining 75 marks available are for your individual role and the way in which you perform it – so you need to spend some time thinking about how you will work in the group.

Obviously, everyone in the group will have different strengths and weaknesses. Bear in mind, therefore, that everyone is likely to want to include their own 'party trick' – the thing they do best – and if you allow that, the overall piece could end up looking like a piece of variety entertainment rather than a coherent and continuous piece.

Here are some tips to help you think about your role:

Equal exposure for all

The piece is expected to allow everyone the equivalent of five minutes' worth of exposure. This would be easy to define if the piece was simply a set of monologues bolted together, but we strongly recommend that you avoid this, as it will be difficult for you to demonstrate any group interaction. In most pieces, there

---

In the rush and excitement to show your performance skills, it's easy to forget that the style of the piece is an important consideration.

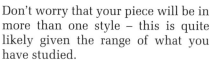

Tip

Don't worry that your piece will be in more than one style – this is quite likely given the range of what you have studied.

Tip

Never forget the audience. As well as demonstrating your practical skills, you are trying to entertain them, even if the piece deals with disturbing material.

Tip

There could be a tension between working as a group and trying to get the best mark for yourself. If everyone pulls their weight, this is unlikely to be an issue. If you feel that someone is not pulling their weight, you should discuss it with your tutor immediately.

will be some ensemble sections and some scope for solo work. This means that if seven performers are on stage for the whole time, your piece need not last the whole 30 minutes, because the examiner will have seen everyone during the entire piece. Remember that a shorter piece can sometimes be more powerful than one that is dragged out.

Some of the commissions look as if they almost require you to focus on a central character. For example, if you devise a piece based on the cellist Jacqueline du Pré, it is quite likely that someone will play the role of the cellist herself. That does not automatically mean that this person will score higher marks than anyone else in the group: they may not be a very impressive performer, after all. However, it may mean that there will be less scope for the other members of the group to demonstrate their performance skills. If the lead character gives a mediocre performance, it will also have the effect of depressing the work of the others, so be careful about this.

You may find that there is a struggle in your group over who plays which roles. Almost certainly, this is likely to concern points where the focus is on drama, for it would be unwise to keep changing the person playing that role. In the case of dance or music, it would be straightforward to have different people doing similar things at different points in the piece without confusing the audience.

Just as there may be some prima donnas, there may also be one or two shy and retiring members of your group who want to take on peripheral roles. For example, in the sample commission above based on Wendy Cope's poem, the line 'whose friends are few' might suggest that someone lacking in confidence should play such a role. We suggest that this would be a mistake. It is crucial that you do not end up with a role that simply reinforces your own personality. It doesn't matter whether you're naturally confident or shy, loud or quiet. You need to avoid being typecast – in other words, being given a role that people think resembles what you are like in real life. This is a performance, not reality TV.

Group dynamics are hard to gauge. There is no such thing as the principal performer in your group and no one should be encouraged to act as such. You need to be a generous performer – someone who is able to lead where necessary and follow where necessary. As the piece emerges, make sure that you have some points at which you lead the ensemble. It's probably best if this is a section where you have some real skills and can successfully help others to give their best. For example, if you have strengths in dance work, you could help choreograph a section within the piece and then help everyone to do their best in that section. Of course, there will be no extra marks for doing that, but think about the alternative: your high level of performance in that section will be undermined if no one else is able to do anything to support you.

Tip

If you look back at the example of working structure, you'll see that it doesn't make any reference to which of the sections could include solo work. Now is the point to consider that in more detail. How much scope is there for anyone to have any solo exposure?

Tip

Examiners are looking for generous performers – that is, people whose style encourages others to give their best. Mean performers are those who crush others rather than encouraging them. Watch out for the prima donna. It's a well-known saying that everyone wants to play Hamlet but a less well-known fact is that playing a spear-bearer can demonstrate as much performance ability in the right context.

Tip

Be democratic over who gets which roles. Don't sit and seethe because you didn't get the role you wanted – talk it through with the group and base your group decision on hard evidence of who is best suited to which role. Ask your teacher to intervene and advise if necessary.

Lead and follow

On the other hand, you may know that when it comes to singing, for example, you need other people to support you in holding the melody. In this case, it would be foolish to try to sing a solo passage because this will simply undermine everyone else's singing. Play to your strengths in terms of skills: look again at your skills audit and make sure that you offer your strengths to the group.

You could hold a workshop to help you all to be honest about what you can do. Although this type of workshop can be painful, it can also be a huge help in getting everyone to be realistic and supportive of the needs of every member of the group.

Being realistic and generous in devising roles

In this session, everyone comes prepared with a copy of the rough structure of the piece and talks through what they can contribute to the piece. This will include:

➢ Knowledge about how to turn the commission into a piece

➢ An honest appraisal of their performance strengths

➢ What contribution they could make in each of the art forms (even though ultimately they need to include only two)

➢ The specific contribution they could offer to each section – where they could lead, where they would be happy to be in the ensemble

➢ What support each person thinks they may need

➢ Any concerns that anyone has about the piece and the way it's going

➢ A final agreement on a working plan in which everyone has enough exposure of a high enough quality.

> **Tip**
>
> We know that some groups find it difficult to get on. If you think this is the case, why not ask your tutor to chair the session to ensure that everyone gets their say?

At least two art forms

It is essential that you demonstrate your performance skills in at least two art forms. It's no good just devising a role in drama and then singing a short song or doing a little movement work. This will almost certainly create an imbalance between the art forms. Examiners are told to look for **tokenism**. Put simply, this means that they will be checking to make sure that you attempt to use both art forms to broadly the same extent. Obviously it would be impossible to do an exact calculation as to the balance between the art forms but a good test is to calculate exactly how much time you spend on each one. If your skills are unbalanced, you will lose a lot of marks.

> You do not have to tell the examiner which art forms you are working in. The examiner is assessing a performance and will simply mark whatever you choose to present.

Some candidates make a mental decision to ignore one of the art forms completely. This is very unwise and we strongly recommend you avoid doing it. One of the most depressing things an examiner can be told in the discussion before the performance is 'we don't do music' or 'we've dropped dance'. The whole point of performance studies is to encourage you to bring the performing arts together and to make natural links between them in your performance work.

Even though the exam board requires you to work in only two art forms, you will find the whole experience more rewarding and enjoyable if you think naturally about embracing all three art forms of dance, drama and music.

When devising your role, it is not just your skills that you need to think about. Everyone brings different levels of energy to a piece. This can vary according to physical size, vocal power and natural levels of confidence. You need to know how your level of energy can contribute to the piece. Some people have too much energy and will need to control it – other people have little natural energy or presence and will need to work at increasing it.

If the energy levels in the piece are unbalanced, everyone will suffer. As you work though the roles you will all take, make sure that you work together to balance energy levels.

As we have already seen, most of these decisions will take place during the improvising phase of the work. All decisions at this stage, however, are preliminary and you need a level of honesty to be able to revisit them in the rehearsal phase if there is anything that is not working properly. Remember that your teacher can intervene at any time and it is wise to ask their opinion as to how the roles are working at every rehearsal.

Use your energy

> **Tip**
> Don't be afraid to video your rehearsals. It can be a very useful tool to allow you to see the balance, pacing and contrasts between the roles, just as your audience will see them.

Case studies

Over the following pages, we'll take you through some case studies so that you can see how former students have approached this unit, and the problems they faced. Don't take these as rigid models for your own work – use them as inspiration, note what they did well and learn from their mistakes.

Hansel and Gretel

With six candidates in their piece, the group had decided to work almost at the maximum group size allowed (seven candidates). While this meant that there was plenty of scope to cover a wide range of roles, it also meant that there was potential for one or two people to dominate the whole piece, or for some weaker members of the group to end up as 'passengers' with not very much to do. There was also the possibility that there might be divisions if one sub-group of two or three people had ideas that were in conflict with the other members of the group.

The group did not need to spend very long researching around the story since its basic elements are fairly straightforward:

Researching the commission

> Hansel and Gretel are abandoned in the woods by the evil stepmother

> They stumble across the witch's house

> The witch entices them in and takes them captive

> The witch makes Gretel her slave and feeds Hansel with a view to cooking and eating him

> Gretel kills the witch by pushing her into the fire or oven

> Hansel and Gretel take the treasures from the witch's house and return home

> The evil stepmother has died and the father is delighted to see his children return

> They all live happily ever after.

Once they had the essential aspects of the story clearly set out before them, the group moved on to considering the performance, and focused on how this structure could be used. After much experimenting and improvising with roles, they decided to use a parallel story that took the form of a commentary on teenagers ensnared by drugs in contemporary society.

Structure of the piece

Note here that the group has not abandoned the original story of the modern reworking – the two are presented together. If they had abandoned the basics of the original commission, they would not have scored many marks.

The group devised seven episodes that mirrored the episodes in the original story. These were:

➤ A single-parent mother is struggling to bring up two teenage children but cannot pay the rent and forces them to seek employment

➤ The teenagers head for London where the little money they have is tricked away from them in gambling and drugs

➤ They become ensnared in selling drugs in pubs for a dealer and are held captive

➤ They ultimately trap the dealer who is caught by the police and imprisoned

➤ The teenagers take the money and return home

➤ They give the money to their mother who is able to pay the rent

➤ They all live happily ever after.

This structure worked well. They used a short musical motif based on the whole-tone scale (played on the piano) to signify the transitions from the scenes set in the present to the fairy tale scenes. They did not use this device for the return to the present, however, as these transitions were more obvious to the audience.

Individual roles

Once this structure was agreed on, it was decided that everyone in the ensemble would have two roles – one in the fairy tale and one in the contemporary scenario. This would help to ensure that no one dominated the piece. The group could have created parallel roles, but decided against this in order to avoid certain members being doubly advantaged by having two major roles. The roles they devised in the fairy story were:

➤ Father
➤ Stepmother
➤ Hansel
➤ Gretel
➤ Witch.

They then devised the roles in the parallel story:

➤ Mother
➤ Teenage child
➤ Teenage child
➤ Drug dealer/gambler
➤ Drug dealer
➤ Drug seller.

The characters in the contemporary story were more fluid and there was some multi-role playing in these sections of the piece.

At the very beginning, the group decided that they would work in all three art forms, even though they did not have to, as they thought this would give the piece added power. They decided that they would take a very physical approach to the piece and tell as much of both stories through image, spatial relations and episodic structures as possible. This meant that the frequent use of contemporary dance fitted in well with the style, and that the songs they composed acted as a commentary on the action of the piece.

Style of the piece

This was an extremely strong piece. The link with the commission was handled with great sophistication, and the interweaving of the two stories cleverly ensured that the audience was always aware of the commission while thinking about the links with a contemporary scenario. The commission was awarded a very high mark, as were the individual roles for the candidates. Some candidates had more developed performance skills than others, but all candidates ultimately achieved an A grade for this unit.

Commentary

The group summarised all of this very effectively for the programme notes. There are no specific marks for the programme but examiners may take them into account in awarding a mark for the use of the commission.

Programme notes

Hansel and Gretel

A tale retold for our time

Programme Notes

Cast

Jonathan	Hansel, Gambler
Luke	Father, Drug Dealer
Charlotte	Mother, Drug Seller
Emma	Gretel, Teenager
Liz	Witch, Teenager
Jo	Step Mother, Teeenager

There is some multi-role playing which will be obvious as the action of the piece progresses.

Setting

We have interspersed the story of Hansel and Gretel with a modern story about how teenagers can get ensnared by drugs. This is the same way that Hansel and Gretel got trapped by the witch who seemed very plausible and friendly until she had them in her grasp. Ultimately, however, right prevails and just as the witch is killed, the evils of the drug dealers are revealed to the police who intervene and arrest the dealers. In spite of the dark side of the stories, both end happily.

About the piece

We hope you enjoy our piece. We aim to tell the story through dance, drama and music and we have tried to make sure that we use all three equally throughout the piece. Some sections make extensive use of contemporary dance, while others use original songs that we have written as a commentary on the story. We have been influenced by the practitioners we have studied throughout our course, particularly Christopher Bruce, Bertolt Brecht and George Gershwin although we do not simply copy their techniques. The style of our piece is not meant to be naturalistic. We have used an episodic structure and you will know when we move from the contemporary story to the fairy tale by a short musical motif on the piano.

Sit back and let us transport you 'Once upon a time' ...

Once upon **our** time, that is ...

Mistake one

They decide simply to tell the story.

Researching the commission

Mistake two

The group spends far too long on factual research and not long enough on performance research.

Structure of the piece

Mistake three

The structure is predictable and leads them towards drama only.

Mistake four

The dating agency is a cliched device and best avoided.

The wives of Henry VIII

This piece was chosen from the historical events section of the commissions and we've included it so that you can learn from five mistakes that the group made. The choice facing the group at the start of their working process was whether they were simply going to tell the story or whether they could make it original in structure and approach. They decided to tell the story and this dictated everything that they did.

There were five members of the group, four female and one male. This lent itself very easily to the subject matter of the piece. It meant that there was plenty of possibility for multi-role playing by the four female members of the group but that the one male member of the group played the role of Henry throughout.

The group spent a long time on the Internet researching the history of Tudor England. They were particularly interested in the fact that disease and death were a common feature of everyday life in that period. They also became fascinated by Henry VIII's approach to personal hygiene. At times, however, the fascination with these details led the group to become more interested in peripheral details of the commission rather than in trying to devise an effective structure. After four weeks of searching the Internet, the group's teacher suggested that they were wasting time and should get on with trying to structure the piece. They had done little research so far into how they might create performance from the subject matter, although they had stumbled across one website that contained some details on courtly dance. They also discovered that Henry VIII was thought by some to have written *Greensleeves* so they decided to try to play that tune on the recorder in one of the scenes.

The group found that from all their research, they had masses of information about Henry VIII and it was difficult for them to know where to start in using any of it in the piece. After a further two weeks of arguing, the group managed to agree that they would have six scenes in the piece, one for each of Henry's wives. Each scene would be separated by a blackout to enable them to shift the props and change costumes. The structure they decided upon was:

➤ Scene 1 – Katherine of Aragon

➤ Scene 2 – Anne Boleyn

➤ Scene 3 – Jane Seymour

➤ Scene 4 – Anne of Cleves

➤ Scene 5 – Katherine Howard

➤ Scene 6 – Katherine Parr.

The group decided to introduce the idea of a dating agency to move things along. This became a predictable device in which Henry kept being interviewed about his desired qualities in a wife.

This structure did not work especially well. It was predictable and tended to mean that the group simply told the story as it stood. In other words, they merely animated the story. Some of the details they thought of were original (such as the dating agency and points about Henry's personal hygiene) but seemed out of place in the final piece. The whole piece was dominated by a light-hearted (but not especially comical) approach to naturalistic drama.

The composition of the group was something of a straitjacket. It was decided that the one male member of the group should play the role of Henry VIII and he immediately set about designing a sumptuous costume, which took up most of the time he could have used working practically with the group. He also decided early on that he would use his rock guitar skills to follow on from the singing of *Greensleeves*. Although the group thought this was a strange idea, he pressed his ideas against their will and they all built their roles around this caricature of Henry VIII. The four female members of the group multi-roled the dating agency employee and the six wives. They decided that they would build the personalities of the wives around their own natural personalities, as they thought this meant it would be easy to act them out. This undermined much of the drama and meant there was no real need for them to act. The multi-role playing meant that they had less flexibility on costume and the blackouts were intended to enable them to change costume.

Each member of the group had skills in drama but none of them felt especially able to perform in dance or music. This was a real problem because it meant that the whole piece looked like a piece of drama with a song and a dance introduced almost at random. The performance of *Greensleeves* on the recorder with the others singing was under-rehearsed and the rock guitar playing that followed it was unintentionally comical.

Although there were some reasonable drama performances, there was so much more that could have been done by the group. The link with the commission was fairly obvious but the group did very little apart from animate what was already there – in other words, they told the story as it was. This meant that they received approximately half marks for the link with the commission. This was their best mark. The roles were essentially one-dimensional and no ability to shape the direction of the piece was demonstrated. The worst aspect of the performance was that that it was dominated by fairly average drama with only tokenistic amounts of dance and music. The blackouts between scenes slowed down the pace and action of the piece, and, had the group not been so dependent on costume and elaborate props, these would not have been necessary.

Ultimately this combination of factors meant that the members of the group were each awarded a grade D with the two weaker performers receiving a grade E. This was a real shame. Looking back, the group realised that if they had not taken so much time looking on the Internet for factual research but had spent more time working how to integrate the art forms, each member of the group could have received a much higher grade.

Individual roles

Mistake five

Too much time is spent making costumes instead of rehearsing.

Mistake six

The characters were based on the candidates' own personalities.

Style of the piece

Mistake seven

The group fails to integrate two, let alone three art forms.

Commentary

The programme notes for this group ran to six pages as they struggled to incorporate all of the research into the final document. They should have followed the type of layout we gave for the first case study above

Web link

Images of the painting are easy to find on the Internet. Try www.virtualdali.com/37MetamorphosisOfNarcissus.html.

Researching the commission

Web link

See, for example, www.pantheon.org/articles/n/narcissus.html

Here the group could easily have lost sight of Narcissus, but they pulled back from that danger and decided to create parallel characters.

Structure of the piece

Metamorphosis of Narcissus

A group of five girls shared the list of 20 commissions between them, and each member researched three or four. They all brought their findings to a session, and discussed their initial impressions of the commissions and the ones to which they were drawn. Salvador Dali's *Metamorphosis of Narcissus* from the pictures category was a popular choice among the group, so they decided to look more closely at various versions of the myth.

Having found the story on the Internet, each member of the group studied it for five minutes and made their own notes on their first impressions. They then looked at the following aspects of the myth, which were suggested by their teacher:

➢ The spatial and temporal settings (where and when it is set)
➢ Characters
➢ Reflections/mirrors
➢ Themes of self-obsession and self-love
➢ Title
➢ Possible performance ideas.

Having carried out some initial preparation, the group went to the Learning Resource Centre to find out more about the painting and get more ideas on how to develop their initial thoughts.

On investigating Dali's life and work, the group discovered that he was interested in dreams and surrealism. The work of Freud and his analysis of dreams fascinated the group, but they thought that incorporating this in their piece would be moving too far away from the original commission. They decided to focus on three aspects of the myth in order to come up with a scenario around which they could improvise. The three aspects were:

➢ Narrative
➢ Characters
➢ Themes.

The basic theme of a person being self-obsessed was one that intrigued the group, and they carried out further research on this. They decided that self-love was something that many people are guilty of, particularly in this era of the self-made celebrity. They considered shallowness and blindness to the truth to be relevant concepts in contemporary society, and discussed how the characters could be updated from the myth to be given modern-day equivalents.

They hit on the idea of setting the action in an office of a magazine called *Reflections*, which would immediately set the right tone for the commission as it spelt out one of the significant issues in the narrative. There would be lots of similar clues in the other names.

As five girls, the members of the group played five female workers in the *Reflections* office. Their piece begins with a dance scene presenting their journey to work on the tube. This is followed by a series of monologues in the office, where each character introduces themselves and explains their relationships to the others. One of the characters raises the topic of speed-dating, which features in that week's issue of *Reflections*, and this provides a link to the next scene, in which all five girls go speed-dating.

Melanie, the boss, who is the piece's equivalent of the Narcissus character, has no success at speed-dating, but then receives a message from a dating website inviting her to a date at a restaurant. What she fails to realise is that the message is one of her own and has come back to her by mistake. When no one comes to meet her at the restaurant, she gets drunk alone and goes into a dream world, in which she sees her reflection in water and falls in love with herself. She never recovers, and is left alone and miserable. The other performers re-enact the Narcissus myth, showing the pool as a circular blue light into which Melanie gazes. This initial motif is then developed through a series of motifs and variations, expressing the need to be loved and the failure to find a lover. The piece ends with this dance section.

The structure of the piece is thus:

➢ Getting to work
➢ In the office
➢ Speed-dating
➢ Greek restaurant
➢ Drama sequence
➢ Finale – dance ensemble – themes entwined.

Each of the characters has a different role within the magazine that represents some aspect of the themes of self-love and self-obsession. Carol, for example, is the dietician for *Reflections* and represents society's obsession with looking thin in order to attract the love of another. She introduces herself to the audience while weighing herself on a set of scales. While her section of the magazine gives advice to readers on which diet works, she confesses that she has tried every diet going and had success with none of them.

Gina plays the part of Echo in the Narcissus myth – the one unrequited in love. She is the outcast in the office, eliciting the suspicion of the other females because she is a lesbian. They feel threatened and tend to gossip in corners about her attraction to Melanie, who is too wrapped up in herself to notice Gina's attraction.

The piece combines many different styles. The first scene grabs the audience's attention, as they see the five girls on the tube going to work. Each has a newspaper and uses it to add levels and noises to the movement that ensues. The girls eye up men and have reveries as they dance to the Glen Miller song *In the Mood*. Simple gestures such as heads turning, legs flicking or feet tapping were used to good effect by employing unison followed by canon. The group created a good texture in this scene and neatly used the chairs to move quickly and smoothly in to the following office scene, where the chairs, set in a V shape, indicate the positions of the girls in the office. In this scene, each performer freezes into a pose that shows an aspect of office life such as typing, answering the phone or

Individual roles

The relationship between the characters in the piece and the commission was made clear in the programme notes.

Style of the piece

As this was a group of performers who could dance and act well, they chose not to compose their own music but to use pre-recorded tracks instead.

gossiping. Carol is then immediately in position downstage right to deliver her monologue.

The monologues contained many comic aspects, for example with Carol fiddling with the dial on the scales to make herself lighter while she spoke. Her monologue then cuts to Lily who is eating a doughnut. Both characters pronounce the word 'doughnut' at the same time, and Lily then continues with her monologue. This cross-cutting device was used to introduce all five characters, and, although it became slightly predictable, it was effective in keeping the pace up and conveying the information in a slick manner.

As a transition to the dating scene, Gina states that she does not know how to behave around men, so the other girls give her a lesson in seduction, with *Hey Big Spender* playing in the background. Comic movement is used as Lily 'walks in the joint' and falls over. By the end of this excerpt from the song, the girls have moved the chairs back into a line upstage centre and are sitting in a row facing the audience ready to be speed-dated. A soundtrack of couples having conversations plays, and a bell punctuates the transitions between the dates, which last only 30 seconds each. The audience hears the actors on stage asking and answering questions that are full of double entendres in order to add humour to the piece. The performers deliver their lines as if speaking directly to the audience.

In the Greek restaurant scene, the group varied the dance style by using Greek dancing. One member of the group came from Cyprus and was well acquainted with this style. She taught various steps and movements to the rest of the group who perform as an ensemble once the restaurant has been set up. The girls don aprons and bring in bottles and plates in order to signify food.

The style of the last scene was taken from watching Christopher Bruce's work – in particular *Swansong* for the lifts – and Matthew Bourne's *Car Man*, in which there are scenes with couples dancing in a provocative manner.

Commentary

There is a high entertainment factor throughout, but the link with the commission remains evident, particularly when Melanie goes into the dream world, and because of the clear links in characterisation.

The success of many of the scenes depended on a fast pace with quickfire lines, as well as strong diction to ensure that the audience could appreciate all the jokes. Facial expression was used well and the comic moments worked well throughout.